THE LIVINSKI SAGA

-THE EXCURSION-

Don Moggs

Pen Press Publishers Ltd

Published in Great Britain by
Pen Press Publishers Ltd
25 Eastern Place
Brighton
BN2 1GJ

ISBN 978-1-906206-36-9

Cover design Jacqueline Abromeit

Dedication:

To my Wife, Diana, who listened and helped each day while
I read what had been written.

About the author

Don Moggs was born in London's East End, the son of an engine driver on the L.N.E.R. After early schooling in the West Ham and Dagenham, he won a scholarship to Romford Royal Liberty School, later moving to the grammar school in Enfield.

Pre-war, he worked as an office clerk and during the war served in the RAF as a pilot and an accountant Officer. After the war he qualified as an accountant, going on to become Financial Director of a public company. He has also worked as a consultant in industry and as administrator to an international firm of architects and consulting engineers.

Don Moggs currently lives in Surrey, where well in his eighties he continues to write. Previous publications include; *Dad's War*, an account of his wartime experiences, *The Moscow Contract*, and *The Takeover*. A second edition of the latter two were published by Pen Press who also have published three further novels: *The Adventures of Diana and Harry*, *Incident 1986* and *The Turin Contract*.

Prologue

In the dictionary the word excursion is defined as 'a journey or ramble with intention of returning to starting point' or 'pleasure-trip of number of persons'. In the twentieth century the word was generally associated with trains when railway companies ran special trains at much reduced fares to encourage the public to ride with them. Thus in the thirties and immediately post World War Two there were in England many Sunday excursions to the seaside, exhibitions or renowned beauty spots, whilst on Saturdays special trains would take people to important football games.

Since the demise of steam on the railways, the advent of motorways and the tremendous increase in the use of the motorcar, the popular railway excursions offered today are those generally associated with nostalgia with people travelling, often uncomfortably, in old carriages pulled by steam engines, which although lovingly restored by railway enthusiasts, are mostly unlike the real trains of the time The nostalgia urge is the same in America where such nostalgic journeys are known as fan trips.

Contents

PART ONE

Chapter 1	1937	1
Chapter 2	The Seaside	14
Chapter 3	The Livinski story begins	23
Chapter 4	First days in Brooklyn	42
Chapter 5	Manhattan and Central Station	44
Chapter 6	Decision time	56
Chapter 7	The Opportunity	61
Chapter 8	Shall we go?	65
Chapter 9	North Conway and Jackson	77
Chapter 10	Work allocation	84
Chapter 11	Early days in Jackson	93
Chapter 12	Christie's show interest	99
Chapter 13	Back from New York	107
Chapter 14	Sold	109
Chapter 15	We pass on the good news	115
Chapter 16	Two strangers arrive	118
Chapter 17	Choosing a house	125
Chapter 18	The wedding	129
Chapter 19	We start a family and plan the future	133
Chapter 20	Munroe helps again	141
Chapter 21	Hotel owners	142
Chapter 22	Century ends	145
Chapter 23	Sad news from home	149
Chapter 24	The age of the motor car	150
Chapter 25	The Mount Washington Hotel	152
Chapter 26	A new enterprise	155
Chapter 27	The first decade of a new century	159
Chapter 28	Indecision and Suffragettes	162
Chapter 29	World War I	167

Chapter 30   Post War   173
Chapter 31   World changes and great sadness   178
Chapter 32   More Romans?   183
Chapter 33   Progress in the air and on the ground?   184
Chapter 34   The Excursion ends   186

PART TWO

Chapter 1   Little Warley   191
Chapter 2   Returning the favour   198
Chapter 3   Found?   202
Chapter 4   Samantha   212
Chapter 5   Getting to know her   217
Chapter 6   Preparing to go   226
Chapter 7   Passports   228
Chapter 8   The Davis family and Warley church   234
Chapter 9   To America   237
Chapter 10   New York   242
Chapter 11   Jackson, I'm back!   244
Chapter 12   Introduction to the Washington Valley   250
Chapter 13   To Return?   256
Chapter 14   Back to England   264
Chapter 15   Storm clouds over Europe   266
Chapter 16   Returning to America   272
Chapter 17   Disaster   276
Chapter 18   Work in America   282
Chapter 19   New Year Party   286
Chapter 20   The war goes on   292
Chapter 21   Leon and Joseph   294
Chapter 22   Samantha and Kirk   296
Chapter 23   December 7th   298
Chapter 24   In the Marines   308
Chapter 25   A surprise visitor   312
Chapter 26   The victors return   318

Part One

The American Dream

Chapter 1

1937

Leon Livinski had come a long way to try to find his granddaughter and on this Sunday in 1937 had determined to start early in his quest. He had arrived at Southampton the day before and caught the boat train to Waterloo and there boarded a taxi to be taken to his hotel he had booked before leaving America.

"I want you to take me to the Russell Hotel but I would like you to drive via Tower Bridge, if that is possible."

"As you like, guvner, but it'll cost you more." The driver got out of his cab and helped Livinski with his luggage. "No business of mine but any particular reason?"

"As a matter of fact there is. This is my first visit to London since many years ago I was on a ship that docked here and tied up by the side of the bridge. Men were still working on it then and I learnt since that it was opened that year. I just would like to see it again."

"When was that, guvner?"

"The year was 1893."

"Cor blimey, you do surprise me, if you had asked me I would have thought the old bridge had been there for a hundred years or more."

"Yes, I imagine a lot of people think it to be much older. No, I can assure you it was opened in 1893, the year I went to America."

"All right, guvner, off we go to Tower Bridge."

The driver did not cross the nearby Waterloo Bridge but kept south of the river and at the Elephant and Castle turned up the road leading to Tower Bridge. He slowed as he approached the bridge and called back to his passenger.

1

"Here we are, guv, Tower Bridge."

Livinski looked out of the window and relived that day over forty years ago.

"Thank you, driver. Now I have seen it, just take me to my hotel."

Arriving at the hotel a porter came out and carried the luggage into the hotel whilst Livinski paid and thanked the driver. At reception his booking was confirmed and before being shown to his room, he asked for an early call and breakfast in his room.

He was a man who had been used to rising early when required and although staff in the hotel may have thought it strange for him to order breakfast in his room for seven o'clock on a Sunday morning, he thought nothing of it.

The next morning he had washed and dressed when the expected knock came on the door.

"Come in."

"Your breakfast, Sir."

"Thank you, put it over there." He paused and then, "Before you go, can you tell me the best way to get to Liverpool Street station?"

"Well, if you are in a hurry and this time of day, being a Sunday, I would go by taxi, otherwise take the underground. There's a station just round the corner, Russell Square, catch a train to Holborn and change onto the Central Line. It'll take you, I reckon, about twenty minutes, or a bit more, depending on trains. But by taxi today, ten minutes."

"Thank you, I'll go by taxi. I wonder could you arrange for a taxi to be outside at eight o'clock?" Livinski fished in his pocket and pulled out some silver coins and pressed them into the waiter's hand.

"Thank you very much, Sir, I'll see the cab is there for you."

He left his room on the fourth floor and was in reception just before eight. The doorman called out that his taxi had arrived. The roads through to the City were empty and in just under ten minutes the taxi drove into the station, Livinski paid the driver and walked to the nearest booking office.

"I would like a return ticket to the nearest station to a village called Little Warley."

"Sorry, I don't know where that is."

"I am told it is in Essex."

"Most of our trains go to Essex but sorry I still don't know." Livinski stood there not moving. The booking clerk could see the man did not know what to do and continued, "Your best bet is to go to a library, they'll tell you, but of course they are not open today, it's Sunday."

Livinski appeared to wake up and smiled. "Thank you, I'll do as you say." By this time two people had fallen in behind him. He backed away allowing them to buy their tickets. What should he do? He had promised himself that he would make an early start in his search and on the first full day in England he had been thwarted. He had been told by the Army in Washington the name of the village where his son had got married and that this was in the county of Essex. An officer nearby having overheard the information being given to him interrupted.

"I couldn't help overhearing what you were just told. I was stationed in England for some time and happen to know that all Essex is served by the London and North Eastern Railway whose trains leave from Liverpool Street station. It is right in the City of London. I assume you will be staying in London?"

"Yes, I intend to."

"Well, you get yourself to Liverpool Street and I am sure the man you buy a ticket from in the booking hall will tell you which station you want."

Yes, the officer was right, the booking clerk had confirmed Liverpool Street did serve Essex, but obviously not all villages were known to booking clerks. 'I guess I was naïve to expect they would,' Livinski said to himself.

He pondered what next to do, perhaps he should ask some other traveller at random, or maybe just leave it until he could get to a library. At that moment his eye caught sight of a board nearby which read in big letters:

EXCURSION TODAY
CLACTON-on-SEA
A Day at the Sea for 5/-
Children Half Price
Train leaves at 8.30

Livinski looked at his watch, it was 8.20, the two people who had been behind him had bought their tickets so he was clear to walk up and speak to the booking clerk again. Thoughts raced through his mind as he walked up to the ticket desk, it had been many years since he had been to the seaside and nineteen years since he lost his granddaughter, it would surely not be so terrible to start the search for her tomorrow, why not take a day at the sea?

"Oh it's you again, found out where it is then?"

"No, I want a ticket for the excursion advertised just there." He pointed to the board that could be seen by the booking clerk.

"Oh decided to take a day at the sea instead. Don't blame you, it's going to be a lovely day. But you better hurry; it goes in a few minutes. That's five shillings. Go to platform 15."

Livinski handed over a pound note, grabbed the change, thanked the booking clerk and started off to where he could see platform 15. He got to the ticket barrier at just after twenty-five past eight.

"You have just three minutes to find a seat, so hurry along," the ticket collector urged. Livinski hurried down the platform and about halfway along he thought he saw a few empty seats. He climbed aboard and walked along the corridor to a compartment occupied by a man, a lady and two children, there were two empty seats. He hesitated before sliding the door. Supposing these people wanted to be alone or that they were saving seats for someone else?

The people inside the compartment were in fact the Davis family from the East End. Mr Davis, an engine driver on the railway, had seen posters advertising the excursion and had purchased the tickets the previous day at Stratford station, his depot. He knew that although the train would not be stopping at his station the tickets purchased would cover the cost of the short journey to and from the London terminus.

There had been great excitement that morning in the Davis household. Dad was only entitled to one week's paid holiday a year so extra outings to the seaside were special. Of course the Davis children were not alone in their parents only getting a short holiday each year, indeed they were more fortunate than many children living in their part of London as it was not unusual for the father's holiday to be unpaid when the factory or other place of work simply closed for a week. Many children they knew at school had never even seen the countryside or been to a seaside. Although Mr Davis often worked at weekends to earn more money he usually managed to take his children out on one day on those weekends that were free. Sometimes it was to the country, sometimes to the shops in the West End, and occasionally it was a trip to the seaside. John was proud to tell people he had even been taken to the Empire Exhibition at Wembley, although he was really too young to remember much of that, and he and his young sister had been on a number of train journeys, Mr Davis making use of the three free railway passes granted to him each year. Once or twice in most years they had spent a day at the seaside and once even stayed away from home one night in a bed and breakfast house.

Mrs Davis had early on that Sunday morning prepared sandwiches to be eaten on the sands and she had baked a fruitcake the evening before and cut off some slices to eat with a flask of tea, which they would take with them.

They had set off from home just after seven thirty in the morning to catch the seven fifty-five from Stratford which would get them up to Liverpool Street in time to catch the excursion due to leave at eight-thirty. It only took a few minutes to walk to the station, the weather was fine and everything promised to be a wonderful day at the seaside. The train arrived on time and soon they were on their way to the terminus stopping en route at two stations, Coburn Road and Bethnal Green, to pick up more people The Davis family arrived at the terminus with twenty-five minutes left to get across to the excursion train leaving on platform 15 close by.

Eileen, the younger of the two children, was obviously very excited and could not stop chattering, whilst her older brother remained calm although inwardly he too was thrilled at the idea of going on an express to see the sea again. Several other children carrying buckets and spades were making their way with their parents to the same train and Mr Davis told his party to hurry along or they might not get seats together. Passing the ticket collector, who greeted Mr Davis as a friend, they hurried on down the side of the train searching for an empty compartment, Eileen running ahead.

"Here's one," she shouted excitedly. The others soon came along and stepped up into the corridor and made their way to the empty compartment the young girl had found.

Trains at this time usually had first, second and third class compartments, but this one had been made up so that all seats were third class, which on main line trains in any event were generally quite comfortable having only three seats either side of a compartment next to a corridor running the whole length of the train. The two children, John and Eileen, took the two seats next to the big outside window, each parent sitting next to a child.

They had only just got seated when the sliding door to the corridor was pushed open.

"Are these seats taken?" the question came from Livinski, an elderly man with white hair, wearing an old green sports jacket, a white shirt and a green tie.

"No, they're free," Mr Davis answered.

"Thank you. I hope you don't mind me joining you?" he said in an accent which the Davis's recognised was definitely not English.

"Not at all, we expected the train would be crowded anyway – are you on your own?"

"Yes, I am quite alone. But I like trains, and of course the seaside, so I thought I would treat myself to the excursion as what I had originally come out to do did not work out. I thought that if I went back to my hotel there would be nothing much to do on a Sunday and there is, I am told, not much on the wireless, unless you are a churchgoer. This is my first excursion for a long time; in fact it is many years since I was last on a train for fun."

"We came last year," the young boy said. John had earlier that year had his fifteenth birthday and but for the fact he had won a scholarship to a Grammar school would have already been expected to have started work. He continued, "But the weather was nasty and it was no fun at the seaside was it, Dad? Do you remember when Mum's umbrella blew inside out?"

His dad smiled at his wife, "You were right, Jean, when you said I bet one of them will remember the umbrella."

"I should have guessed it would be John," Mrs Davis replied.

Many people were now passing along the platform and whistles were blowing accompanied by much slamming of doors. Then there was a slight jerk and the train started moving slowly forward. As they cleared the train on the next platform one could see right across to the far side of the station where other trains were waiting.

"It's a big station," Livinski remarked.

"Yes, it has eighteen platforms and there are at least eight or nine other big stations like this in London," John said.

"Show off," Eileen spoke for the first time since sitting.

"Well, I think it's good to know these things," the newcomer said. "London is so big and I do remember reading that there were so many railway companies last century wanting to build a terminus in this city that big stations were built everywhere. I doubt there is another city in the world that can boast so many big stations."

"My encyclopaedia says London is the biggest city in the world with a population of well over eight million, according to the 1931 census, and it is still growing," John added.

"New York is also growing fast too and they tell me in twenty years time it will be bigger than London, nevertheless it only has two big railway stations," Livinski said.

The train was now gathering speed, had passed Bethnal Green Junction and was fast heading back to Stratford.

"You'll see our house soon," Mr Davis said.

"I'm going to wave as we pass, I want Mandy next door to see me," Eileen said.

"There, there it is."

"My goodness that was fast, I wonder if she saw me?"

"Where do you live, Sir?" John asked.

"You shouldn't ask such questions, John, it's rude," his mother said.

"Oh that is quite all right I don't mind, I enjoy talking to people." He paused a moment as if thinking hard, "I come from America, I live in a state called New Hampshire – a part of America known as New England. But I am over here to try to find my granddaughter. I have only just arrived so haven't started my search yet."

"I thought I recognised your accent from films I have seen, but I was not sure."

"That is probably because I am originally from Europe and have not completely lost that additional accent."

"Where was it you were last on a train?"

"Oh that was in America but I have travelled on trains in Canada and years ago in Austria, Germany and Poland. I travelled a lot on trains at one time when I was young and on some very long journeys."

"Are you foreign?"

"You shouldn't ask the gentleman that, John," his mother said.

"That's quite all right, madam, I guess I still have another accent beneath my trans-Atlantic one. Yes I was born in the old Austro-Hungarian Empire, my parents were Polish, Cracow was the nearest big town. But when I was quite young I went with a friend of mine to America."

"Are you an American now?" John asked.

"Yes, I became an American citizen many years ago."

"I think you should stop questioning the gentleman and let him enjoy the journey."

"I really don't mind, the lad is interested, he seems a bright lad. Perhaps he could tell me something about where we are and where we are going. I only saw the poster advertising this excursion a few minutes before I bought my ticket and hurried to the platform, I don't even remember the destination, I just know it was to the seaside and as I had never seen a British seaside on the spur of the moment I thought I would go. Anyway, young man, where are we going and where are we now, I see we keep passing stations?"

John was only too pleased to tell the gentleman all about the journey and looking through the window as the train rushed through another station he said, "That was Forest Gate and the next one will be Manor Park – look up there above the seat opposite and you will see on that chart all the stations we will pass, of course they are all close together in the suburbs but once we get past Chadwell Heath they are more spread out."

"Yes, I see, but where are we going?"

"Clacton-on-Sea – there you are, right over there." The boy pointed to the extreme right of the framed diagram, which was next to two similar size glass frames showing pictures of towns or villages served by the London and North Eastern Railway.

"When do we expect to be there?"

"At this speed I should think we should be there in about another hour," Mr Davis said.

"You speak as if you know about trains, Mr er…"

"Davis is the name. Yes I should know I have been working on this line for the railway since before the war."

"My name is Livinski, Leon Livinski. What is your work on the railway, if you don't mind me asking?"

"Not at all, I am an engine driver."

"I know what you mean, we call them engineers in the States, I think the name the English use is more appropriate."

The conversation lapsed for a while until – "We just passed Chadwell Heath and now we will be going into the country," John said, "I like the country – do you, sir?"

"Yes, I do, I was born in the country and have spent much of my life away from large towns."

They were now passing many of the small fields typical of the English countryside at that time. Fields of wheat, cabbages, sugar beet, carrots, etc. some with sheep or cattle, others lying fallow or with tall grass, almost ready for cutting, to be used as animal feed the following year. Occasionally the train passed a farm and then the odd village next to a level crossing or a bridge.

"It is very pretty, just as I was told it would be."

"Have you checked the speed?" Mr Davis addressed his son.

"We're doing just over sixty."

"How did you know that?" Mr Livinski asked.

"I've been looking at the mileposts on the side of the line and checking with my watch. You can also do it by telegraph poles but it is not so accurate."

Three more stations were passed and then the train noticeably slowed.

"We are climbing Brentwood Bank," Mr Davis said.

"I take it that is a big incline?"

"Not particularly big, especially compared to what I have seen in pictures of America, it's only about three hundred feet high, but it is a big pull in a short distance for one engine with fourteen coaches, it only takes a few minutes, unless you stop like Mike O'Reilly did."

"That sounds like a story – tell us, Mr Davis."

"Well, Mike was driving the Boat Train to Harwich, the harbour where passengers board a ship to The Hook of Holland. Mike was a nice fellow but he had a strange way about him, they said he read a lot and it had been noticed by his fireman that in recent trips he had been becoming less talkative and would stay silent for long periods. Charlie Lavender, his fireman, that's the man who keeps the fire burning, said Mike was a good driver and a meticulous timekeeper. But on this day," Mr Davis paused as if thinking back, "let me see, it would now be five years ago, Charlie told me they had made good time to Brentwood Bank; they had fourteen coaches, ten of them the white or cream Pullman Cars, when suddenly Mike started to apply the brakes whilst going up the Bank. 'What's the trouble Mike?' Charlie said he asked. 'We can't go any further,' Mike replied, 'Why what's the matter?' 'There are Roman soldiers crossing the line up ahead.'"

"Roman soldiers?"

"Yes, poor old Mike really believed he could see them."

"What happened?"

"Charlie said he couldn't get Mike to move the train for some ten minutes, in which time the guard had made his way up through the corridors to the engine and climbed down onto the track to speak to the driver as he could see they had the road – that is what we say if the signals are down or green as with the new signalling. Charlie said Mike told the guard about the Roman soldiers. The guard clearly didn't know what to do but managed to say, 'Alright, Mike, let's get going now, they've crossed now.' At this Mike moved the train forward and he actually managed to complete the journey to Harwich on time, where of course the guard reported the incident – Charlie said Mike had not spoken since he restarted the train and nothing more was said about the Roman soldiers. 'I kept quiet until we reached Harwich and he made no further mention of the Romans.'"

"What happened then?"

"I'm not exactly sure, except I know Mike ended up in Brentwood."

"What is Brentwood?"

"Oh it's a mental hospital."

"Is he still there?"

"I don't really know, he hasn't come back to work so he probably is. It looks a nice place and I'm told they look after sick people very well."

John and his sister had listened with interest; Mrs Davis had heard it all before.

"How do we know he didn't see Roman soldiers?"

"Oh come on, John, this is 1937, the Romans left here over fifteen hundred years ago," his dad said.

"Some people claim to have seen ghosts and according to a teacher at school the Romans did a lot in Essex, he told us Colchester, not so far from here along this line, was their main Roman town for many years, I expect their soldiers marched all over Essex, they could easily have marched where the railway line is now."

"That is true but if they were ghosts the train could not have hurt them. Mike must have thought they were real. Anyway the medical people would not have put him away for just this one incident, they must have found out other things and realised he was a sick man," Mr Davis said.

"Do you think we will see any Romans when we get to Colchester?" Eileen asked.

"Shut up, Sis, we are having a serious conversation."

The train had reached the top of the hill and once again picked up speed as it rushed through Brentwood station.

"No Romans today!" Mr Livinski said with a smile.

Chapter 2

For the next ten minutes or so no further words were spoken, it was as if Mr Davis' story had caused each person to think and remain quiet. Even Mrs Davis who left school at thirteen had a Roman story. Her mind had wandered back to when she was young and out walking with her uncle near Waltham Abbey in Essex, and he had shown her the place where legend had it that Queen Boudicea took poison after fighting bravely against the Romans. Of course, young Eileen's knowledge of Romans was limited, but she remembered Ronnie Dickson being a Roman soldier in a school tableau with Jesus, and the story her father had told for a moment puzzled her, what were Romans doing in England, she thought, but she said nothing. Her brother's mind on the other hand had gone back to school, he liked stories of Rome but he did not like having to learn Latin. Livinski sat looking at the passing countryside and pondered over stories he had heard of psychic phenomena.

Mr Davis broke the silence, "Looks as if we are stopping at Chelmsford," he said.

The train had noticeably slowed as it rattled over points where the main line was joined by lines from sidings and was soon running alongside a platform and coming to a gentle stop. There were several people on the station platform but no one was attempting to board the train as if they had been forewarned not to.

"We were not scheduled to stop here, I expect the local was running late," he added.

"Or there are more Romans on the line?" John ventured.

"Who's being silly now," his sister replied.

14

Just then there was a slight jerk and the train started moving, gathering speed quite quickly as if the driver was trying to make up for lost time.

"When do we branch off the main line, Dad?" the young boy enquired.

"Soon after Colchester, the next big town, barely twenty miles from here, it is not long then to our destination." Mr Davis took his watch from his pocket, "We should be there by 9.45."

"How long before we have to return?" the stranger enquired.

"I think the train is due to leave at six o'clock – gives us quite a good day, usually long enough for me and quite long enough for young children after spending all day on the beach."

"Would you mind very much if I came along with you to the beach, assuming that is where you will be heading when we get to that place on the map. Sorry, I've already forgotten its name."

"Clacton-on-Sea; you will be very welcome to join us," Mrs Davis said.

"Thank you, I won't bother you once we get to the sea."

"You are welcome to stay with us if you like; it's not very nice being on your own."

"That is most kind of you, I accept your offer."

The twenty miles or so to Colchester was soon covered with the train, according to the boy, speeding for much of the time at nearly eighty miles an hour. The conversation in the carriage had lapsed and Mr Davis had closed his eyes. Outside the sun was shining brightly and the Essex countryside could not have looked better. As the train slowed and started rattling over points Mr Davis opened his eyes.

"We are scheduled to stop here for a few minutes and sometimes we change drivers, the local drivers being used for the runs to Clacton and Walton-on-the-Naze."

"What happens to our driver?"

"Well, if they do change, he and his fireman would take back to London either one of the trains coming from where we are going, or a mainline train coming say from Norwich, the Norwich driver and fireman returning to their depot by taking another one from London."

"Not a very long journey to change drivers – what about the mainline trains from Kings Cross to the north?" John said.

"I did say sometimes they change here, it can save a driver and fireman having to stay overnight at the end of their journey when they would then take another train back the following day. As for longer journeys the same thing happens, although on the non-stop run to Edinburgh by the Flying Scotsman the drivers and firemen are changed half way along by means of a corridor built in the engine tender."

"I never thought of that before, I suppose the same sort of changes are made on the long journeys in Canada and America, although I would think the business of a corridor in a tender is unique to your non-stop trains. That is most interesting."

The train stopped in the station and John went into the corridor to look out of a window and see if the drivers did change, he came back excited.

"I saw them change, you were right, Dad."

Very soon the train was on the move again.

"How much longer, Dad?" Eileen asked.

"Not much longer, about twenty minutes I would think."

In fact the train rolled into Clacton station at twenty to ten, and as soon as it stopped doors were opened all along the train and children and their parents poured onto the platform surging towards the exit, with the noise of spades and buckets hitting each other mixed with the voices of children and parents trying to control their excitement.

The Davis family were soon on the platform amongst the other families making their way to the exit, Mr Livinski followed close behind. The ticket collector was hardly looking at the half tickets being handed to him.

"Make sure you only give up half of your ticket, you'll need the other half for the return," Mrs Davis addressed the American.

Mr Davis handed his four tickets to the collector and the American followed.

"It's not far to the beach, the children know the way, anyway you just follow the crowd. It is certainly a fine day. The tea rooms won't be so happy, they like a shower or two as people usually rush for shelter and a cup of tea," Mrs Davis said. "I expect it's the same in America."

"I imagine it is, people are much the same all over, however, since I have never been on a day excursion to the sea I cannot speak with authority. This for me is a first."

Having passed a few shops and crossed one or two roads they saw the sea.

"It looks very calm, it'll be good for paddling." Again Mrs Davis spoke.

Sure enough as they came up to the sands there were many in the sea paddling, mostly children but also men with their trousers rolled up to the knees, some still wearing their jackets but most in shirt sleeves and braces – many still wearing a cap.

"It looks as if we will have to sit on the sand, I can't see any free deckchairs – do you mind sitting on the sand, Mr Livinski?"

"I'll do what you do."

They made their way onto the sand and found a vacant spot.

Eileen, who had brought a small bucket and spade with her, started to dig in the sand but John did not join in as he was conscious of the fact he was fifteen and in his mind an adult. The American, however, had no such inhibitions and got up to help the young lady.

"Come on, John, your sister needs a little help," the American said. John who really wanted to help got up off the sand and came over to give a hand, literally in fact, as he started digging with his hands. Soon they had made a good but small castle with a moat which they took turns in filling with water collected in the bucket, though it never stayed but gradually disappeared through the sand.

"Who would like an ice cream?" Mr Davis asked. There was a general chorus of 'me' or 'I would'.

"Let me get them, come along with me, young ones, we will bring them back for your parents." Mr Davis settled back on the sands and off went the American and the two children. Some five minutes later they came back just in time as far as the ice cream was concerned as it was already beginning to run down the sides of the cones.

After the ice cream, they sat back on the sands and talked until Mrs Davis started to unwrap the sandwiches and cake she had brought along. She passed a sandwich to the American.

"Thank you, I will take one as they look so nice but I do hope I am not depriving anyone. I'll take you all for a tea later – we passed what looked like a good café on the way down to the beach."

Everyone enjoyed their short break and as there was no wind they were able to eat what Mrs Davis had brought without having to eat sand as was often the case when eating sandwiches on the beach.

The day passed and the sun shone, and after everyone had had a paddle, including Mr Livinski, they decided it was time to leave the sands and find the tea room the American had mentioned. They found the café and were soon eating scones and jam followed by a large plate of fancy cakes.

Leaving the tea room at five thirty they made their way to the station. The train was in the platform ready to leave at six o'clock and with ten minutes to spare they boarded the train and found an empty compartment.

"That was a very enjoyable day, thank you so much for letting me join you, I have had a great time."

"So have we, we've enjoyed having you with us, I know the children have too, I'm sorry the day has to come to an end," Mrs Davis said.

"Well we still have the train journey, we must enjoy this too," the American added.

At six o'clock precisely and after the whistles had stopped and all doors were closed, the train moved slowly out of the station. It was not long before they were rolling in to Colchester where they stopped and a few people boarded the train.

"Do you think the train was scheduled to stop, Mr Davis?"

"I don't rightly know, I would think the driver had been told to stop before he left Clacton – there may be some problem up the line making it necessary to take on the people from this station. But I am surprised there was room for them."

"Dad, I thought the train looked longer when we got on, I think they had added a coach or two before we arrived."

"Oh I guess that is the answer. We should be clear now to London."

The train soon picked up speed and sailed through Chelmsford, hardly slowing at all.

"I like it when we rattle through stations," John said.

Ten minutes later and still going at the same speed the train was racing through another station with John looking hard outside to see if he could read the station name.

"It's going too fast, I couldn't read it," he said.

"That was Shenfield, son," Mr Davis said. "The next station will be Brentwood."

"Ah, and soon the famous Brentwood bank, am I not right? But this time we will be going downhill," the American said.

"Yes that is it, won't be long now before we are back in London."

He had hardly finished speaking when they flashed through another station.

"That's Brentwood that was," John laughingly said.

Suddenly there was a screech of brakes, the occupants of the compartment lurched forward or were pressed to the back of their seats as the train lost speed and some quarter of a mile further on came to a stop. Mr Davis, nearest the door, opened the window to look out.

"I can't see anything, the line looks clear, the driver must have suddenly got a red, he should have seen a yellow to warn him before entering Brentwood, must have missed it. The signals are on the other side, I'll go across to the corridor and look out there."

Mr Davis slid open the door to the corridor and walked down to the nearest door having a window he could open. Other people were looking out of windows all along the train. He came back to the compartment.

"The signal is green, I don't know what has happened but I expect we will be off any minute now."

But the train did not move.

"Strange, perhaps someone was on the line. It happens sometimes, people do sometimes get knocked down by trains, usually purposely."

"Oh, Bert, don't say that, it is horrible, I do hope that is not the reason the driver stopped," Mrs Davis said.

"Perhaps it is our Roman soldiers again, I hope it is, wouldn't it be exciting."

"Don't be ridiculous, John," his sister said.

Still the train did not move.

"I'm going along to see if I can find the guard, he'll be able to tell me what is happening." Mr Davis left the compartment and began walking to the rear of the train, about eight coaches back. He had gone through just one coach when he met the guard, who he knew, coming towards him.

"What's the problem, Sam?"

"No idea, Bert, I'm just going up to see what is happening." He passed Mr Davis and hurried forward. Mr Davis returned to his compartment.

"The guard does not know what has happened, he's just gone forward to find out."

"Have you ever been on a train that has stopped for no apparent reason?" John addressed the American.

"I can't say I have, although occasionally I have been shunted into a siding to let an important train pass. This usually happens if you are travelling on a stopping train on a main line used by expresses, or if you are on a single track. But the stops are generally very short."

John went over to the compartment window to look out.

"I can see a couple of men up near the engine but nothing else except other people poking their heads out of windows."

"Would anyone like a piece of cake, we didn't eat it all?"

"I would, Mrs Davis, it was so nice, I expect you baked it yourself. Nothing like home-baked cake. My wife used to cook one for us on a Sunday."

"There you are, I'm afraid it is a little broken, been shaken too much in my bag. Where is your wife?"

"Oh I'm afraid she died a few years ago, I'm on my own now."

"Oh I am so sorry for asking."

"This stop is most unusual, I wonder whether Sam has found out anything yet. He ought to come along and tell people what is happening."

"We're not the only ones on the train, Bert, I expect he is telling people right now and will soon get to us. We'll know soon enough."

She had hardly spoken when the door to the corridor slid open and there stood the guard.

"Hullo, Sam, what did you find out?"

"I can't tell you now, but Fred had to stop and it'll be some time before we can get away. He's a bit shook up."

"How long do you reckon, Sam?"

"Could be a couple of hours or more, sorry about that but there is nothing more I can do at present – the fireman is hurrying back to the station, it's about half a mile."

Sam pushed the door closed and carried on down the train telling people it would likely be quite a long stop.

"Two hours, or even more, what shall we do to pass the time?" Eileen asked.

"I know what I would like to do."

"What is that, young man?"

"I would be most interested for you to tell us about yourself – how you went to America and what happened. I think Mum and Dad would like it too, wouldn't you, Mum?"

"Yes that is a nice idea but perhaps Mr Livinski does not want to talk about it."

"I really don't mind but whether it would be interesting enough I don't know. Now let me see where do I start?"

Chapter 3

"Tell us what you remember of America. The guard told dad it could be at least two hours before the line is cleared, I'm sure we would all like to hear, wouldn't we?"

"Well, we are not going anywhere, so if the gentleman is of a mind to tell us I am sure we would all like to hear, particularly young John."

"Here then is my story."

My life was fairly unremarkable until my friend and I set out to emigrate to America. I will therefore start by telling you what it was like approaching our destination all those years ago. Try to imagine the excitement of passengers, mixed of course with apprehension, as our crowded ship neared the end of its journey on a date I well remember – the 4th of April 1893.

On that day, the SS *Dresden*, our weather-beaten single funnel steamer, slowly passed through the Verrazano Narrows and made its way up the Hudson River towards its final destination, New York. It was eighteen days out of London, having started its journey in Hamburg. Most of the passengers were hopeful immigrants travelling steerage below decks in cramped and unhealthy conditions. The remaining passengers, those the owners of the ship called first class, had had a more comfortable voyage but nevertheless were generally unhappy with the service they had received and at various times during the voyage had complained bitterly to the captain about the attitude of the crew and the poor accommodation with which they had been provided. Nevertheless their food had been satisfactory unlike us below decks who had to fend for ourselves on what we could scrounge.

All the steerage passengers had come aboard in Germany and the ship had left port on the evening of the 15th March. Two days later the vessel in thick fog, heading for London, picked up a pilot and edged carefully up the River Thames, finally docking next to where a new bridge, complete with Gothic towers on either side of the river, was being built, which you now know as Tower Bridge. A few first class passengers disembarked to be replaced by an equal number of new arrivals being waved aboard by friends and relatives on the dockside. The ship had sailed that evening, and two days later whilst south of Ireland we met the first of the bad weather that continued for the remainder of the voyage, averaging less than eight knots – which I am sure you know, John, is about ten miles an hour – indeed until we met calm waters outside New York. During the voyage we in steerage had entertained ourselves as best we could. Several passengers had brought their musical instruments and many a night there was dancing and general merrymaking which passed the time very well. Unfortunately there were of course some passengers who never really got their sea legs and were thus unable to join the fun.

However, the voyage was nearly at its end and as we slowly made our way up the Hudson River most of the first-class passengers on board, having just finished breakfast, had by this time occupied positions on the ship's rails to get a better view of the unusually tall buildings that occupied the New York skyline on what we learnt was Manhattan Island ahead. However, instead of sailing to the main docking area on the west side of Manhattan, the captain, guided by his New York pilot who had been picked up at the harbour entrance, was heading towards a small island close to the mainland on the west of the river. The engines almost stopped. Slowly the ship pulled alongside the wooden jetty, whilst ropes were thrown over to dockers on the shore who made sure the ship was properly held in position. Steerage passengers without American papers and some would be immigrants in first class were being told by megaphones to disembark and take their luggage with them.

Gangplanks were lowered and on shore customs officials directed us into a large building where we were told to join the many queues waiting to be seen by officials who would examine any papers we immigrants had and ask many questions. Such as, where do you come from and where do you intend going, have you a trade, what work do you expect to do, have you any money, what is your general health, etc. etc. It was obvious judging by the number of people in the hall that other ships had arrived before the SS *Dresden* whose crew were now making sure that all immigrants had disembarked. This completed, the ship untied and soon was making her way to dock further up the river on the west side of Manhattan where she would take on more passengers, coal and provisions ready for a return voyage to Europe.

I, Leon Livinski, and my friend Joseph Birkowski, carrying canvas bags slung over shoulder, joined one of the queues in the building. I was 24 years of age, six feet tall, with a somewhat freckled face and auburn hair, but I was told that to women I was a good looking young man. Joseph of the same age but slightly shorter, had dark hair and a tanned appearance gained from working on the land since leaving school. Our journey had started weeks before in the small town of Wieliczka in the Polish part of the Austro-Hungarian Empire, which no doubt you know is no longer there having been dismantled after the First World War. In early February we had said goodbye to our families and, armed with a few belongings and money saved over the past year, set off for our initial destination, Cracow, the nearest big town. My widowed mother had given me a necklace, which she sewed into my coat pocket and told me, "My grandmother was given this by a Polish Princess for whom she worked; I think she was a lady-in-waiting. It is very old and I believe it could be worth something. If you get into difficulty you may find the necklace could help you. I have no further use for it."

I thanked her and said I hoped I would see her again.

"Did you see her again?" interrupted John.

"No I am afraid I did not, she died in 1900."

"Oh, I'm sorry."

Anyway to save money, we walked rather than take the stagecoach, which left our village twice weekly. In Cracow we bought rail tickets to Berlin, which we were assured would take us all the way even though we would have to change trains several times on the way. Much of the rail journey was in Germany which, in spite of Bismarck's efforts to unify Germany in 1871, still had railways not yet fully integrated and in certain states, holding on to railway independence, trains were notoriously slow, particularly the section through Saxony. However, after spending two nights and a day on trains we arrived in Berlin. Here we found cheap lodgings and the following day found work doing odd jobs for a department store in the city centre. This we did for almost four weeks, earning sufficient to book a passage, without touching our savings, on the SS *Dresden* sailing from Hamburg to America. We travelled by train to Hamburg and joined the many other people seeking a new home in that country.

I could speak passable English, learnt while at university in Cracow, but my friend Joseph, who had had little schooling, only knew the little I had taught him since we had decided to go to America the previous year.

"You went to university? I have never met anyone before who went to university." John said, being obviously impressed. At this time in the thirties there only existed two universities in most young people's mind and these were Oxford and Cambridge, and they were there simply because of the annual boat race. At state schools, even those with grammar school status, a pupil going to a university was

very rare indeed, certainly as far as John's schooling was concerned no one had ever mentioned a university.

"Yes I went and I obtained a degree in Engineering and later studied Accountancy as I was told such a combination would be very rare."

"I believe our masters at school went to universities as they all wore black gowns, but they never mention any of us going."

"That's enough, John, questioning the gentleman, let him get on with his story, I am finding it very interesting," Mrs Davis, who had been looking out of the train window as if not listening, surprisingly said.

"Yes let me see, where was I. Ah I remember, I was telling you about us waiting to be seen in the immigration hall. I remember Joseph was getting very agitated."

He had vowed he would keep close to me when we disembarked.

"If we ever get out of this building, where do you think they will send us, Leon?" he asked.

"Don't worry, we'll get out and when we are passed I am sure they will tell us where to go. That custom official over there told me we are on Ellis Island and if we are allowed to enter the country we will be taken by ferry to either New York or to another town nearby, I think he called it, Joisey." I later learnt the town was called Jersey City but at that time I was unfamiliar with the New York accents.

Most of the many people crowding the hall, including us, were poorly dressed and many looked decidedly dirty, particularly those from the Dresden, who had not had proper washing facilities since leaving Hamburg over three weeks before. In this particular shipment the predominate language seemed to be German, with Polish and Russian coming a close second. There were, however, several interpreters on hand whilst some immigrants, hoping not to be rejected, tried hard to show the American officials they had acquired knowledge of the English language.

The building in which we were waiting was obviously quite new and I learnt from the customs official I talked to that it was only in the previous year that Ellis Island had been chosen as the point of entry for immigrants when the previous site had become overwhelmed with the numbers arriving. All the buildings on the island had been purpose built.

It was some two hours before we were seen and another hour before we were both finally given papers in the Registration Hall showing we were permitted to enter the country. We were shown where in the building we could change our money into American dollars and where we could buy rail tickets to take us to other destinations. We changed our money but decided not to buy rail tickets at that time even though we had previously decided we were unlikely to stay long in New York. After changing money we were directed to join another queue, waiting for the next ferry to arrive.

Whilst being processed we had sadly seen two or three people we recognised from boarding the ship in Hamburg taken from the hall and it was understood refused entry and would be sent back to Europe. However, we were told that the vast majority of people at this time were being accepted, often several thousand a day.

Joseph and I managed to get aboard the next ferry and were taken on the short trip across the river to New York, the ferry docking on the south of Manhattan in an area known as The Battery. On shore, awaiting each ferry, were people hopefully looking for friends or relatives who might have been aboard the latest ships to arrive, others touting for people to come and rent their accommodation or offering to exchange foreign currency for those who had not taken advantage of the facilities offered on Ellis Island.

"Here we are, what do we do now?" Joseph asked.

I suggested we get away from the mob near the shore and see if we could find someone to help us when we were away from the crowd.

We therefore made our way through the jostling people to a place where there were fewer people and where we could look around and consider the next move. Neither of us had a watch but according to a clock outside a building close to the open space around the ferry terminal, it was almost three o'clock in the afternoon. We had arrived on Ellis Island at just after nine that morning and by then most of the immigrants on SS *Dresden* would have been processed and New York's population that day would have increased by several hundreds, at least temporarily as many no doubt intended to move on to somewhere else. However, unless one had a definite destination or had relatives or friends to meet you the chances were, so we had been told, one would end up staying in the place you first landed.

"It looks as if we shall have quite a bit of time to find somewhere to stay before it gets dark," I remarked, pointing to the clock. "I think our priority should be to find somewhere to stay for the night, we can then decide what and where we go from here – we have a few hours of daylight left."

"Well then what should we do?"

"I suggest we get out onto a street and see what we can find. I read New York has had trolley cars running all over the city for many years." I thought it enough to say just this, as I thought Joseph might get a little fed up with me spouting my University knowledge. I could of course have said New York was the first city in the world to introduce 'street railways', that is trams pulled by horses, as far back as 1832, which I knew had recently been converted to electricity.

"Perhaps," I continued, "we should take ourselves to the end of one of the many lines and look for accommodation there. What do you think?"

"I go along with you," he replied.

We made to walk to the road on which we had just seen a trolley car go by when a young lady approached us looking as if she wanted to speak.

"Excuse me," she said in Polish, "are you looking for somewhere to stay?"

"Yes we are. How did you know we were Polish?" I asked.

"You obviously never noticed me on the *Dresden*, but I remember passing you on the lower deck once and heard you speak to your friend, I too am Polish."

"Now I remember, it was just after we left London, you were with another young lady, but I didn't see you again – is she with you?"

"Yes, she is over there. We have an address to go to and from what my friend said there are a number of Poles living in the building and they can usually find temporary accommodation for friends. Would you like to come along with us?"

"That is very nice of you to offer, my friend and I were just deciding where to go. How about it, Joseph, shall we go along with the ladies?" I said.

"Sounds good to me."

"Have you any idea how far away this place is – eh – Miss – what is your name?" I asked.

"I'm Tanya. My friend told us it would be easiest to try and get a carriage, not too expensive if there is more than one of you, better than struggling to find where to go, you can use the trolleys when you find your bearings, he said."

"Sounds good advice, where do we get a carriage?"

"Just over there, that is if there are any left after the first-class passengers have filled them. Let's see what we can find."

We walked over to where Tanya's friend was standing.

"This is Anna, and your names are?"

"I am Leon and my friend is Joseph."

Tanya a girl of about twenty years of age, some five foot three inches tall, had a dark complexion and black hair gathered together and pinned on the top of her head. She wore a long black coat, a white blouse buttoned to the neck and a large black brimmed hat. Her friend was similarly attired, both wore boots laced to above the ankles but Anna's hair was brown but seemed similarly gathered under her brown brimmed hat, she too looked about the same age and was slightly taller than Tanya.

"There's a carriage over there, I'll go and ask the driver how much to take us to the address I'll show him."

"You speak English then," Joseph said, "I wish I did."

"Yes I speak a little but you will soon learn. Anna is making good progress."

The driver of the carriage was standing next to his horse when Tanya approached him and showed him the address she had on a piece of paper.

"How much to take us four to that address?"

The man looked at the address and then at the four young people.

"That'll cost you a dollar."

Tanya looked at the others and repeated in Polish what the man had said. They nodded approval.

"I believe the trolley cars are only 5 cents but it will be worth the extra to get somewhere without having to worry," Tanya said.

We climbed up into the open carriage and seated ourselves, the men facing the two ladies. The driver seated himself and spoke gently to the horse and off we went. The afternoon was quite mild with the sun shining brightly as we wound our way through what the driver told us had become the financial district of the city, and then to the East River which we crossed by the tremendous Brooklyn Bridge, built, the driver informed us, in the last decade, which you will remember was the 1880s. The address we were heading for was in Brooklyn, 'near Prospect Park' Tanya's friend had told her.

The carriage continued on for another mile and then the driver, after turning off the main road, pulled up outside a large house, part of a terrace of houses, built probably since the War between the States.

"Did you learn anything about the American Civil War at school, John?"

"No, our history didn't cover that, but I have learnt something from films, but not much."

"One day I recommend you take a book out of the library, you will find it very interesting."

Anyway, the houses we had stopped at had four floors and a basement, the front doors being raised from the sidewalk by six steps. The driver had applied the brake to the carriage but the old horse seemed to want to go on further and jerked forward as we were getting out carrying our bags.

"Steady, old girl, I'll take you home soon," he said, then turning to his passengers, "I live a couple of blocks further on this way and I think she thought we were going home. That'll be one dollar."

We had already passed to Tanya our share of the fare and I had added a small tip for the driver, which I knew the stagecoach drivers back home always expected.

Tanya handed the fare over; the driver thanked us, wished us well in our new country, and left.

"This doesn't look too bad, better than I expected," Tanya said, "I better go and see if Kas is around – he could be at work."

She went up to the front door and knocked, we waited on the sidewalk with our bags. There was at first no reply. She knocked again and shortly a middle-aged lady opened the door.

"Yes, what is it?"

"Is Kas Poloschanski in? I am a friend."

"He don't live here no more. I think he gone up to Canada."

"Oh dear, he told me there were Polish people living here and that we might find somewhere to stay."

"You want rooms – I got two empty; two dollars a week in advance."

"I'll have to speak to my friends. Are there any Poles staying here?"

"I don't ask where they come from, long as they pay the rent."

Tanya called down to us on the sidewalk.

"My friend is not here but the lady has two rooms to let at two dollars a week. Are we interested?" Tanya said in Polish.

"We don't have much choice, the place seems alright and not too far from anywhere, I think we take them, but have a look at them first," Joseph said, the three of us nodded in agreement. Tanya turned to the lady, "I think my friends would like to take the rooms but they would like to have a look at them first."

"OK follow me, you can leave your bags in the hallway. The two rooms are on the third floor at the back of the house."

We heard what the lady said, so climbed the steps and followed as the lady made her way up the stairs to the third floor.

"There is a washstand and basin in each room and the John is at the end of the corridor. You provide your own bedclothes and there is a meter for the gas."

By this time they had reached the first of the rooms, the lady opening it with a key tied around her waist. The two girls walked in, neither said anything but just looked at each other. There was one small cane chair, a washstand with jug and basin and a double bed. A sash window with a thin cotton curtain overlooked further buildings quite close by. The second room was just the same as the first and the two men like the girls said nothing until they met up in the corridor.

"I suppose these will have to do," Anna said in Polish. "We haven't much choice – we ought to see if she can let us have some blankets."

"You bet she'll charge us for them. What do you say, do we tell her we'll have them?" Tanya asked.

"Yes we'll take them," I replied.

Tanya told the lady that we would take the rooms and asked if it were possible to borrow blankets.

"I can let you have blankets, I charge a nickel a night for each," she paused, "payable in advance."

"I seem to remember the currency people on Ellis Island telling us about nickels and dimes but I have forgotten which is which, do you know Tanya?" I said.

"A nickel is 5 cents and a dime 10."

"So that will be 35 cents a weeks for each blanket," I said in Polish so that Anna and Joseph knew what was going on.

"Again we have little choice, but if we stayed here long I expect it would be cheaper to buy our own. Shall Tanya tell her we will have a blanket each for the week?" Joseph said. We were all obviously in agreement and Tanya told the landlady.

"In total that will be three dollars and forty cents for the week. I'll give you the blankets and keys to the rooms when you pay me. Come down and I'll get them for you."

"Where do we get water for washing?"

"There is a tap at the end of each corridor, next to the John."

We walked down to the hall and between us raised the money to pay whilst the owner opened a locked cupboard under the stairs and took out the blankets. She fumbled with the keys taken from her apron pocket and somewhat embarrassed said, "I charge 50 cents for the keys, paid back when you return them to me. I lost too many not to charge."

I gave a knowing look to the others whilst delving in my pocket for the 50 cents which, when found, I handed over to the lady without saying anything, she in turn gave me the room keys plus two keys for the front door. We collected our bags and took them upstairs, the girls taking the first room at the head of the stairs.

It was now many hours since we had had anything to eat or drink and although no one had said anything, probably because each wanted not to waste time eating when the top priority was to find accommodation, now we were settled each suddenly seemed to become aware of the need for food and drink.

"I'm starved; we ought to have asked the old girl where we can get some food. Let's see if the girls have any ideas," Joseph said.

I let him know I was just as hungry and agreed we should go along and talk to the girls. We knocked on their room and Tanya opened the door.

"We thought it was time we ate. Have you any idea what we can do?"

"Yes, we were thinking the same thing. I suppose we can ask the lady where the nearest café or shops are, or maybe she can give us some food." smilingly adding, "at a charge!" We decided we would all go down after first freshening up and making use of the small room the lady had called the John.

Half an hour later the girls collected their coats and we four went down to see the lady who had retired to her rooms on the ground floor. We knocked on the most likely door and after a pause it was opened, but not by the lady, instead we were faced with a giant of a man who looked menacingly at us.

"Yeah?"

"I'm sorry we wanted the lady of the house," I said. "We've come to the wrong door."

"What do you want?"

"We were going to ask where we could get something to eat."

The man turned and yelled back into the room.

"Sadie, it's dem new guys, they want to know where to get something to eat."

"Tell 'em to go to Murphy's joint in the next block, I ain't got nothing to give 'em now."

"You heard the lady – take a left outside and at the next street you'll see some shops, you can't miss Murphy's." He closed the door.

"Phew I wouldn't like to meet him on a dark night. Do we all go to where he said? Or perhaps you prefer to go on your own," I asked.

"If you don't mind we would like to go along with you now my friend is no longer living here. I am sure Anna and I would feel safer going along with male companions, especially after seeing that man. We will of course pay for what we have."

I translated for Joseph's benefit and he looked pleased.

"Well come on then, off to Murphy's."

It was a short walk to the next street, I walked with Tanya and Anna with Joseph, the latter two talking all the time in Polish whilst we conversed in our best English.

"It is good that we talk in English, this is to be our new country," Tanya said. "Where did you learn to speak so well?" she asked.

"I was at Cracow University and I had an English friend whose father was a diplomat, a consul or something, I never really understood what he did. However, we shared a room together for two years, I taught him Polish and German and he taught me English. We had a fine old time together, especially when we went down to Vienna. How about you, where did you learn your English?"

"My mother was English but she died when I was quite young, but I was old enough to learn to speak to her, but of course if she had lived longer I would be quite fluent without an accent as I am sure I have now."

"You speak very well," I said.

"Ah I see Murphy's – across the road there." I pointed and we crossed over, Anna and Joseph followed happily talking away to each other.

"Let's go inside and see what they have to offer."

I pushed open the double doors and went inside, the others followed. It was now near to six o'clock and no doubt early to eat as the place was nearly empty. Five or six wooden tables and chairs looked lonely and the only customers were two men sitting at the bar. Murphy's was a pub. I walked across to the bar and addressed the man behind it who had been watching us as we came in, the other men seated turned quizzically.

"And what can I do for you?"

"We are looking for some food, what have you got?"

"I can recommend the Irish stew, made by my good lady's own fair hand – as good as you're get outside the Emerald Isle."

"I don't know what you mean but I think we are so hungry we could eat most anything. What do you say?" I asked turning to my friends. Tanya translated what she had heard the man say and it was agreed they would try this Irish stew.

The man called through an opening by the side of the mirror behind the bar, "Molly, we got four guests here who would like to sample your masterpiece," he said with a chuckle. "That'll be 80 cents. And would you be wanting something to drink?"

"What are we going to have to drink?" I asked at the same time, making as if to pour a drink to my mouth.

"Anything you like," Joseph said in Polish.

"How about you ladies?"

"Anna and I don't want alcohol but we would like coffee if they have it. You go ahead and have beer if you want to."

"A beer?" I looked at Joseph who raised his right thumb.

"Two beers and two coffees please."

"That'll be a buck, friend."

"What's a buck?"

"You must be new here, buddy. A buck is one dollar. Where are you from?"

"Yes we are new, arrived this morning. We are Polish, my friend and I are from Galicia."

"Where's Galicia?"

"Part of greater Austria."

"I thought they spoke German in Austria."

"It's our second language." Whilst they were talking the others had sat at one of the tables and the man behind the bar, who could be Murphy, poured the beer and called through for the two coffees. I took out a dollar and passed it to 'Murphy' and then carrying the two pints of beer seated myself with my friends.

"How much was all that?" Anna asked.

"It came to a dollar."

The young ladies fished in their handbags for some coins.

"Twenty-five cents each, that's right isn't it?" Anna said handing the money to me.

We four carried on talking in Polish until a young lady brought the coffee to the table.

"Two coffees, Ma's heating the stew – it won't be long. You new here?"

"Yes, arrived today."

"You going to stay around?"

I took it upon myself to answer the inquisitive young lady.

"For a time I think, we haven't decided what we will do."

"You gotta get away from here or you'll never leave. I know, I've seen it. I'm going when I get enough money."

"Where are you going?"

"I don't know – just want to get away." She started walking back to the kitchen, then turned, "Maybe out West."

Tanya translated for the benefit of Joseph and Anna. It certainly was not what we, the new arrivals, wanted to hear but it at once changed our conversation.

"Where do you plan to go?" Anna asked looking at the boys.

"We are not sure. I have worked on a farm all my life so I suppose that is all I can do.

I don't know too much about America but I know there must be many farms, Leon is the one who knows about places," Joseph said.

"What about you ladies, what do you want to do?" I asked.

Anna understood what I had said although I had spoken in English.

"Tanya told me her friend had warned her to be careful where she looked for work and try not to take work making clothes. He said that he had known women working in these places and they worked very long hours for very little pay, better to work in a shop. But until I can speak better English I could not work in a shop. What about you, Leon?"

"I am not sure. I am not keen to live in a city but since I thought I might work in an office, become an accountant or a lawyer or something, I suppose that is where I could end up, for that is where the work is. But I would like to travel before settling permanently, that's if I can scrape together enough money."

"We all have to find work quickly unless we already have enough money to take our time and decide what we want to do or where we want to go. Anna and I saved for a long while and have enough to last us a few weeks or get us away from New York."

Before either of us could reveal our financial status, the conversation was interrupted by the arrival of the stew, brought to them by the young waitress on a huge tray complete with four huge chunks of bread.

"Enjoy your meal, mind the plates they are very hot."

Hardly a word was spoken for the next ten minutes as the stew and bread were eaten.

The portions were very generous but the plates were cleared.

"I enjoyed that, it was very good," each uttered this or something similar.

The boys' glasses were not yet empty but the coffee had been drunk.

"Would you like another cup of coffee while we talk or do you ladies want to go back?" I asked.

"I would like another coffee and so would Tanya, wouldn't you?"

Tanya smiled, "It looks as if we want to stay. Now tell us what are your plans for the next few days?"

"We haven't got too many dollars but I have something I could sell that should give us funds to last a while longer, that is if we do not find work or decide to buy a rail ticket to somewhere else."

"Your 'something' sounds mysterious, but you need not tell us," Tanya said with a twinkle in her eye, "I like mysteries."

The four of us sat talking until after seven and when we decided to leave some of the other tables had been occupied by men who the waitress told us had just finished work at the engineering factory nearby. The noise level in the bar increased further as someone put a coin in the Pianola tucked in the corner. The man behind the bar was indeed Murphy, as the young waitress told us earlier, and he waved as we left and shouted something which none of us could quite understand.

"What did he say?" I asked.

"I couldn't hear – probably hoping to see us again, he was certainly being friendly," Tanya replied.

"Are we going back to the rooms or would you like to go anywhere, it is still early?" I asked in Polish.

"I would like to go somewhere but I am really very tired, it's been a long day and I'm looking forward to sleeping on a bed for a change, even if there is only one blanket, I'm going to have to say no this time," Anna spoke. "You go if you want to, Tanya."

"No I think you are right. Thank you both for escorting us to Murphy's – I enjoyed it very much, but I think I'll go back to the room."

"We'll walk along with you and we probably won't be long before we turn in too. What do you say, Leon?"

"OK, as we Americans say."

Chapter 4

FIRST DAYS IN BROOKLYN

It was still light when we reached the house but already the gas street lamps were being lit by a lamp lighter who passed by carrying the long pole used to switch on each lamp in turn.

"That reminds me, we will need some matches to light our lamp in the room – have you any we may borrow?" Tanya asked me.

Luckily both Joseph and I had some and so one box was handed over to the girls.

"You know how to light the gas don't you?" Joseph asked.

They assured him they did as Anna said her mother's house in Warsaw had similar lamps.

"Shall we see you tomorrow?" Joseph asked.

"Yes, if you would like to – we will have to find somewhere to get some breakfast. If I see the landlady I'll see if she gets breakfast for any of her guests – if not I suppose we will have to try Murphy's."

The girls said goodnight and went in the house. Joseph and I decided to go for a short walk back towards the Brooklyn Bridge. After walking a short distance we spotted a row of shops down a street we were about to cross so we turned to investigate. The shops numbered about ten and included a general store, where it looked as if one could buy almost anything, but of particular interest to us was a shop with the big facia board announcing Sam's Diner. Looking through the window we could see men sitting on high seats eating in front of a long counter.

"This is where we could try for breakfast tomorrow if the landlady does not serve it."

"Sounds good to me, but what are we going to do then? We have to start looking for work or plan where we go next, we cannot afford to stay where we are and do nothing."

"You're right, I suppose meeting up with the girls has thrown us a bit, it's been pleasant and too easy, we have got to make decisions. They are very nice but we must not lose sight of the fact they could become a distraction," I said, giving Joseph a knowing smile, "I noticed you being quite friendly with Anna – she seems a nice girl."

"All right, as a first step we talk to them tomorrow and let us see if they are staying in New York or are planning to move on. That young waitress was quick to tell us we should not stay around."

"Plenty of people have though, the place is growing fast."

We took one last look at the shops and returned to the house. As we passed the room occupied by the girls the door opened.

"We were listening out for you coming up the stairs. We thought we would tell you that the landlady cannot help us with breakfast so we will have to go out."

"Thanks, we think we have found a place that might be all right for breakfast –it's not far away. We'll show you if you like."

"That would be nice. What time would you be going?"

"How about eight o'clock? Oh I forgot we haven't got a watch."

"I have one, shall I knock on your door at say seven-thirty?"

"Tanya says she'll knock on our door at seven-thirty, that all right with you, Joseph?"

"That's fine."

Chapter 5

Tanya up bright and early the following morning had completed her ablutions before knocking on our door at about seven-thirty. Joseph was already out of bed and straightway went along to collect water from the tap at the end of the corridor. The tap was fixed to the wall over a small basin some two feet below where wastewater disappeared down a drain. At least there was only one other room on the floor besides the two we had rented so there would unlikely be much of a queue for the tap or lavatory. Washing in cold water was no fun and shaving was decidedly painful but we had become accustomed to this for the past few weeks so the shock was not so great, although we had hoped that when we reached land things would be different. Having washed and shaved we were pleased to be able to put on a clean shirt and underwear having decided to save these whilst on board ship, but what to do with the discarded dirty clothes was something we would have to deal with soon. The ladies were no doubt in a similar position.

It was past eight o'clock when we left our room and knocked on the ladies' door, which was opened almost at once.

"Are you ready, ladies?"

"Yes, just about. We are certainly ready for some breakfast."

"How did you sleep?" Joseph asked.

"I think we slept quite well although it did get a little cold at one time – that is until we got up and put our coats on the bed. How about you?"

"Much the same." The four of us walked down to the street door. "Shall we try the place Joseph and I found last evening?"

"Yes we are happy to come along with you, which way do we go?"

"This way."

It was a bright sunny day with hardly a cloud in the sky. Several people were on the sidewalks hurrying along whilst the road was busy with all types of carriages and other horse-drawn vehicles. We walked on, Joseph and Anna deep in conversation, until we came to the street where we had found the diner.

"There it is, just across the road. We have to sit up at a counter, let's see if they have room for four starving Polish Americans!" I led the way and we were able to sit four together at the counter and were soon drinking coffee and tucking in to fried eggs, bacon and sausages. Not much was said during the meal but on their second cups of coffee I thought it was time for us to decide what each wanted to do.

"We have paid to stay in the house for a week but of course we do not have to wait until the end of our week if we want to move on. Have you ladies thought what you will do next?"

"Well we talked about it in bed last night but came to no firm conclusion. If my friend had been here it would have been different, I suppose we would have stayed on, but now we feel unsettled. I would have liked to have found out where he went to and why."

"When was it you last heard from him?"

"Oh, it was last year, he wrote a letter to my big sister trying to get her to come out to America, it was she who gave me the details. She did not want to come over here and wasn't too keen on him anyway. She probably wrote and told him she wouldn't be coming. He would have had no idea I had decided to come."

"Perhaps one of the other tenants may have some idea where he has gone, might be worth asking if you want to find him."

"I am not really very bothered, but as he has been over here for at least three years he could have given me a better idea of where to go and what to do. I will as a matter of interest ask someone on the second floor who I heard speaking Polish, if they knew him or where he had gone. But I think Anna and I would listen to any good suggestions as to what to do."

"Joseph and I think we ought to get out of New York but where to go we are not sure. Joseph ideally would like to get away from big cities, as he can't think of what he could do to earn a living other than work in the countryside. I on the other hand probably need to find a reasonable size community in order to stand a chance of getting the type of work I think I could do. But I think although we are for getting away from New York we haven't yet got much idea where to go."

Anna had understood a little of what Tanya and I had said at the beginning but soon found it too difficult to keep up and instead turned to Joseph and told him what they were talking about.

"I guessed that was probably what they were talking about. It is important we decide what we are going to do. What would you like to do, Anna?"

"Ideally I would like to find a nice rich husband and not have to worry about finding a job," she said smiling, "but since that is most unlikely I suppose I will have to find any work that is going. I am going to try hard to improve my English and then I might be able to work in a shop. I am of course a skilled machinist – dressmaking I mean."

"Well at least you have that, I am sure you could soon find that sort of work in New York but I expect you would have to be careful what type of place you worked in. I only know about farming, I'm happy with cattle or horses, so I will have to leave the city."

"There are hundreds of horses in New York, I am sure there are plenty of jobs with horses – you could drive a carriage like the one we came down in," she said smiling.

"Not much use if I cannot speak English – I'll have to get some lessons or I won't get anywhere."

Turning to Tanya and me she asked, "Have you two come to any conclusions?"

"Nothing really, other than Leon and Joseph will probably leave New York, but to where they don't know."

"May I suggest that today we go over to Manhattan, find the main rail terminus, buy a map of America, then see what the fares are to various places, at least then we will be able to see where we could go," I said.

Tanya translated for the benefit of Anna and Joseph.

"That sounds a good idea, at least it might help us make our minds up," Anna replied.

We left the diner and walked to a main street we remembered crossing in the carriage where we had seen a trolley car, but instead of taking a ride we opted to walk towards the Brooklyn Bridge. It was another nice day and we four chatted as we walked, Tanya with I talking in English and Anna and Joseph mostly in Polish but with attempts now and again to speak in English. It took us about fifteen minutes to get to the bridge we had seen towering above buildings long before reaching it. At the bridge we found there was a powered cable car that could take us across. We stood watching it cross the bridge and a man standing near to us who must have seen our interest told us it had been in use since just after the bridge was built some ten years before. He said the cable car went from Sands Street in Brooklyn across to Park Row on Manhattan. We thanked him for the information but decided to walk across the bridge, save a few nickels and enjoy the sunshine.

Across the bridge Manhattan was busy, everyone walking seemed to be in a hurry as were the many carriages, trolley cars and heavily loaded carts pulled sometimes by four horses. We walked on, somewhat in awe at the size of the buildings and the sheer activity of everyone, and after walking north for some considerable time we managed to get a person to stop long enough to direct us to Central Station.

When we got to the station we immediately took the opportunity to rest on one of the many seats in the entrance hall.

"Well here we are, what do we do now? I wonder where we can best get information on the trains?" I said in English.

"There is a bookstall over there – that might be a good place to start, but I must rest my feet first, we have been walking for quite a while," Tanya replied.

I volunteered myself to go to the bookstall and looked along the display of papers and books but did not immediately see anything that might give details of train times and fares. For much of the time the two sales assistants were busy serving the endless stream of people entering this busy station, but at a suitable gap I asked one if they had a book on train times and fares.

"Try the booking hall," the assistant said, pointing to double doors at the end of the entrance hall.

I thanked her and made my way in the direction she had pointed. Through the open double doors I saw there were five cubby-holes in the wall at the far end where people were buying tickets and as soon as one became vacant I made my enquiries.

"You will find local time tables on the walls but if you are looking to travel farther then we have a few pamphlets giving some fares and special offers from various rail companies. Do you want to go farther?"

"Yes, sir, I do."

"I guess you are new here, just a minute I'll collect a few for you."

He returned with a small bundle of papers. "You might find what you are looking for amongst this lot." I thanked him and returned to my friends.

"This is what they gave me – at least there is plenty to look at." I shared the papers between the other three.

"It's all very well having all these papers but how much does anyone know of the geography of America?" Tanya said speaking in Polish.

"Shouldn't we get a map?" Joseph suggested, "I know Leon knows a lot about America but I for one would be wasting my time looking at the names of places on the pamphlets without the aid of a map – quite apart from the fact they are in English!" he laughed.

"I have an atlas in my case back at the house and I know that in there are two or three maps of North America, I think most of the main towns will be shown. So I suggest we take our papers with us and look at them together when we get back. We don't need to buy a map until we have decided where we think we are going, then see if we can get one of the area," Tanya said.

"That is an excellent idea. We can then perhaps decide what we all want to do and whether we stay together or go our separate ways," Anna added.

We all nodded agreement.

Anna had said something that she thought everyone had so far been avoiding. She had, I guessed, enjoyed being in the company of two men but must have reasoned she and Tanya hardly knew us or we them. They surely had their own ideas as to what they wanted to do, as indeed we had earlier thought we had.

"I don't think we should today venture any further north on Manhattan or we will find it too difficult to walk back. Shall we go back the way we came?" I asked.

"Yes, but let's go back on the other side of this road, if we can get across!"

We left the station and eventually crossed over the road, Joseph continued to walk with Anna, and I with Tanya. We talked a lot, looked enviously in several shop windows, marvelled at the crowds filling the sidewalks and strained our necks looking to the top of many buildings on our route.

When we arrived back across the river it was mid afternoon and we'd had nothing to eat or drink since leaving the diner earlier that morning.

"We had better get some food and drink, it has been a long day and I for one am tired and hungry," I said.

"How about we go to the same place as we had breakfast, I thought the food quite good. That's if I understood correctly what you said," Joseph said.

"There you are, Joseph, you are beginning to understand the new language."

"I guessed most of it from his facial expressions, particularly as I am feeling the same, as I expect you girls are too."

We made our way to the diner and ate and drank heartedly before walking back to the house.

"I feel like putting my feet up for half an hour before we have our talk. How about it, girls?" I asked.

"We feel the same, shall we say we meet at five o'clock in our room?" Tanya said.

We agreed.

In our room we talked about what we would say when we met the girls.

"How do you feel about allowing the girls to tag along, Joseph?"

"I was going to ask you how you felt but I would not have put it quite the same way, maybe they think we are tagging along with them. Are we?"

"You are of course right but I wasn't sure quite how to put it, I don't know whether you like their company. I get on well with Tanya but I would not want you to have to suffer Anna if you were not at all interested."

"I don't suffer Anna, I think she is a very nice person – yes I like her and her company."

"Well then that's settled, so at least for our part we are prepared to carry on our friendship and perhaps see whether we can find somewhere in this new country that suits all of us. Is that how we approach it?"

"Yes."

Both of us then lay back on our beds to rest.

Some time later Joseph woke me as I had fallen asleep.

"It's about time we went along to see the girls."

I found I was very tired and it was a while before I realised what I was next supposed to do.

"That walk took it out of me – I'll be alright in a minute," I said.

Five minutes later we walked along to the girls' room and knocked on the door.

"Come in."

"I fell asleep, how are you girls?"

"We feel better after resting for a while, but it was a long walk."

Tanya had opened her atlas on one of the beds and arranged some of the brochures alongside; the atlas was showing a map of the eastern United States and part of Canada.

"I see you have been looking at where to go," I said.

"Well hardly, but we have found out where one or two places mentioned on the brochures are located. I found this brochure by the Canadian Pacific Railway most interesting; it mentions so many places all over North America and indeed the world.

"Some places I had never heard of but between us we have found quite a few – we guessed how far they might be by the size of the fares quoted, all of which as you see are from Toronto in Canada. This I am sure will give us a good idea how much fares for similar distances might be from New York."

I hurriedly translated for the benefit of Joseph what Tanya had said.

"Give us an idea of what you have found, sounds interesting," Joseph said.

Tanya picked up the Summer Tours 1893 brochure and pointed to St John, New Brunswick, which showed a return fare of $35.00 from Toronto.

"I measured very roughly the distance from Toronto to St John, which I made about 700 miles, I reckon it is about 500 to Toronto from New York via a town called Buffalo – so the return fare to Toronto might be say $25.00 return."

I interrupted, "On that basis I reckon a single fare to Toronto might be $15 to $20, that is if it is anything like railway fares where we came from, the single fare never being half the return," I paused thinking, Tanya said nothing, I continued, "This is good, now we have some sort of a measure and at least will know where we cannot afford to go. Have you ladies any ideas?"

"Anna and I have decided that we do not want to go anywhere from which we could not return or at least move on because we had run out of money. So we don't want to spend all our money on train or stagecoach fares."

"Makes sense to me, now I would like someone to give me the options and at the same time I should like to be clear whether we are setting out as a party of four or whether we go our own ways," Joseph added. Each one understood what he meant and there was a lengthy pause whilst the other three waited for someone to speak.

I spoke first, and since I wanted to be sure everyone understood I spoke in Polish, "Let us list the possible ones when we have some idea how much each of us would be happy to spend, on say a train journey, bearing in mind what you girls have decided as prudent. I could afford to spend $50.00 and I believe Joseph would be able to spend the same – isn't that right, Joseph?" Joseph nodded agreement. "Now how about you girls?"

Tanya replied, again speaking in Polish, "I know Anna and I would be willing and able to spend the same."

"Now we have some idea, taking your Canadian Pacific yardstick, how far we might go from New York. I think we should take say two-thirds of the return fare as likely being the cost of a single fare. Do you agree?" I asked.

They all agreed and thought it might be possible to travel say anywhere between a 1000 and 1500 miles.

"That means we could easily go as far as Chicago and on the outer limits perhaps to the centre of Canada, say Winnipeg."

"Or we could go south."

"I do not particularly want extremes of weather; I think it might be too cold in the winter and too hot in the summer if we go to the middle of Canada," I remarked.

"Going south might make it more difficult to find employment," Anna said a friend had told her.

"Well what about north east of New York, this I remember learning at university was where the British established a big colony many years ago and was indeed where the war of independence started."

"I am afraid I am ignorant of the history," Anna admitted.

"So am I," Joseph added, "We will have to let Leon enlighten us, I know he has been studying it for some time – do you know anything about American history, Tanya?"

"Very little, but I am willing to learn if Leon would like to tell us."

"Now come on, I am not trying to show off my knowledge, such as it is. I enjoy learning about a place, of course it is not necessary but it might help to understand certain things," I said.

"We don't think you are showing off, Leon, it could be interesting, don't you agree, Tanya?" Anna said smiling with her friend, "Anyway where are these places you are talking about?"

I told them I was thinking that as people settled there two or more hundred years ago and fought to call it their own and are still there, it must be a good place to live. I went on to say that the biggest and most important town was Boston but of course there were many other towns and villages and that the whole was known as New England. I then pointed to the area on Tanya's map. I continued, "If we think it worth a try we must decide where we should head for and then think hard as to what we will do when we get there."

"Of course you are right," Tanya said, "but it is really no different from our situation on arriving in New York – we must have thought something about what we would do when we got here," she hesitated, "or perhaps we didn't. Perhaps we left it to chance, or in my case to the man I had expected to meet."

"She is right; I suppose we may have assumed things would just fall into place. We were on a big adventure and, having arrived, everything was bound to be all right. But of course things are not necessarily like that, we have to have some plan and act on it as best we can." Joseph, the one that maybe the girls had thought followed whatever I did, had shown he had a mind of his own. He continued, "We may find that the place we choose may not be suitable to all four and in that case we have to decide whether to split or find somewhere else. Leon and you ladies, I suggest, choose the place to head for as I really haven't a clue as to where to go, however, I am sure we will soon discover whether that town or the community will allow us to settle or whether some or all of us will have to move on. My only contribution is to say, you pick a medium size community, not a big metropolis, and then ideally seek accommodation on the outskirts, as I am sure it will be cheaper, but at the same time consider, on the assumption work is available, how we expect to travel to and from that work."

"Good old Joseph, that makes good sense!" I added, "Agreed girls?"

Both of them nodded agreement.

"Well then, where shall we head for?"

"Why don't we list a few of the towns that are shown on the map in fairly heavy print and then find a reference library and see if we can read about them. It may help us decide the right one." Anna said in Polish of course, "I have a notebook, now who is going to give me the first town?"

Over the next hour we listed five towns – Portland, Manchester, Albany, Springfield and Berlin. The last town was not in particularly heavy print but Joseph having spotted it reasoned that with that name surely some German people must have settled in that area and perhaps some still spoke the language, which of course was his second language.

"Now we should find this reference library and read up about these places," Tanya said. "I believe it is too late to find anywhere tonight, it must already be past six. I think we have to leave it until the morning. What do you think?"

"You are right, we leave it until after breakfast tomorrow. Now I suppose it is nearly time to eat again. Let's be adventurous and go round to Murphy's," I said.

This we did and spent nearly two hours in the bar before returning to our lodgings.

Chapter 6

The following morning Joseph and I were up and washed before we heard the girls making their way down the corridor. Joseph opened the door and called out to them.

"Shall we meet you down in the hall in say half an hour? On second thoughts could one of you knock on our door when you are ready, I forgot we haven't got a timepiece." The girls said they would.

Having met in the hall, we set off in the direction of the shops reasoning a library would likely be somewhere near that area. In the diner for breakfast we asked where the nearest library was situated and sure enough were told there was a small branch just two blocks away.

In the small library we were directed by one of the staff to the reference section housed in a small room at the rear. The assistant also showed us the two books in which we could find details on the towns we had listed. The first two towns in alphabetical order, Albany and Berlin, were in the first book whilst the others were in the second. Joseph and I looked at the first book whilst the two girls read the second. After ten minutes or so Tanya and I had read and translated to the others what it said about the towns chosen. Portland, in the state of Maine, seemed to be quite big but we thought it had a lot going for it as it was on the sea, which attracted us since until making our trans Atlantic crossing we had never seen the sea. Berlin we discovered was clearly the smallest of those chosen, it was in the state of New Hampshire and we read near to the White Mountains which seemed to be a popular destination for holidays. Manchester on the other

56

hand was listed as a growing industrial town after its namesake in England; it too was in New Hampshire. Albany was obviously very old having been a centre for the British in the early days of the colonies, it was the capital of New York State and therefore, we assumed, quite big. Springfield was the only one chosen in the state of Massachusetts but as the book did not have too much to say about this town we crossed it off the list.

The library assistant asked us as we were leaving if we had found what we wanted.

"Yes we have thank you but I am not sure we are any nearer deciding what to do."

"Perhaps I can help," she said.

"Well we are trying to decide where to go to settle and find work – we have decided that New York is not for us so thought we would have a look at what you call New England as finances will not allow us to go too far."

"That sounds good to me, some parts of the country there are very nice, I went up there once to visit an old aunt of mine, who lived right amongst the White Mountains in New Hampshire. I would love to have stayed and made a home there but I think it would not have been easy to find a job as librarian at that time in the area she lived. The White Mountains are very popular for holidays for wealthy people from New York, Boston and Philadelphia, particularly in the summer when it gets hot in the cities. I believe there are lots of grand hotels. I am sure there ought to be work there even if it is mainly in the summer. It is not difficult to get to as there seemed to be plenty of trains to the station where my aunt met me, I was surprised. I really think it might be worth a try."

Leon quickly translated the gist of what the lady had said so that Joseph and Anna knew what was going on.

"Why don't you have a look at the job adverts in the papers over in the reference section, you will find employment adverts in all the papers, it'll give you an idea where work might be found out of town."

"Sounds a good idea – what do you say Tanya?" I asked.

Having explained to Joseph and Anna, we all returned to the room at the back of the library and sat down to look at the papers displayed in the big centre table. The employment ads covered two or three pages in each of the papers, there certainly did not seem to be a shortage of work in New York, but those away from the city and its suburbs were far fewer. We spent half an hour looking and were just about to leave when Tanya spotted the words White Mountains.

"Just a minute here is an advertisement for something in the White Mountains. I haven't read it yet. Ah here it is, it is from a hotel, 'The Wentworth Hotel, Jackson, New Hampshire'. They want additional staff for summer work. It says telegraph enquiries to Wentworth Hotel care of North Conway Rail Station. Shall I take a note of the address?"

"I know nothing of hotel work, let's see what the others think." I was not very keen but thought it fair to ask Joseph and Anna, so we told them in Polish what Tanya had read.

"Hotels probably have horses and carriages so I might find work with such a place."

Joseph said, "What about you, Anna?"

"I suppose I could be useful in a kitchen, or as a seamstress, or even a maid. Would you think it worth trying, Tanya?"

"I have never thought about working in a hotel but I suppose there maybe something I could do. My mother always used to say I was a good cook. It could be worth finding out more." Then turning to me she said, "What about you, doesn't sound like your kind of work?"

I told them I would not wish to spoil anyone's opportunity and then laughingly added that in any case they might want me for an hotel manager.

"Well then I vote we send a telegraph and find out whether there is anything for us," Tanya said.

Before leaving we waited to speak to the librarian, she saw us standing by the counter and came over.

"We have found something that might be worth following up, can you direct us to the nearest telegraph office."

"I am glad you have found something, where is it?"

"It is in an hotel in the White Mountains."

"Well that is a coincidence. I hope you are not disappointed after me making the area sound so good. Anyway, the Telegraph Office is just a short way along on the other side of the street; you'll see the sign Western Union. I wish you luck."

We left the library and made our way towards the Western Union office.

"We have to think of what to ask them to send, any ideas?" I asked.

"I think that first we tell them we are two hard working men and two equally hard working women newly arrived from Europe seeking work. The women can cook and sew, the men, one a countryman can handle horses, the other a university graduate is prepared to try his hand at most anything," Tanya said.

"Those ideas are excellent but we will have to be shorter and crisp when sending a message."

We came up to the telegraph office and crossed the road. Joseph pushed open the door of the office and allowed the ladies to enter before him.

I went over and addressed the clerk who was sitting behind a glass partition, his hand moving rapidly on a Morse key. He was in shirtsleeves with two sparkling armbands and a green shade over his eyes. He suddenly stopped and without looking up spoke, "Yes?" he enquired.

"We want to send a message to a rail station in New Hampshire, could you let us have a piece of paper to write down what we want to say?"

"You tell me and I can write it."

"We haven't got what we want to say quite right yet – it would be helpful if you could let us have a piece of paper and lend us a pencil."

The clerk tore a piece from the pad in front of him and handed me a pencil.

I thanked him and turning to the others, "Now let us see if we can summarize what Tanya said."

I wrote the address copied from the newspaper at the top and followed with 'Four hardworking young people (two female) newly arrived from Europe seek work. Skills include cooking, sewing, gardening, cleaning, skiing and experience with animals and horses.' I then translated it for the benefit of Joseph and Anna.

"What do you think?"

"Sounds impressive, but why skiing? Who knows how to ski?" Anna asked.

"I do a little. Well it is a holiday hotel and I can't imagine that wealthy Americans haven't yet caught on to Alpine skiing. I would be pretty certain that at these latitudes where there are mountains there will be snow in winter. My English friend at university took me to Switzerland one winter and I learnt to ski – it is great fun," I replied.

"OK, then we include skiing – sounds good anyway. I say send it as Leon has written. Agreed?" Anna said.

There was general assent and I handed the note to the clerk who looked at it and said, "That'll be a dollar."

I fished in my pocket and handed over the money.

"I assume you want them to reply here? In which case I need a name."

I told him to sign it Leon.

"When do you think we should get a reply?"

"Come and see me tomorrow, you could be lucky."

Chapter 7

THE OPPORTUNITY

Having made the decision to find out about the vacancies in the White Mountains we were naturally anxious to get a reply.

"Is there anything else we ought to do?" Tanya asked.

"I suppose we ought to assume we get a favourable reply and in which case it would be useful to know the fare to this place and a little about the time it takes to get there."

"So you think it would be a good idea to go again to the central rail station?" Tanya asked.

"Yes, it will at least give us something to do today, we could try going a different way," I said and then in Polish to Anna and Joseph, "Do you all want to walk over to Manhattan and see what the fare is to this place and the time of trains?"

"I am game – how about you, Anna?"

"Yes I would think that a sensible idea, but let us go a different way, if we can."

"Leon has just suggested that," Tanya said.

"Right then we are all agreed, let's go."

The walk to the rail station was much the same as before, the streets were just as crowded and crossing the road was hazardous although many of the crossings had new electrical arms telling you to stop or go. At the station they left me to make the enquiries. I was told that the main route was via Boston and then to transfer on to the Boston and Maine Railway, which would take us to North Conway via Portland. I learnt that the fastest train to Boston was The New England Limited, taking six hours to cover the 230 miles and that the remaining 200 or so miles would take a little longer, since that train would stop several times en route. The single fare was fifteen dollars, the return twenty-two.

I relayed the information to the others who were sitting talking in the main station hall.

"I suppose the fare is about what was to be expected, but if we do go we must decide whether to buy a single or return, the return ticket I understand lasts one month," I told them.

"We'll have to wait to see what the hotel says, if they do reply. The journey takes longer than I expected, it doesn't look that far on my map back in the house," Tanya said.

I interrupted her, "Oh, I forgot to mention the fare I was quoted included an extra dollar for travelling on the New England Limited, which I am told is a crack train where, if you want to spend the money, one can get a four-course meal for 75 cents."

Tanya translated this in Polish.

"I think we will take sandwiches," Joseph said smiling.

Walking round one of the back streets on returning to the bridge we found another diner similar to the one in Brooklyn and so we had a midday meal. The afternoon was bright and sunny and we spent time, and a lot of energy, looking around south Manhattan, returning to our lodging tired out in the early evening. Later, when we had recovered, we once again went round for a meal and drinks in Murphy's bar.

Once again Murphy's stew was the favourite and the waitress who had advised us not to stay in New York asked us whether we had thought any more about what we were going to do. Tanya told her about the possibility of a job in the White Mountains.

"Oh the White Mountains, I've heard about them, a rich gentleman came in here one night and told me, they're up north somewhere, he said, and very beautiful. I have never seen a mountain; well not that I remember, mam tells me there are mountains in Ireland, but we left when I was only a babe. But I shall see some one day, I hope."

The few words spoken by the waitress approving, through her gentleman friend, their proposed destination made Tanya hope they would get a favourable reply to their telegram.

"It's good to know a stranger approves of where we might be going, don't you think?"

I smiled in agreement and translated for the benefit of the others.

"Let us hope we get a reply or I can see we are going to be disappointed."

We spent an enjoyable evening eating, drinking and listening to music and even joining in the singing when a fellow customer on the next table taught us some words in one of the songs.

The following morning we made our way to the diner for breakfast and then went on to Western Union. On entering the office we saw the same clerk seated, as on the previous day, behind the glass partition, wearing the same shirt and armbands as if he had not moved from the previous day. Two other people were waiting to speak to him so it was some five minutes before he was free.

Eventually I addressed him, "Have you by chance a message for Leon?"

The clerk looked up, "I remember, you are the man applying for work in New Hampshire. I wouldn't mind going up there myself but got four kids at school. Anyway you have a reply, it came through last evening, my colleague took it down." He shuffled through some papers, "Ah, here it is."

I thanked him and took the piece of paper across to my friends all anxious to know what it said.

I read it out loud and Tanya translated it for Anna and Joseph.

'Have several vacancies, recruiting now. Will provide board and lodging for two nights whilst you and we decide

63

whether The Wentworth is place for you. On arrival North Conway hand this note to Station Master to call for carriage. The Wentworth Hotel, Jackson, N.H.'

"Well it looks as if we have a chance. Now we have the offer we must decide whether we go through with it. Are we still of the same mind?" I asked, and Tanya translated the question. They all nodded in agreement.

"Now I guess we had better get the tickets and decide when to go."

Chapter 8

SHALL WE GO?

It was decided that since I had volunteered I be allowed to take the long walk to buy the tickets and if necessary book seats on the New England Limited for the following morning. We had decided over a cup of coffee at a nearby diner that they would gamble on getting the work in New Hampshire and thus only buy single tickets. Since each of us carried all our money on our persons I was able to collect the contribution from each before leaving.

"You trust me with all this money?" I said laughing, "I reckon I could get to California and still have some to spare. Anyway I am off now, I will see you in Murphy's about one o'clock."

I strode off in the direction of the Brooklyn Bridge whilst the others walked towards the nearby park with the intention of looking at the spring flowers and perhaps sitting on the grass.

I bought the tickets and found that I did not have to book seats as the journey was on a Thursday. The booking clerk was very friendly and asked what were we going all the way up to North Conway to do. I explained what we hoped to do.

"What time does the train leave?"

"It leaves at 8.30 but the gates open ten minutes before so it is worth getting here early to join the line and get a good seat. Best of luck to you, bud."

It was near one o'clock when I finally arrived back in Brooklyn and straightway made my way to Murphy's saloon arriving just after my friends who were already seated.

"Here you are – one ticket each to North Conway, I decided California was not for me."

"Did you book seats?"

"No, apparently there are not so many people travelling on a Thursday so the booking clerk did not think it worth it. He did say that in order to get a good seat we should arrive early; the train leaves at 8.30."

"We had better tell our host we are off tomorrow early and give back the keys. Do you think we should order a carriage, it is much too far to walk with baggage, don't you think?" Tanya said.

"I agree, if we can get a carriage, and it is not going to cost the earth, we had better order one, after all we have saved something on not having to book seats on the train."

Joseph suggested they enquire, whilst in Murphy's, how to organise transport for the morning.

They asked the young waitress if she knew anyone who knew about organising transport, as they had to go to Central station in the morning.

"You are going away? Good for you, tell me all about it after I've had a word with Mike, he'll sure to know the best way to get there."

Mike Murphy came over to speak to them.

"I understand you want to get to Central station tomorrow morning. At what time?"

"We would like to get there very soon after eight."

"I tink your best bet is to get a lift to Manhattan and then get a trolley car the rest of the way, otherwise you'll be paying too much. Providing you are staying near here I can arrange to get you over the other side of the Brooklyn Bridge – that's if you don't mind riding in a milk cart and haven't too much luggage."

"We are near here, we are staying just along the road at number 675."

"Oh I know the place, she has been taking people in for years, charges for everything I hear. How about your luggage, I don't expect you got much, have you?"

"No we have very little luggage, but how can you manage to take us?"

"I have a milk float and my man finishes his morning round before seven. I could get him to pick you up just before seven. You should then have plenty of time to get a trolley car up to Central station before eight."

"How much will that be?" Leon asked.

"This one is on the house, but of course you can give the driver something. The very best of luck to you all."

"Thank you so much, Sir, that is very kind of you, we are overwhelmed and you make me feel sorry that we are leaving Murphy's behind."

"Ah, tink nothing of it, I remember what it was like when I first came over here."

We spent an hour or so eating and drinking, thanked Murphy again when we left and said we would call in this evening for a meal and confirm his man would be coming for us in the morning.

On returning to our lodging we informed the proprietor we would be leaving early in the morning.

"Don't forget to hand in your keys, just knock on the door, I'll be up."

That afternoon I asked Tanya if she would like to take a walk with me over the nearby park we had passed when walking to the bridge. She asked Anna if she minded and found that Joseph had also suggested a small shopping trip with him. Apart from when I went to Central station on my own, this was the first time the four of us had separated since arriving in New York.

"We'll meet up at Murphy's at six this evening?" Tanya asked.

"OK, as Americans say, I'm sure Joseph will agree."

We found there were very few people in the park and the only sound was from the many birds in the trees and from our own footsteps on the gravel path as we walked slowly down towards a small lake we could see in the distance. The park was obviously well maintained with many well-manicured lawns and beds of spring flowers in full bloom. The sun shone in an almost cloudless sky and to us everything was beautiful.

"It is so peaceful here, I think this is the best I have felt since I left home, one could so easily imagine being far into the country and yet we are so near to a large city. What do you think, Leon?"

"Yes, I was thinking much the same myself – it reminded me of walking to a farm near my village when as a boy I used to go there to help with the haymaking – not spring of course, but cloudless skies and so much silence."

"Are you looking forward to seeing the place we are going?"

I told her I was but that I was a little apprehensive as to what sort of work the hotel might find for me to do.

By the lake there were two or three seats and Tanya and I sat on one by the water's edge. We continued talking and must have sat there for nearly an hour. I learnt she had once had a boyfriend in her home town but he had gone in the army and never kept in touch with her. She told me too, that her friend Anna had said she liked Joseph, I said it did not surprise me as it was easy to see from the way they walked and talked that they were quite happy together.

"That just leaves us," I said. Tanya smiled and said she hoped I liked her.

"You must know I do, or why would I ask you to walk with me in the park."

She looked pleased and on our walk back she held my arm.

We all met at Murphy's at six o'clock as arranged and during our meal Murphy confirmed that his man would be at our lodging just before seven the next morning. Before we left we thanked him again. It was quite late that evening before we walked back to the house and as it was important we were ready early next morning I asked the girls to give a good knock on our door when their alarm woke them up, which they did.

The next morning we were all washed and dressed well before seven and met downstairs in the hall carrying our belongings and the blankets we had hired.

The lady of the house had opened her door as she heard us coming down the stairs. We handed over the blankets and returned the keys and I collected my 50 cents, but it came as no surprise that no offer was made for return of rent since we had paid for a full week.

As promised the milk float was outside when the landlady opened the door, it was five to seven. The milkman was a big man dressed in a black jacket, a peaked cap and blue and white striped apron.

"Here, ladies, you climb aboard here, I'll take your bags. Stand close to that churn and leave room for your two friends. That's right. Now you two, you'll have to squeeze up a bit or there won't be room for me. By the way my name is Sean, but everyone calls me Paddy. I'm afraid we will have to go slow all the way or else the old horse will soon get tired, he's not used to carrying such a load."

Once we were all settled Paddy urged the horse forward and we moved off.

"Mike tells me you're going up north somewheres. I never been further than Yonkers since I came here twenty years ago, but one day I tell Molly – that's my wife – we will have a holiday and perhaps see a little of the country. I never went far in the old country, until I came here, I suppose I am not the travelling kind. Where you folks from?"

I told him where we were from and where we were going.

"The White Mountains, sounds as if it could be cold up there, but I guess that is in the winter, you should be alright at this time."

It was fortunately level ground to the bridge as the horse seemed to be struggling a little after the driver had to pull up at a crossing. There were already a number of carts and carriages crossing the bridge, all seeming to be in a hurry but Paddy kept the horse at a steady fast walking pace much to the annoyance of many drivers forced to overtake in the already crowded highway. It was twenty past seven when we finally were over the bridge.

"This is where you get off, you can get a trolley car over there."

We thanked him for the ride and gave him a dollar which we had previously agreed would be the tip. He helped us off the platform at the rear and wished us luck. We joined a line of people at the trolley car stop along the road but it was the third one to arrive before there was room for us.

"Does this car go to Central station?" I asked a man in the line.

"Yeah, I think so," he said.

We boarded and the conductor confirmed we were on the right one. We arrived at the station before a quarter to eight, in good time to get our train, which we found was leaving from track nine, the gates to the platform below opening at eight o'clock. As we had not had any breakfast we walked over to the snack bar across the hall where we bought sandwiches, some to eat as soon as we were settled in the train and others to keep us fed during the rest of the journey to Boston, we also each quickly swallowed a cup of coffee before making our way down to the gate where people were already in line. At eight precisely the gate was opened and we hurried down to the train. Several of the coaches were reserved but we soon found the unreserved ones and boarded. The coach had tables on both sides with four seats to each table, we were the first in the coach and chose a table half way along as Joseph and I remembered from our journey in Europe that sitting over the wheels at the end was less comfortable. It did not take long for the coach to almost fill up and very soon the conductor was calling out 'All aboard'. As far as I could see before boarding there were at least fourteen coaches and a very big engine up front, and at half past eight the train slowly moved from the station and entered a tunnel.

"We have six hours now to Boston, it would be nice to know the route the train takes – can you get your atlas out, Tanya, so we can see?"

"I don't think it will be of much help as the scale is too small, anyway I'll get it."

Tanya produced her atlas and we could see that the distance from New York to Boston represented less than two inches on the map and thus only one or two intervening towns were shown, but at least it would give us an idea where we were if we stopped on the way.

We were very soon running through the New York suburbs and then out into the country, at first much like the countryside we are now going through. I suppose the train was going along at something near the speed of this train but I seem to remember the coaches swayed more than the ones we are now riding in. Although the sound of the train was different for a good part of the journey from the rhythm we now hear.

"What do you mean?" John asked.

"Well I didn't know at the time but it seems quite a bit of the track had been welded whereas the track we are now running on has not and therefore instead of a continuous rhythm we get di di di dah as the wheels cross the joins in the line."

"I wonder if the LNER will ever weld rails – I hope they don't, I would miss the di di di dah," John added.

Leon continued his story.

Our journey to Boston was really quite uneventful, the train stopped twice, I think, one station I remember was New Haven but I cannot remember the other.

Shortly after two o'clock the train slowed and started running through a built-up area which we guessed must be the suburbs of Boston and just before two thirty it glided into Boston station and came to a halt. Joseph had fallen asleep in the last half an hour and looked so peaceful.

"We better not leave him," I said, "But it does seem a pity to wake him."

Anna shook his shoulder, "Come on, Joseph, we are here."

Joseph sleepily opened his eyes and looked around, "I was having a lovely dream – I suppose we are in Boston?"

"Make sure we leave nothing behind," one of us said as we left our seats. On the platform most people seemed to know where they were going and so we followed the crowd. We found a station official at the barrier and asked him where we would get the train to North Conway.

"The Portland and Maine platforms are over there, you'll have to ask again." He pointed to the far side of the station. However, we were in for a bit of a shock as we were told the next through train to North Conway would not be until eight o'clock the following morning. We learnt that the journey would take nearly eight hours.

"What do we do now, any suggestions?" I said.

"Well we can at least have a look at Boston, but of course we will have to decide what to do tonight. We either have to find a place to stay in the town or we ask the station officials if the station stays open all night," Tanya replied. The last conversation had been in Polish so that Anna and Joseph understood what was going on.

"It might not be easy to find accommodation for one night unless we went to a hotel and that will cost us more than I am sure we would want to spend. I think we should see if we can stay at the station, it is going to be uncomfortable but I think we have little choice," Joseph said.

We agreed this was the best option and sought out an official to see what the situation was as regards the station remaining open.

"Officially the station will close after the last train arrives just after midnight and reopens in time for the first train to leave at six. However, although all lights will be turned off when the last train is in, the waiting room over there is not locked and I guess you could stay in there, but don't say I said so. I go off duty after the last train and lock the main entrance which remains closed until about five thirty when a colleague of mine comes on to work. After he arrives I suggest you stay where you are until you see other passengers arriving, in that way he will probably not know you are there."

We thanked him and said we would be going out for a few hours and would return later.

It was now just after three in the afternoon and the weather was fortunately still fine and sunny. We had not expected to have time in Boston and except that I had once by chance read about certain events leading up to the war which gave America her independence and remembered reading of the Boston tea party, none of us knew anything about the city. As we stood outside the station wondering which way to go I told them that I believed Boston had been a very important city at the time America gained independence from England, and that this being so there were likely places of historical interest to visit.

"That's all very well but we do not know where or what to see. What do you suggest we do?" Joseph said.

"I am easy," I said, "I mercly mentioned it because that is all I know of the city."

"If there is anything worth seeing then surely we can find out from someone where to go. Why don't we ask one of the carriage drivers over there?" Tanya said.

"Before we do, and just in case we get carried away with a visit to somewhere, we perhaps ought to decide if we want to spend money on seeing something of Boston, and if so how much," Anna said.

"Sensible thinking," I said, "I am happy to go along with what you all decide. For my part I reckon I can spare a couple of dollars for food and anything else that might help us pass the afternoon, but I would be pleased to spend less."

The others indicated that they would be prepared to spend the same.

As when they first met in New York it was Tanya who volunteered to speak to one of the carriage drivers. She came back all excited.

"The driver says there are many places to go and see. It seems that many Americans and people from Europe spend time in the city visiting places of historical interest. He says he will take us on two-hour tour for three dollars – that'll be 75 cents each and he will take us afterwards to a diner where we can eat cheaply with only a short walk back to the station. What do you say?"

We all agreed to spend the 75 cents, particularly as we had no idea how else to spend the next few hours.

The tour turned out to be most interesting and we all learnt something of the Revolution which, apart from my chance reading, was all that any of us knew of what happened in the late eighteenth century. We were shown where citizens first fought the British in Lexington and Concord in the year 1776 and I was pleased also to be shown where the Boston tea party took place – this was a demonstration against a tax imposed on tea when a hundred or more citizens dressed up as Indians tipped cases of tea from ships into the sea. The driver appeared to be very knowledgeable and we all learnt a little of the War of

Independence and also how Boston was the first big British city to be built in America. We arrived at the diner about six that evening and made our meal last as long as possible before walking slowly back towards the station. Shops were still open and we spent time window-shopping and then found a seat in a nearby square and just sat talking. When we eventually arrived back at the station there were still people about as local trains were due to leave every half hour until midnight. The waiting room was not, however, occupied and we entered and sat on the wooden seats facing an empty fireplace, it was only ten o'clock and we knew we had another ten hours to wait for our train. Over the next two hours only four people came into the waiting room but just before midnight the friendly official poked his head round the door.

"I am just about to go home and the lights will go off in a few minutes. Just remember to stay in here until you see other passengers in the station. I hope you have a good night."

We thanked him once again before he left.

It was a very long dark night and we were pleased when the first passengers arrived on the station soon after six o'clock. Whoever opened the station before six o'clock had not come into the waiting room and so our friendly official of the night before would have nothing to explain. We had all managed a small wash in the station toilets and were able to have a hurried snack for breakfast when the station kiosk opened shortly before our train was due to depart. Armed with sandwiches to eat later, on what would be quite a long journey, we boarded the train.

According to Tanya's atlas the rail line to Portland followed the coast and so we chose seats on the right-hand side of our carriage in order that we could perhaps see the New England coast. The train left on time and we were soon moving quite quickly through the eastern suburbs of Boston and into the country.

Whether the train did run near to the coast so that a view of the sea was possible we never did find out as we became either engrossed in conversation or from time to time each of us falling asleep due largely to the almost sleepless night we had had on Boston station. The train I believe stopped several times before we reached Portland. According to Tanya's atlas we had left Massachusetts and crossed over into the state of Maine. From Portland the train would cut inland and into New Hampshire which was the state of our destination, North Conway. I do remember how the country changed as we went further inland, passing en route a number of lakes many with boats of all shapes and sizes. Later on the journey we could see hills or mountains in the distance and we guessed we were nearing our destination.

Chapter 9

NORTH CONWAY AND JACKSON

Just after four in the afternoon the train pulled into the station that the conductor had told us would be North Conway; we had arrived. The area around the station was flat but not far away was the high ground forming part of the White Mountains which at this time of the year were anything but white. We climbed down the steps placed there by the conductor, and said farewell to him as the train slowly pulled away to finish its journey further up the line. Half a dozen people had alighted before us and had soon disappeared leaving us on what appeared to be a deserted station. We made our way to the part of the building where we had seen the others leave and inside found an empty booking hall. We walked towards the door to the road outside and as we did so an old man appeared from a door in the hall.

"You folks look lost, I didn't hear the train arrive, guess I must have fallen asleep. We don't get many strangers coming to North Conway this time of year. How can I help you?" he enquired.

"We were told to hand this note to you and you would arrange for a carriage."

The old man put on a pair of glasses and carefully read the note.

"Oh I see, you looking for work at Wentworth – it's a nice place and nice folks up there. Wait there and give me a minute and I will be able to talk to them." He disappeared into his office and reappeared some five minutes later.

"They're sending a carriage but it'll be a while before it gets here. Where you folks from?"

I told him and he proceeded to tell us how his family had been some of the original settlers in this part of the country. "My grandfather was with Washington at Valley Forge and later at the surrender at Yorktown," he said with obvious pride, "But I guess you folks don't know what I'm talking about." I told him I did know a little about how the people fought to be independent of England and this seemed to impress him.

It was nearly an hour later before the carriage arrived. The driver was a young lad with a shock of ginger hair and a freckled face.

"You the folks wanting to go to Wentworth?" he asked as he got down from his driving seat. "Sorry it was longer than usual but Doris here didn't seem to want to pull the carriage today, she's like that sometimes. Anyway, climb aboard, it'll take about twenty minutes, if Doris doesn't mind an occasional trot." The lad helped pack and secure the small amount of luggage on the rack behind the carriage, climbed aboard and took the reins. The railman who had arranged the transport and who we had learnt was the station master, came on the road to see us off.

"I hope you find what you are looking for; I expect to see you again."

The carriage pulled away, turned and headed down the dusty road to the left.

"By the way, my name is Adam," the lad proclaimed, "I help out sometimes when I'm not at school. You folks specting to stay long?"

We told him we had no idea as we were seeking employment.

"You'll find the owners are good people, they've been there since before I was born."

He went on to tell us that there were only a few people employed at present as there were only two people living in the hotel at this time. However, he said that it would not be long before the summer rush started and many more staff would be needed.

We passed several good looking shops and about a mile along came to what could be a main road junction and Adam kept the carriage going straight ahead. Whereas the road to the junction was open with a number of houses on either side, and as stated near the station several shops, the road we were then on was wooded on both sides. All the way along Adam talked to us about Wentworth and how it was ideally situated in the midst of beautiful mountains.

"We have Mount Washington on one side and Kearsarge on the other, then there are Black Mountain, Spruce Mountain, Tin Mountain and many others, all within easy reach, plus the Wildcat and Glen Ellis rivers and of course Glen Ellis Falls. Inside the hotel we also have a billiard parlour and a big ballroom where people dance regularly." It was obvious the way he talked that Wentworth was a very big thing in his life.

We were heading towards the mountains in the distance and some ten minutes later the woods on the right ended and we saw habitation which we guessed was our destination, Jackson. As we approached, the first building to come into view was a wooden structure painted a bright red with a slanting roof.

"What is that?" Anna asked, speaking out to a stranger for the first time in English.

"That's our bridge, the building on it protects it from winter snow."

The bridge over a stream was the only entrance to the settlement from this side.

"What do you think of our bridge?" Adam said proudly.

"Very impressive, you obviously get a lot of snow in the winter," I said.

"You'll find other bridges in the White Mountains but none better than ours."

Over the bridge we passed a number of attractive timber houses on both sides and after a short while as the road turned to the left there appeared an unusual and very impressive building.

"That is Wentworth, what do you think?"

We all turned our heads to look.

In the front and around the side of the building on the ground floor there was a long extended covered veranda with a green tiled roof, above were two further floors stretching the entire length of the building with all the windows on these floors being sheltered from the sun by impressive striped awnings or shades, whilst in three parts of the building there were higher windows indicating one other floor above. All parts of the slanting roofs were tiled in green.

"It is a fine building," Joseph said.

Adam drove the carriage along the drive in front of the hotel and turned in a gateway on the far side which led to a yard with stables and a shelter for the carriage.

"I'll help you with your luggage. We'll go in over there." He pointed to a single door under a canopy of wisteria. As we walked to the door it opened and a plump middle-aged lady stood there smiling.

"Welcome to The Wentworth, you must be tired after your long journey, come inside and I'll get you something to drink. My name is Martha." She moved aside as we walked through the door. "I expect Adam has told you a little about The Wentworth, it's a great place as I am sure you will soon find out."

Martha told us to take a seat, in what was a large kitchen, whilst she poured us lemonade from a huge jug. "Most of our folks like my home-made lemonade, especially in the summer." Adam came into the kitchen whilst we were drinking.

"I've put the carriage away, Aunt, and Doris in her stall; I'm going off home now."

Martha thanked him as he left.

"See you folks later."

I was at that time a little puzzled as to who Martha was, other than Adam's aunt, and I am sure the others were wondering too.

"Did Adam tell you who I am?"

"No, he was so keen to tell us all about Wentworth itself that he never mentioned people who lived and worked in the hotel. He surely likes the place."

"Yes I know, there's not much else around here to interest a young boy, he enjoys helping out, he's a good lad. Well, I'm the general cook, I look after all the cooking in the off-season period, with the help of Jenny, who you'll meet later. We have a chef from Boston who joins us for the busy season. Mr and Mrs Donald, they are the proprietors, also employ two other locals all year for cleaning and washing. Then in the season they hope to take on at least ten more people, two or three who will likely be locals."

Tanya quickly told Anna and Joseph what Martha had said.

"Oh I see you don't all speak English. That could be difficult, but depends on what work they do, anyway I'm sure they will soon pick up the language. Where you all from?"

I explained where we came from and how we had met. I told her that Joseph was a countryman used to working outside, he understood horses and would be a very useful man for odd jobs as he was skilled with his hands. I agreed his not speaking English could be awkward at first but felt sure that he would soon learn enough to get by in the work he was likely to do. I said I would like the ladies to speak for themselves and was honest enough to tell her that I might be considered the odd man out as I was not sure what work I could do that would help the running of an hotel. "I am a university graduate in engineering and accountancy, so you can see my difficulties," I said. She said it was not up to her but that the proprietors were good people and would surely try to fit me in somewhere. She then asked Tanya about herself and she in turn said what she and Anna were capable of doing.

"I will show you to the two rooms we have set aside for you and when you have had a chance to settle in come down and I will take you along to meet Mr and Mrs Donald."

We were taken up three flights of stairs and shown two rooms at the back of the hotel on the top floor. Each room was well furnished having two single beds in each, a dressing table, bedside cabinets and two chairs. In each room there was a wash-hand basin and jug, and a chamber pot. At the end of the short corridor was a flush toilet next to a bathroom with a full size bath and washbasin. The girls took one room and Joseph and I the other. We told Martha that we would clean ourselves up before coming down to see her and be presented to the owners.

By the time we went down to the kitchen it was close to seven o'clock and we were feeling terribly hungry only having had the sandwiches we bought in Boston early that morning, we were also very tired. It was with some relief therefore when Martha told us she had spoken to the proprietors and they had suggested it would be better for all concerned if the meeting with them was delayed until the morning thus giving a chance for the new arrivals to get fed and have a good night's rest. She told us to sit at the table in the kitchen and she would give us some food. Tanya and Anna offered to help her but she refused and soon put before them a big meat pie and a stack of potatoes and cabbage. You can imagine how that pie was soon consumed with nothing left to throw away.

"That was the finest meat pie I have ever taste," Joseph said which Tanya translated for Martha who beamed all over her face. We all thanked her and said we would like to go for a short walk but would soon come back to get a good night's sleep. The four of us walked through the village ending up at the bridge leading to the main road, and on the way we passed a number of local people some sitting on verandas others in groups talking. Most acknowledged us, passing the time of day and generally being friendly. We strolled back the same way as we had come and entered the hotel through the back entrance and into the kitchen. No one was about so we went up to our rooms and for my part I was soon in bed and asleep.

Chapter 10

The following morning the girls knocked on our door and told us it was seven thirty, Joseph and I had in fact been up and washed some time but not having a timepiece could only guess the hour. We knew we were hungry and Joseph went along to the girls' room to see if they were ready to go down to get some breakfast. They were, and so we went down to the kitchen and found Martha there accompanied by a young girl of about sixteen.

"Morning, did you sleep well?" We all said we did.

"Well help yourself to what you can find over there and come up to the table." She pointed to a large kitchen range on which at one end on the hot plates was a pan of sausages and eggs whilst at the other was a saucepan of porridge next to a huge loaf of freshly baked bread. On a small side table next the stove were plates, cups and cutlery plus two jugs, one full of coffee the other milk. Truly a feast which we knew we would enjoy.

"Don't be afraid to eat, there is plenty more. This young lady is Jenny, she lives in the village and helps me when not at school."

We smiled and said hullo to the young lady and started to fill our plates for breakfast. The food was excellent and I know we all enjoyed it, especially I remember the fresh bread that Martha had baked that morning. Young Adam came into the kitchen while we were eating.

"No school today, Adam?" I asked.

"It's Saturday, we don't go to school on this day," he replied.

I had lost track of days and had quite forgotten it was Saturday

"Of course not," I said, "I had forgotten it took us two days to get here, I was thinking it was Friday."

"Where did you set out from?" he asked.

"We left New York early on Thursday expecting to get here that night but we had to stay overnight in Boston."

"I'm going to Boston one day. I am trying to get a scholarship to Harvard."

"I wish you luck," I said. "I too went to university but not in America." I could see he was interested to know more but Martha called over to him.

"You better see Doris is fed and cleaned out, young man, then come and have your breakfast." Adam winked at me and as he went out the door and I said I would speak to him later. "I'll go and see when the proprietor will see you," Martha added.

Whilst Martha was out of the room we asked Jenny if she knew Mr and Mrs Donald.

"Yes, I know them very well, everyone in the village knows them, they are very nice people."

"Are you going to stay here?" she asked.

"I think we would all like to but it depends if the owner wants us to stay."

Martha returned to the kitchen and told us the owners would like to see us in five minutes.

"Do they want to see us all together?" Tanya asked.

"Yes, certainly at first but they may want to see each of you individually later. Of course you Anna and Joseph will have to have one of your friends to translate for you." It looked as if they understood but Tanya repeated what Martha had said in Polish, just in case.

We all helped Jenny clear the table and then Martha told us it was time to go. She took us into the main entrance hall, which was most impressive, then up a central staircase to the first floor and down the corridor on the left to the end. She knocked on the door and entered, beckoning us to follow.

"These are the young people – this is Tanya and this Anna, Tanya speaks good English, and this is Leon and Joseph, Joseph has only a few words of English but Leon is fluent."

Mr and Mrs Donald were seated in two armchairs next to an open fireplace.

"Do sit down somewhere. Thank you, Martha, we can manage now."

We found seats facing the owners, Martha left the room and we waited for the questions to begin.

"Tell us about yourselves, where you come from, what you did before coming to America, what you hope to do and how you think you could help us in our hotel. I suggest the lady who can speak English start."

Tanya first explained how we met in New York and emphasised the men were not tied to them in any way, although all had found they got along very well together. She then told them where she had lived and that she had learnt her English from her mother. She went on to tell how she and Anna had come over on the German vessel *Dresden* and then how they had met Joseph and I. She told them her mother always said she was a good cook.

They next suggested Anna talk about herself and let Tanya translate. When Anna finished it was my turn. I told them that at university I had studied Engineering and later took a course in Finance. I said I did not think I had much to offer them in hotel work. They, however, thought they could have something for me to do which would at least give me the opportunity to look around and decide if there was anything more I could do in the area. They were very nice people and seemed to like us. Joseph was next and through me he told them of his experience on high quality of service farms and with horses. They seemed impressed and it was obvious they wanted to employ him.

They then told us a little about the hotel which had been opened over twenty years before. The hotel had proved popular with many people from Boston and New York, with some coming regularly from as far away as Washington. They explained that they expected staff to be smartly dressed whilst in the hotel and to be courteous at all times.

"People pay a lot of money to come here and we must give them a very high quality of service. In two weeks' time we will be employing our regular summer chef who comes from Boston, he, with the help of Martha, always ensures our guests are well fed. Cleanliness is very important, all rooms must be spotless, bedclothes are changed regularly and there is a daily run to the laundry in Conway," Mrs Donald said.

I remember we listened as the lady continued to say how they wanted the hotel to be run. Poor Joseph, and I believe Anna, hardly knew what was going on until we explained after the meeting. Mr Donald did not say a lot but it seemed he always acted as manager, although in truth he looked as if he should retire.

Finally Mrs Donald stopped talking and her husband moved to say something.

"Now you have heard my wife tell you how we expect to see the hotel run, I wonder if you are still interested in working in such an environment." I thought it best I answered.

"I know nothing of how a hotel should be run but what Mrs Donald just said made sense to me and if ever I was in a position to advise on such matters I certainly would have tried to say what your wife said, although perhaps not so eloquently. I would be surprised if Tanya thought any differently." I looked at her and she nodded in agreement. "I am sure when we translate for Anna and Joseph they will be in accord with us. Yes I think we would be happy working in such an environment should we be offered the opportunity to work for you."

Mr Donald looked pleased and smiling he said, "I expect you would now like to know what if any work we can offer you. I suggest you go now and talk among yourselves and we will call you back individually after lunch to tell you what we propose. Of course I realise the two who do not speak English will have to have a translator with them. I suggest we start at two-thirty. Thank you for coming."

We of course told Anna and Joseph what had been said by the owners and we all agreed it seemed as if it would be a good place to work. We returned to the kitchen and asked Martha if there was anything we could do to help her but she declined any help. So we said we would take another walk in the countryside, this time going in the opposite direction to that of the previous evening.

"Lunch is at 12.30, now don't be late," Martha called as we crossed the yard.

I had no idea what if anything the owners would find for me to do. We told Joseph that he was the one they were most eager to employ, both Tanya and Anna knew that they were likely to be employed helping in the cleaning, making beds, carrying water to bedrooms, and perhaps work in the kitchen, neither of them were expecting to be asked to serve at table.

Lunch passed and we sat in one of the lounges waiting to be called to the owners.

Joseph was first and I went along with him to translate. It was as we thought, they wanted help in the yard, someone to look after the horses and carriages on a regular basis; they would of course still be using Adam when he was free, but they wanted someone to replace the full-time man who had left them last year. Joseph would get full board and lodging and three dollars a week plus any tips he might get from the guests when he collected and returned them to the station in one of the carriages. I translated what they had said and he seemed satisfied. They suggested he leave and they would proceed to talk to me.

"Mr Livinski, we know you have studied to be an engineer and I am afraid we have nothing at the moment to offer you in this respect, however, you mentioned you had also taken a course in finance and this is of interest to us. I am assuming you have some knowledge of accounts, at least you know what accounts are intended to achieve."

I said I did and Mr Donald continued. "For the last many years I have taken it upon myself to manage the hotel and with the help of Mrs Donald prepare accounts to make sure the hotel is not being run at a loss. However, it occurs to us that you could help in this respect, take some of the burden off our shoulders and at the same time learn about managing a hotel. I could train you so that you became my assistant. If you enjoyed the work this would give you the opportunity of taking full responsibility at some time or, at least, allow you to apply for such work elsewhere. It might even take over from any thought you may have of engineering as a career. What do you think?"

I told him I was surprised and very pleased with such an offer, it was much more than I had hoped. I said I would certainly do my best to be of value to them.

"We will give you five dollars a week and your full board and lodging." I told him I was happy to accept.

"One more thing, Mr Livinski, I see from the telegram you sent us that you mentioned skiing – who skis?"

"That is me, sir, I thought that since this is a mountainous region that there might be skiing and that to be able to ski might be helpful in an hotel. I have done very little but was taught by an Englishman friend at university. I went with him to the Alps and though I say it myself I learnt very quickly."

"Skiing was introduced in the Washington Valley a few years back and we get a few guests who like to partake in the sport, I think it might be useful you having some knowledge. Do you have your own skis?"

"No, sir, I only borrowed or hired some."

"We have one or two pairs for the use of guests – if they fit you, you would be very welcome to use them. If you then became more proficient you may be able to help beginners."

"I would like that but it is quite a long while since I skied so I certainly would need to practise some."

He asked me to tell Anna and Tanya to come along to the office and I left.

I am not sure exactly what happened at their interview but they told us afterwards everything went well and they were both offered work. Anna was to help the general maid and would be expected to do running repairs to clothes, bedclothes etc., and ensure laundry was regularly collected and taken to the laundry in North Conway. Tanya was to help in the kitchen and would be trained to serve at table and, as her English was good, she would learn the work carried out by the receptionist, a vacancy yet to be filled. Both appeared to be happy with the offers made. We would all continue to occupy the same rooms on the top floor. Martha said we were lucky as some of the staff to be recruited would have accommodation found for them in the village, she said there were more people coming for interview the following week.

So far we had not seen the two people who Adam had told us lived in the hotel, but on returning to our rooms via the main staircase we passed them on the stairs. They smiled and made their way to the lounge for afternoon tea. Both were getting along in years, Mrs Brunel was the widow of a shipping magnate and Miss Haverford was her sister. It seems they had been in the hotel for over a year and looked as if they were going to stay, so Martha told us. Their room was on the first floor.

Before leaving Mr and Mrs Donald we were each told that our work would start on the following day. Tanya was to report to Martha, and Anna to Maggie Braithwaite, a lady who lived in the village. Initially they would start work at eight, although later, when more people arrived, they would have to make a much earlier start. Joseph was also to report to Martha but later would be expected to work on his own with the help of Adam; he was urged to hurry and learn English as it would certainly be necessary when collecting guests from the station. As for me I was told to report to Mr Donald at nine.

We were all up bright and early the following morning, and went down to the kitchen to get breakfast at 7.30. Martha and Jenny were already there and breakfast had been prepared. By eight o'clock all had been cleared away and Joseph and the girls ready to start work. Joseph managed to make it clear to Martha that he would go into the yard to look after the horses where he was joined by Adam. Tanya was given tasks to do in and around the kitchen and then taken to the restaurant where Martha showed her how to set a table in the Wentworth way. Maggie Braithwaite, who had come into the kitchen whilst they were eating breakfast, took Anna to show her around the hotel and tell her what she was expected to do. I sat at a table with a cup of coffee feeling a little awkward as everything was going on around me whilst I still had time on my hands waiting for nine o'clock to arrive.

At nine Mr Donald called me to the reception area and took me into a small office behind the reception desk.

"This is where I keep all the hotel paperwork with which I want you to become familiar. We buy much of our food from local farmers who invoice me monthly, but of course we also buy from businesses elsewhere, this mostly arrives by train. Martha orders food and checks it arrives in the winter months but as soon as more guests arrive much of the responsibility for ordering food is done by our chef, with of course Martha assisting him by checking it in and ensuring that appropriate invoices are received. I pay accounts promptly, that is within 30 days, and because of this I get good service. I will show you the bookkeeping records which I would like you to study. I am hoping that at some time you would be able to take over the work from Mrs Donald."

He spent a good time explaining what exactly he expected me to do and although I at first felt overwhelmed with it all, I knew I would soon learn and indeed thought I would enjoy doing this new kind of work. He left me to look through papers and in the afternoon introduced me to hotel management by setting me certain tasks to do. I had seen the girls and Joseph at lunch and they all seemed to be pleased with what they had been given to do.

Later, after our evening meal, I asked Tanya if she would like to take a walk with me around the village, and, as if taking a cue from me, Joseph asked Anna whether she would like to go along with him. Martha overheard me ask Tanya, "It's a nice walk towards the falls," she said, "it is not too far, cross the bridge and turn right, you'll soon see them. Have a nice evening and mind what you get up to."

Chapter 11

EARLY DAYS IN JACKSON

The early days at Wentworth were enjoyable; I found work most interesting and the others seemed equally satisfied with what they had to do. The chef arrived from Boston and the first of the summer guests. I spent most of my free time with Tanya as did Joseph with Anna. Joseph, with the help of Adam, was beginning to understand and speak a little English, whilst Anna, helped by those she worked with, was quickly becoming fluent. Martha had told us that until it got really busy we could excuse ourselves some evenings, always providing others were covering as necessary for us, and take a trip into North Conway where she knew sometimes there was a dance. When we asked her how we could get there she said that villagers occasionally took a wagon in and for a small fee, she was sure she could arrange for us to go with them, providing there was room; she would make enquiries. We heard nothing more for quite a while but in the meantime we did manage to get one or two afternoon trips into the town in order to buy a few clothes and odds and ends, on these occasions either young Adam or Joseph was the driver of the carriage we had got permission to use.

The hotel began to get busier over the next few weeks and Joseph was regularly meeting the trains driving one carriage with Adam often driving a second. May and June passed almost without me noticing, we had all settled in well to our new life and although I do not remember us saying it at the time we had indeed been lucky. I had become quite familiar with the paperwork Mr Donald had shown me and I, in a new suit he had arranged for me to have made, was often to be found greeting guests and telling certain staff what they should be doing. We now employed some ten people from the village and had taken on people from as far away as Portland. Those needing accommodation were found this close by, either in houses in the village or in the case of a few men in a log cabin built in the hotel grounds. There were now more horses for Joseph and Adam to take care of as not only did one or two men living within riding distance leave their horses to be looked after whilst they worked in or around the hotel, but also horses began to arrive for the use of guests. In June Joseph had been given another young man to assist him and also received a rise in pay to compensate him for the increased responsibility and extra work; he had become a very important employee and the proprietor was obviously very pleased with what he did.

During these first few weeks I had become very close to Tanya and we met frequently after work and by arrangement with Martha managed one or two dances in town, taking the local four-wheeler carriage with others from the village, the fee was 25 cents each. It was in late June when Tanya and I were out walking near the falls when I asked her if she would marry me and she accepted. We agreed we would not tell anyone until we had decided what to do about starting a home, which we knew would not be easy. Ideally we decided we would like to buy a piece of land and build a small house and although the money we had brought with us to America had not been reduced too much we knew it would be nowhere near enough to contemplate buying land. Nevertheless we began to make enquiries in North Conway when we were able to get there; we discovered that plots were being sold in two or three areas in that town and money could be borrowed on favourable terms from a small savings and loan society set up by an ex-bank employee. Nevertheless, although I was able to get the promise of a loan, the amount I wanted to borrow for a plot of land I had my eye on, was more than the society was prepared to lend. But talking to Tanya one evening about our life back in Europe I mentioned the necklace my mother had given me, and it occurred to me I should ask Tanya what she would think if I tried to sell it.

"My mother gave it me for use in an emergency and I would feel a little guilty selling it in such circumstances. What do you think?"

"Did your mother indicate she would like it back at some time?"

"No, she said she had no use for it."

"Well then I think it would be quite acceptable to her if she knew you had used it to help you settle in the new country. Why don't you ask her when you next write?"

And so I did, my mother was very happy to learn I was going to get married and said in reply about the necklace that she would be very happy to know that what she had given me would help me in setting up a proper home.

Having now settled my conscience with respect to the necklace, I now had to consider where best to get a valuation. I asked Mr Donald for his advice and when I showed him the piece he said I needed to go to a city to get a proper valuation as it certainly looked as if it could be valuable. He suggested that although one might succeed in getting a valuation in Portland or Boston, in order to be sure the piece was properly looked at by experts it may mean a visit to New York.

Tanya and I discussed what Mr Donald had told us and came to the conclusion that it might be a very long time before either of us could get to a big city so we decided to talk to the local jeweller in North Conway and see if he had any suggestions. So on the next free afternoon we got Joseph to take us in as we knew he had two guests to pick up at the station. He dropped us near to the jewellers and went on to the station where we said we would see him all being well before the train was due to arrive with the guests.

The jeweller looked at the necklace and confirmed what our boss had told us.

"This is a very fine piece of jewellery; I would hesitate to give you a value as from what you have told me there may be an important piece of history to go with it, which could enhance the value considerably. If you are unable to get to New York may I suggest you have it photographed and together with a resume of what you have told me we send the photograph to Christie's representative in New York."

"I am not aware of who this Christie is?" I said.

"Christie's is a very reputable auction house in London, it has been operating, I believe, since the eighteenth century. They have representatives in all the major capitals and sell practically anything in specialised auctions – for a fee of course, but if your necklace is valuable, I can assure you, you would hardly get a better price."

"What sort of fee would they charge, and what would you charge for helping?"

"I have never used them but in my studies at university I learnt auction houses charge anything between ten and fifteen per cent. My charge would be say the cost of the photo and postage plus let us say one per cent of the sale if and when made?"

I looked at Tanya and she nodded as if she thought it the thing to do.

"I agree, but I would like to be present when the photograph is taken, the necklace is not insured and I feel it should be with me all the time, it is my responsibility and it would be unfair to pass this to somebody else. Unfortunately we have to get back now to the train station to pick up our lift back to Jackson."

"I understand, sir, I will arrange for the photograph to be taken when you are able to come. Shall we say next week at the same time?"

I told him I would be there.

From now on I began to worry about the necklace which had been hidden in my jacket since leaving home in Europe and about which I had thought little until two respected men had agreed it was valuable.

We managed to get back to the station before Joseph met his guests and the train arrived about the time he had been told to expect it. The guests were an elderly couple from Boston who had been to Jackson a year earlier. Tanya and I introduced ourselves to them and hoped they did not mind sharing the carriage with us. In the course of the short journey to Jackson I remember we had a most interesting conversation with them. The husband told us he had made his fortune in railways and that he had played a big part in the setting up of the *Pennsylvania Limited*. Neither of us knew to what the gentleman had referred and I admitted we did not know as we had only recently entered the United States. He then proceeded to tell us he was talking about a train which had started a few years back. He said, with obvious pride, that it was a crack train which ran from New York to Chicago in twenty-four hours.

"The rival New York Central Railway is about to introduce a train on a different route that they claim will cut four hours off our time, but I can assure you it won't last," he told us. So, in order to appear interested in what I could see meant a great deal to the gentleman, I asked him why he thought it would not last.

"There's a big exhibition in Chicago this year and they are trying to cash in on the number of people travelling, but our train already averages 49 mph and it is going to take one hell of a schedule to consistently beat that," he replied.

"That's enough rail talk, dear, these young people know little about railroads," his wife interrupted. "Where do you people come from?" she asked.

Tanya explained to her and had managed to give her some idea of how we got to Jackson when Joseph pulled up the carriage outside the main entrance to the hotel.

"It's been interesting talking to you, if you have occasion to want to know anything about railroads I would be available to help. I expect we will see you around." With that they left us while we walked to the yard and into the side entrance.

I told Mr Donald what the jeweller had said and what I had agreed with him.

"I am so pleased he thinks the necklace valuable and I think the idea of getting an agent from Christie's involved is great. You said you want to get to town at the same time next week. I'll make sure that someone is around to take you."

I thanked him and when later we met up with Joseph and Anna I explained what had happened.

The following week never seemed to end but eventually the day arrived for me to go to North Conway. Mr Donald had arranged for Joseph to take me and I arrived at the jeweller in good time for the meeting with the photographer. I had during the previous few days written all I knew about the necklace and handed this to the jeweller who was going to send it with the photograph to New York. We both went along to the photographer's studio to await the developing of the photo. It came out well and was indeed a fair representation of the necklace. The jeweller said he would send it off that afternoon on the evening train to New York.

"How long do you think it will be before we hear anything?" I asked.

"I couldn't rightly say, but as soon as I hear something I will get in touch with you."

Chapter 12

It was almost two weeks later when I went along to North Conway with Adam driving the Surrey, he picking up guests later whilst allowing me to call into the jeweller's shop. The jeweller greeted us warmly.

"Good afternoon, I was about to get in touch with you. I had a reply from New York yesterday."

"Oh good, what did they say?"

"They are interested and would like you to take it to New York."

"I cannot get to New York; I hoped they would send a representative. What do you suggest I do?"

"I think the fact they say they are interested means the necklace is considered valuable. I think it may be worth your while to talk to your boss and see if he will allow you time to go there. It is clear now they will not come all this way to give you a valuation, I hoped they might but I think now it is up to you to try and get there."

I left the shop feeling a little let down but after talking to Tanya in the evening when she had said I should do as the jeweller suggested, I resolved to talk to Mr Donald, which I did the following morning. He was very sympathetic and said he would give me three days to try to get it settled and that he would cover for me on any of the hotel management duties but I should make sure everyone would be aware of my absence and keep their routine queries until I returned. I thanked him and said I would start right away arranging the visit.

By chance, following the meeting with Mr Donald, I met the railway gentleman on the staircase. He said good morning and as I passed it occurred to me that he would be a good person to ask about trains to New York. I turned and followed him up the stairs.

"Excuse me, sir," I said, "I have to go to New York and I wondered if you could tell me the best trains and what ticket to buy."

"Be glad to, my boy. What are you off to New York for?"

"I want to get a valuation and sell a necklace my mother gave me, and the jeweller in town and my boss say I should take it to Christie's who have expressed an interest."

"You need the money I guess."

"Yes, I have my eye on a piece of land and want to build a small house."

"Good for you, lad, nothing like investing in property. When do you want to go to New York?"

"The boss says I can take three days off for the journey. I would like to go as soon as I can get it arranged."

"Leave it with me, young man, I still have some influence, I shall enjoy fixing it for you. Give me your name."

I gave him my name and he told me he would let me know when he had something to tell me. I thanked him and straight way made sure, by checking the hotel register, that I had his correct name so that I could tell Mr Donald of what had happened. Mr Donald was not at all surprised when I told him what the gentleman was going to do.

"Cyrus Munroe lives railways; I have known him for years. I reckon you could have made his day – any excuse to get back into railways and Cyrus is a happy man. He'll certainly arrange something for you. Just let me know when you are going."

It was two days later that Mr Munroe asked for me at reception and I went along to the lounge where he said he would meet me.

"I have arranged for you to go tomorrow on a train that leaves North Conway at seven in the morning, you will pick your tickets up at the station. You should get to New York Central at nine in the evening, changing at Boston."

"Thank you, sir, I'll make sure I am at the station in good time. How much do I owe you for the fare?"

"You owe me nothing, I said I have influence – it'll cost you nothing."

"That's most generous of you, sir, I feel guilty having asked you for help, I never expected this, thank you so much."

"I have also fixed you up in an hotel for two nights – you'll be met at Grand Central Terminal by a cabby who will display a board with your name on it. He will take you to your hotel and you can arrange with him what time to pick you up in the morning to go to the Christie office. Use him to take you back to the hotel and also the following morning when he will take you to Central Station to catch the seven o'clock train to Boston. I'll leave you to make your own arrangements for someone to pick you up at North Conway that evening – the train should get in at 9.30."

"I don't really know what to say, Mr Munroe, your kindness overwhelms me."

"Think nothing of it, I had fun fixing things for you, make sure you come and see me when you get back."

"I will, sir."

I told Tanya of my good fortune and said I wish she had been coming with me. She said there would be plenty of other times in the future.

I had a word with Joseph for him to arrange to have someone drive me to the station in the morning and he said he would do it himself as it would be early, he said he would get the carriage ready for 6.30. That evening at supper I told Anna and Joseph exactly what Mr Munroe had arranged for me and they both wished me luck. Before going to bed Tanya and I went for a walk and on getting back I packed my haversack ready for the morning.

Joseph and I were both up before six and he went down to the yard to harness a horse to one of the carriages, and true to his word was ready to leave at 6.30. After a good trot we were at the station by ten minutes to seven. I picked up my tickets from the station master who said Mr Munroe had personally told him to look after me.

"Mr Munroe is an important man; you have first-class accommodation and will get meals on all the trains. Just show the conductor this pass." He handed me a gold card with the words printed in black 'Special Service – guest of A.J. Munroe'.

According to the station clock the train arrived at two minutes to seven and left right on time. The journey to Boston went quite quickly as I seemed to be drinking coffee or eating meals much of the time and after Portland fell into an interesting conversation with two older people returning from a visit to their son who lived in a town near Bar Harbor further up the coast in Maine. I changed trains in Boston and once again the service I received was excellent and shortly after nine we arrived in New York. As Mr Munroe had told me, a cabby displaying a board with my name was soon found and off we went to a hotel on Fifth Avenue. The cabby said he would be ready to pick me up at ten the following morning if that was a convenient time. It suited me well as the jeweller when giving me the letter from Christie's office had said it would be best to get there before eleven.

The room I was given in the hotel reminded me of the best rooms in the Wentworth and in the morning the choice for breakfast was unbelievable. I sat in the lounge until almost ten and then went outside to await the cabby who very soon drove up. He took me to the address I gave him and I was soon in a well furnished building and talking to reception.

"I have this letter from your office and would like to see someone."

"Just a moment, sir, I'll see if Mr Owen is available, if he is not I will get someone else to see you. Please take a seat."

Five minutes later I met Mr Owen who had written the letter.

He said he remembered the photograph and would be pleased to examine the necklace if I would follow him. He took me to an office on the first floor and closed and turned the key in the door.

"We take all precautions when examining what could be a valuable item."

I could not help thinking of how I had really not bothered about the safety of the necklace when travelling from Europe; I had often left my jacket lying about on the ship, not even considering the necklace sewn within. I produced the necklace which I had secured by a button in my inside jacket pocket and laid it on the table close by.

"This is even more beautiful than I had imagined, the colours make all the difference. Yes this could be an important piece."

He picked it up and closely examined the stones through a glass, "I seem to remember your agent said when he sent the photograph that the necklace had been given to your mother by a Polish princess."

"No, that is not quite right, my mother was given it by her grandmother and it was she who received it from the Polish princess. I think my great grandmother was lady-in-waiting to this princess and was given it when she left to be married. I guess that would have been in the early part of the century. I am afraid I know no more. I have, however, brought with me a copy of the letter my mother wrote recently saying she would be happy for me to sell it in order to buy a home in America." I handed him the letter, "It is of course in Polish."

"Would you mind if I got someone to translate it for me?" I understood his caution and told him I had no objection. He took the letter and unlocking the door left the room. It was some ten minutes later that he returned.

"Sorry to have kept you," he handed me back the letter. "It is a very nice letter. On the assumption you want us to sell the necklace would you mind if we wrote to your mother and asked her a few more questions about the necklace. If she could fill in as to who the princess was it would help in the sale, you could write to her first to warn her we might write."

I had not expected this and I wondered if they thought I had acquired the necklace dishonestly. I did not answer right away but thought a little. "I have no objection," I said somewhat hesitantly.

"Mr Livinski, I hope you do not think we are suspicious as to your ownership, I have no doubt in my mind that the piece is rightfully yours, however, it would be helpful if we could discover who the princess was – there could well be a link with other jewellery belonging to an old royal family of Poland or indeed of Russia."

I said I understood.

"If you let us advertise this for a future auction I am sure you will get a good price. With your permission I will try to ascertain who was the princess and armed with this I could let you know when the auction would take place. We may even send it to London. It will be insured for say $10,000 whilst in our hands and I will give you a receipt before you leave. How about it, are you happy to leave it with us?"

"Yes of course, I too would be interested to know more of where the necklace came from now that it seems it might be important. I do not think it will be easy to trace back to its original owner, Poland has suffered partition so many times over the years, parts being given to Russia, Austria and Prussia. I wish you luck."

"We will do our best and the start will be with your mother. If you come with me I will give you an official receipt and the standard insurance certificate. But first I will put this in a safe place." He picked up the necklace put it into a small linen bag he had brought with him, wrote on a label he took from a drawer in the table and tied it to the bag. He then walked to the door and I followed. We went down two flights of stairs into a basement and after he opened a cage door we passed into a room with four big wall safes. He dialled the combination on one and opened the door. Inside were three shelves and on each were bags similar to the one my necklace was now in.

"This is where it will reside until we get more information. Is there anything further you would like to know?" I told him I could not think of anything. "Well we will be in touch – shall I write to you direct or to your agent?" I told him I would certainly like him to inform me and perhaps send a copy of any correspondence to the jeweller in New Hampshire; "that is the one," I said, "you refer to as my agent, Mr Owen. I have agreed a fee with him of one per cent of the sale value," he noted this and asked for my address which I gave to him.

Leaving the office I was most surprised to find the cabby still waiting.

"Where to, sir?" he asked. I said I would like him to take me on a short tour of Manhattan. "Not too far that it tires your horse, and then you can drop me back to my hotel."

We had a fairly comprehensive tour of south Manhattan going as far north as Central Park. I was back at my hotel in time for lunch, having advised the cabby that I would have to get to Central Terminal in time to catch the seven o'clock train to Boston.

"You should be outside at six fifteen, the traffic starts building about that time and I would not want you to miss your train." I told him I would be outside waiting.

After a good lunch, that the receptionist had advised me was to be paid for by Mr Munroe, as indeed were to be all meals, I sat in the lounge thinking, and occasionally getting into conversation with other guests. After a short walk before dinner I retired to my room, having previously made sure I was called early in the morning; I was still without a watch.

The following morning I was up good and early and having had breakfast left the hotel and found the cabby waiting. We arrived in good time at Central Terminal and I thanked him, offering him a tip which he would not accept as he had had strict instructions that nothing was to be accepted from me. I thanked him and entered the station.

Chapter 13

The return journey proved to be uneventful and the train arrived in North Conway just before ten in the evening, nearly half an hour late, but fortunately Joseph with the carriage was outside waiting. When we got back Tanya and Anna were in the kitchen waiting to hear how I had got along, so whilst Joseph stabled the horse I told them what I had already told Joseph on the way to Jackson.

"It sounds as if you could be a rich man soon, will you still be friends with us?" Anna said with a twinkle in her eye.

"I will think about it," I said.

We had not yet revealed to our friends that we were going to get married but of course if we did get sufficient money to raise the loan for the land and house we wanted to build, then it would be time to tell them our secret, although since we had been seeing a lot of each other they may well have guessed what might happen.

The following morning I made a point of seeing Mr Munroe and thanked him for giving me such a wonderful break.

"Did they look after you on the trains?"

"They could not do enough for me, you must be a man of considerable importance."

"Well I was once and I am gratified to see that I am still remembered. Now tell me about what happened at Christie's."

I gave him the whole story about how they wanted to know where the necklace had come from and that they would be writing to my mother to see if she could tell them more about who originally gave it to her grandmother.

"You could do quite nicely out of this. Are they going to keep you informed?"

"I am sure they will, sir."

"Make sure they send you a copy of the catalogue before the auction date, better still I will ask for a copy to be sent to me here, that is if the auction is to happen in the next three months."

I next told Mr Donald what had happened and he said I could have more time off if I needed to go to New York again. He was not surprised that Mr Munroe had been so generous, "He is a good Christian," he said.

Chapter 14

SOLD

It was now almost August and the hotel was full. All staff were kept very busy and there was little time for leisure activities although I did get Joseph to give me a few riding lessons on one of the horses he used to pull carriages. This I thought would prove useful when I wanted to get to town, particularly as it looked as if transport to North Conway was nearly always in use by hotel guests. Joseph also taught me to harness a horse to a carriage so that in an emergency I could take on the town run.

Tanya and I grabbed what time we could to be together but the pace of work allowed very little. We did manage one visit to the land I had hoped I might be able to buy, it was still available and we called into the savings and loan offices and told them how I was trying to get sufficient money for the required deposit. Since it was through this office that the land was going to be sold the manager said he would put a tentative reserve on it as I said I was confident I would be in a position to buy in not more than a few weeks. I knew I was being a little optimistic but I did not want to lose that particular piece of land.

It was near the end of August when Joseph collected a telegram from the station at North Conway, it was from Christie's and read: *'Received reply from Mrs Livinski. Necklace for auction 9.15.1893. Catalogue follows. Christie's.'*

On reading I straightway went along to show it to Mr Donald.

"I expect you would like to go?"

"In a way yes, but it is a busy time and I am quite happy for them to deal with it, I am sure it will be all right."

"It would be good though to have someone there to look after your interest."

"I will see if Tanya will go in my place, I am sure we can easily find cover for her – would that be acceptable to you?"

"If you would be happy with that arrangement then I have no problem with it."

I thanked him and thought I would next tell Mr Munroe. I found him having afternoon tea in the lounge with his wife. I showed him the telegram.

"Why that is wonderful news, are you going?"

"Well no, sir, it is a very busy time for the hotel and Mr Donald would miss me for a couple of days and I don't think it right – Christie's will look after it all for me, I know."

"I'll go for you son, that's if you don't mind – I'd enjoy the trip, I just love railways, you wouldn't mind, would you my dear?"

"You and your trains, Cyrus, you just can't say no to the chance of a ride. Of course I don't mind, they look after me well here and you'll only be gone a couple of days, no you go and enjoy yourself."

"Then that's settled, you have nothing to worry about my boy, A.J. Munroe will be there."

In a way I would have preferred Tanya to go for me but how could I refuse such an offer, luckily I had not asked Tanya to go for me.

All my friends were pleased to know that the necklace would be in an auction and each had ideas of how rich I would be when it was all settled.

It was the following week when through the post I received the catalogue, and there on the third page was a photograph of my necklace and under it was a description of where it came from. It seemed my mother's grandmother had been a lady-in-waiting to an important Polish princess who had connections with the Russian royal family and the necklace had been traced back they believed to its original owner – the youngest daughter of a wealthy nobleman in the court of Catherine II (Catherine the Great).

Mr Munroe received his copy of the catalogue at the same time and made a point of calling me along to where he was sitting on the veranda.

"It looks as if your necklace is an important piece – I would think there will be a lot of people interested. You should come out of this with a tidy sum."

"Yes, it is wonderful, but it isn't sold yet, I must not, how do you say, count my chickens before they are hatched."

"Quite right, but I don't doubt there will be a lot of interest."

Later that evening I showed Tanya the catalogue and told her that Mr Munroe had offered to go along to the auction.

"Wouldn't you like to go?"

"Yes, of course I would but Mr Donald has already been good enough to allow me to go to see Christie's and we will be at our busiest time that week, I could hardly expect him to want me to go, although I know he would. Anyway old Munroe will see things go all right."

I saw Mr Munroe on the evening of the 13th September and he said he was all ready to go early the following morning. I said I would take him along to the depot. Sure enough he was up and ready to leave the hotel at 6.30 the following morning and I saw him aboard the Portland Flyer at 7.00. All I had to do now was wait.

The next forty-eight hours seemed to drag and I could hardly wait to meet my benefactor off the late evening train in from Portland. She arrived right on time and I don't doubt the driver knowing who was on board made sure that given a clear road he was going to get in on time. Only three people got off the train at North Conway and one of them was Mr Munroe, he walked straight up to the engineer who was leaning out of his cab, and I saw him shake his hand.

"Good evening, sir, had a good journey?"

"Yes very good, nothing like riding the rails, we made good time even though we lost a bit half way along through a durn cow getting stuck on the track – but Buffalo there gave her the gun after that and we got here bang on time. I clocked her at 85 miles an hour for twenty miles, some going eh?"

"That certainly is fast."

"I expect you would like to know, young man, whether your necklace sold. Well it did and there were two or three people interested – one from Europe, but he lost out to a new oil man, one of the men making their fortune based on the predictions some scientists have made on the use of oil in the internal combustion engine invented by those two Germans. Now so many firms are setting themselves up to build this new form of transport that anyone with oil on their land stands to become very rich, or at least that is what they say."

I was certainly interested in what Mr Munroe was telling me but I really wanted to know how much the necklace had sold for and had he brought me any money. However, I did not ask but waited for him to reveal all in his own good time. By this time we were out of the station and I had taken the horse's reins off of the station rail and was helping my friend climb into the carriage. As he seated himself and while I was taking my place on the driving seat he said, "I have some money for you, I have it in a money belt, I will give it to you when we get inside the hotel."

"Thank you, sir, it is really very good of you to have gone to all this trouble for me."

"Think nothing of it, I enjoyed my train journeys and I had a good evening in New York, and saw one or two old buddies."

I stopped outside the main entrance and helped Mr Munroe off the carriage.

"I'll see you in reception when you have taken the carriage round." Fortunately Joseph was in the yard and said he would make sure the horse and carriage were put away.

I thanked him. "Mr Munroe wants to see me in reception, he's got some money for me."

"You go then, I'll see you later."

I met Munroe in reception.

"I think we had better go up to my suite, we don't want people to see the money."

I followed him up the stairs and he knocked as he entered.

"Is that you, Cyrus? I have gone to bed."

"Yes, dear, I am just going to hand over some money to our young friend and then I will come in to see you."

He took off his jacket and under his waistcoat he unbuckled a money belt. From one of the pockets he took out a bundle of notes. "Your money, Mr Livinski." I took the bundle and must have looked lost.

"I expect you would like to know how much there is there. Well I will tell you..." He paused, "$5,760 – you'll find the bill of sale in the middle."

I did not know quite what to say, so much money, I think he must have seen I was dumbstruck and smiling. He spoke again, "I can see you really had no idea what the necklace might have been worth. Well you can see from the bill of sale that someone thought it was worth $7,200, the difference has been taken by Christie's including a sum you apparently agreed for the local jeweller – they must be pleased too." By then I had recovered from the shock.

"I thought the necklace must have been worth quite a bit or they would not have been interested to sell it, but I was thinking in hundreds not thousands. I shall now be able to buy that piece of land and build a house and still have money over – I'm rich! Thank you so much for what you have done for me."

"As you know I was pleased to do it, particularly as I was able to have so much time on the railway. I thought it best to get cash for you, there is nothing like having your wealth in your hand. Of course you must take great care of it and get into town as soon as you can to pay for the land and put the rest in a safe place, I mean in a bank."

I thanked him once again and left for my room still feeling a little bemused. Joseph was coming up the stairs as I walked along to the stairs leading to our room.

"I have just learnt how much my mother's necklace sold for – I've got over five thousand dollars, can you believe it?"

"Good for you, I guess this calls for a party."

"Yes, I am still in shock, but we must celebrate tomorrow if I don't wake up and find it all a dream."

Chapter 15

In the morning I went down to breakfast in the usual way, bursting to tell Tanya our good news. Joseph had already gone down and was sitting eating his breakfast with Anna and Tanya.

"I have not told them how much," Joseph blurted out; the others looked at me in anticipation. I felt awkward saying it in front of everyone so I just said it was quite a lot of money, much more than I had expected. However, I could see the disappointment on the faces of the girls and relented. "Alright then," I said, "It was over five thousand dollars."

"That is fantastic – you are rich, I am so pleased for you," Anna said. "What do you say, Tanya?"

"I think it wonderful, you are very fortunate, Leon."

"Tanya has said I am very fortunate, but she could have said, 'Leon and I are very fortunate' because, as you may have guessed, we are going to get married."

"Congratulations, we wondered when you might tell us. Yes, we had thought you might be heading this way when we were in town with you a couple of months ago and you suggested going round to see where those houses were being built. I suppose now with all that wealth you will be able to set yourselves up."

"Yes, something like that, we have already made enquiries and have a plot in mind."

Having said it I somehow felt guilty, all this money and telling my friends, why had I not kept it to myself, or at least only told Tanya.

After breakfast I took Joseph to one side and in Polish I said, "Joseph, old friend, I have been very lucky and I would like you to have a small share in this luck and therefore I am giving you five hundred dollars."

"You have no need to do that, I earn good money here."

"No, I want to do it, you would have to save for years to get that amount and Tanya and I now have more than enough to buy the land and build a house and still have a sum left over. Take it and put it by for a rainy day. Maybe you will be getting married one day."

Joseph thanked me and I felt very much better for having done this small thing.

Later that day I told Mr Donald of my good fortune.

"Are you going to stay with us or moving on now you have means?"

"Mr Donald, the thought of leaving had never crossed my mind. I need to keep working, and in any case I would not dream of leaving at this busy time and you having been so good to me and my friends. You are stuck with me as Tanya and I are to get married and we intend to build a house in North Conway."

"That is wonderful news; she seems a very nice young lady. You will of course have the wedding reception in the hotel."

"Well we have not got as far as that but when we have fixed a date I will certainly see if your hotel is able to accommodate us."

"Have you told the jeweller in town?"

"I think he already knows as Christie's say on the bill of sale that the amount deducted as commission also covered the fee due to the jeweller to whom they refer to as my agent."

"He'll be pleased, I would reckon."

"I'll go in and see him when I next go to town."

It was almost fall and some of the summer guests had left, there were, however, many who thought the fall, or autumn as you know it, was a time in the White Mountains not to be missed, and stayed on. This reminds me – I have not told you of what guests at the hotel did during their stay, as I have been so full of telling you about myself.

The guests could do just as they please, they could attend meals in the restaurant or have them in their room, they could sit on the balcony or in the lounge – in fact they were left to do as they wish. However, the hotel regularly arranged carriage rides, when either Joseph or his help in the yard would drive the open carriage, pulled by two horses, into the White Mountains along many well known routes. A popular one was to the foot of the railway built to take people up Mount Washington, the tallest mountain in eastern America. The Cog Railway, as it was known, had been built many years before, in fact in 1869, and had been a popular tourist venue for many Americans living in the east. Being a mountainous region there were of course many waterfalls to be seen and guests were regularly taken to view these. But of course in the fall the area was and still is renowned for the spectacular colour of the forest leaves before they finally fall; vast areas as far as the eye can see covered in multi colours from deep red through gold and yellow, many people coming to the area from far away just to see the beautiful colours. Joseph had also arranged for horse riding and had managed to hire extra horses from local farmers during the busy season. In the evenings guests were often entertained by a resident pianist and at weekends by a small orchestra in the ballroom, playing from time to time music for dancing. There was also tennis and a nine-hole putting green, popular with both men and women. For the more energetic a local resident in Jackson, for a small fee and with the permission of the hotel, arranged rambles which started at the hotel, some quite short and others for the extra keen rambler lasting all day.

Chapter 16

TWO STRANGERS ARRIVE

Back to my own story, Tanya and I took the earliest opportunity to go into North Conway to see the man at the savings and loan office.

"I was expecting you, the news gets around, I have heard of your good fortune."

"My goodness," I said, "I have told no one outside of Jackson."

"It of course came from the jeweller, he evidently was advised that your jewellery had sold."

"We are going over to see him after we have finished here."

"Are you still interested in the building plot we talked about?"

"Yes, but I don't think I now want the loan, at least not until I see how far the money I have goes. Is the land still the same price?"

"Of course. I assume you want to build, I can recommend a good and reliable builder. He is just finishing a house on a plot in the same road and I know you would be welcome to look at his work. Why don't you go along and see him whilst you are in town?"

"I think we will, but first let me put a deposit on the land. I imagine the transfer will have to be done by a solicitor which I am sure you can arrange."

"OK, I'll just get you to sign this and pay me one hundred dollars, and I'll get the solicitor onto it today."

Tanya and I left the office and walked down the road to the jeweller. He welcomed us literally with open arms.

"So nice to see you again, the sale was a great success wasn't it – I received a cheque for the fee we had agreed and they are keen to do business with me again. I don't suppose you have other hidden jewels?"

"No I'm afraid not. But I have some business for you, we want wedding rings."

The next hour was spent choosing rings and then we walked to the road where our plot was situated. We found the house the jeweller had mentioned and went to have a look, fortunately the builder was on site and we were able to discuss the building we would like on our own plot. He said he would send us some drawings and quotes based on the size of house we had suggested.

I now had to decide what to do with money that would be surplus to our immediate requirements. There was one bank in town and I decided to go along and talk to the manager who proved most helpful. I ended up opening two accounts, one from which I could issue cheques and the other in effect a savings account but I kept a thousand dollars back to take over to the savings and loan business as I thought it might be best to spread my wealth a little. By the time we had walked back to the station it was almost time for us to meet Joseph who had agreed to bring in the carriage to take us back to the hotel. A train arrived from the east and several people got off and two of them the station master told us wanted to get to Jackson but had not arranged transport. I went over to them and told them that a carriage should not be long as the driver knew we would be waiting.

"The man in the station just told us – would you believe it, the people coming in are going to take a train ride for fun, on a special he said! Why anyone would want to ride a train, unless they had to, I can't imagine, I've had enough of trains to last me a lifetime," the taller of the two men said.

"I suppose you have come a long way today – yes it can be very tiring. How far have you travelled?" I asked.

"Too far, bud, we've been everywhere – New York, Boston, Philadelphia, Washington, you name it. God I'm sick of trains."

I was about to answer when we saw the carriage approaching at a fast trot.

"They seem to be in a hurry," I said to Tanya as the carriage came to a halt. "Any problem?" I called to Joseph as he was getting down from his seat.

"No problem, got to catch a train, it is due any minute."

The four people in the carriage alighted and I recognised my benefactor.

"I might have guessed it would be you, Sir."

"Why is that, my boy?"

"I understand you are taking a ride on the special." The special, I knew, was a train catering for tourists, a train taking the scenic route to Lincoln.

"Yes you are quite right. I am showing my guests here the joys of rail travel in luxury."

I wished him a nice trip and helped Tanya into the carriage.

"These two gentlemen want to get to Jackson too; I guess they can come along with us," I addressed Joseph who nodded his assent.

"Where are you going in Jackson?" I asked.

"We're not sure, we were told it was a quiet place, out of the way where we could relax and be left alone," the shorter of the two answered.

"Well it is certainly a quiet place and yes, it is out of the way, you'll like it there. Have you nowhere booked to stay?"

"No, we just thought we would find somewhere when we got there."

"It is only a very small village, it's not a town, and you will have little choice."

"We'll take our chance."

Joseph drove off up White Mountain Road heading for Jackson. It was not until the carriage was through North Conway that anyone said anything in the carriage.

"I expect you are wondering why we have chosen this village of Jackson and what are we going to do when we do find somewhere to stay?"

"That is no business of ours, we just work in an hotel in Jackson, I was just curious as to where you were staying – we are fairly full at the moment but I think we have one double left, if it's of any interest to you."

"It could be."

The two men talked quietly to each other whilst Tanya and I wondered what these two men would find to do in such a quiet place as Jackson. I was not very familiar at that time with American accents but I noticed they did talk like I had heard many people speak in New York, they must be from a city I thought. Neither man wore a hat, a little unusual at that time, nor had they hardly any luggage, something did not seem quite right. When we eventually drove up to the hotel I asked them if they wanted to try and stay or whether they were going to search elsewhere. They said they would go into the hotel and see if the room I thought was available would suit them. They went into reception whilst we stayed on the carriage until Joseph had driven into the yard.

"What did you think of the two strangers?" I asked.

Joseph said he hardly noticed them but Tanya agreed with me that they were an unusual type to spend time in such a remote place as Jackson. We found they had taken the room and paid in advance, in cash. I then checked the hotel register to see how they had signed. The names had been written in by the receptionist and next to each name were unrecognisable signatures – the names were Andriotti and Loren. We thought nothing more until two days later Anne told us over dinner that when cleaning their room she had found they had put nothing in any drawers or in the wardrobe, their only luggage, which thinking back we remembered, had been a leather bag with a strap round it and a small attaché case. Anne said the bag was by the side of one of the beds but that the case had been slid under the bed.

"Does seem strange, I did not see any razor or evidence of shaving soap next to the wash basin, and I think they both need a shave," Anne continued.

"Perhaps they are going to grow beards," Tanya said smiling.

I suggested that each one of us should avoid giving the impression we had noticed anything as it did seem certain that there was something very peculiar with these men and they might react if they thought they were being watched.

"What do you really think, Leon?"

"I frankly had thought nothing more about them until today but after what you have just told us Anne it is likely they have come away in a hurry, or maybe their luggage has been lost on the way here. They could of course be hiding or at least want no one to know where they are. Anyway it is strictly none of our business and we would be unwise to interfere."

"Don't you think we ought to tell Mr Donald?" Joseph asked.

"I don't think we should do anything for the time being, they are just hotel guests and they have paid in advance to stay one week."

"Whatever you say, Leon."

I did not of course want either of the girls to worry, but inwardly I could not help but think these men could be on the run. Perhaps, I thought, the police were after them and they had come to this remote place to hide away until things cooled down. Should I tell Mr Donald, I asked myself, or should I say nothing as I had suggested to my friends, it would be nice to know what they had in the attaché case under the bed.

That day I carried on with my work as usual, making sure all our guests were happy and that meals – morning coffee and afternoon tea – were served on time. I noted that whereas the two latest guests had hitherto had all meals delivered to their room, on this day they did come into the lounge for morning coffee and later went to the restaurant and were seated by Toni, our head waiter, at a separate table near to the door.

Toni told me afterwards that they conversed some of the time in Italian but although he too was from Italy, he could not hear much of what they were saying. However, they did ask him if he could arrange for them to be taken into North Conway as there were things they wanted to do, he had contacted Joseph with respect to this.

It being Saturday young Adam drove them into town. When the carriage returned I casually asked Adam where they had been. He told me they had been to the barbers and had shopped in the general store, coming away with clothes and a case.

"Did they have much to say to you?" I asked.

"They told me they were from New Jersey; Atlantic City they said. They wanted to know if they could hire a carriage for themselves."

I did not question Adam further as I had no wish to get others involved. I did notice that at afternoon tea the two men appeared, both had now been shaved.

The following day, Sunday, Joseph told me at breakfast that he had hired a small carriage for the two men which they were going to pick up at ten that morning.

"Did they say where they were going?"

"No they simply said they would like it for the day."

"Who did you get it from?"

He told me he had an arrangement with a local farmer who had spare carriages for hire.

"I assume our guests are paying for the hire?" I asked.

He told me they had paid in cash before taking the carriage.

I made a point of being around when the two men came down to take the carriage and I noted they had with them the small attaché case they had when they arrived.

It was early evening when I saw the two men enter the hotel and noticed they no longer carried the small attaché case, Joseph told me later that when he collected the carriage from outside the hotel he was sure the horse had been driven quite a long way as it was obviously very tired.

Chapter 17

CHOOSING A HOUSE

On Wednesday the mailman brought along a small package addressed to me and having guessed what it contained I made sure Tanya was with me before I opened it.

There were two drawings, one showed a house on one floor – it had three bedrooms, a kitchen and one other large room with a big open fireplace plus an indoor toilet and bath – the other was a house on two floors of about the same size but of course not taking up so much ground area. Both houses were timber framed, as indeed were practically all houses built out of towns, quite unlike you have in England today where every one I have seen is built of brick."

"Which one do you like?" I asked. Tanya hesitated a moment but then said she preferred the house with two floors.

"Then that is the one we will ask him to build for us," I said.

"Has he said how much each will cost?" she asked.

"The two-floor house will cost eight hundred dollars and the other is seven hundred."

"Can we afford it?"

"Yes of course, the land was only two hundred and I will still have over four thousand invested in the bank and in the savings and loan."

Yes we were very well off, even after having given money to Joseph and promising myself that I would send a substantial amount to my mother once I had found out how to arrange it.

We had not yet decided when we would get married, but I think both of us were of the same mind that we would wait

125

until the house was built so that this could be our first home together. I checked with Tanya if this was what she was thinking and I was right, all we had to do now was find out when the house would be ready and then fix a tentative date for the wedding. What we had not considered was the time of the year – it was now well into fall and the builder said building work, unless indoors, would be very restricted by the weather, the White Mountain area he said had a lot of snow. He said he did not want to mislead us but felt that he would not be able to start building our house until November and that with the winter upon us, "I reckon it'll be the end of March before I can complete." It was just something we had not thought about, as indeed was how we would get to work from North Conway every day, it even prompted us to think perhaps we should have looked for a home in Jackson.

"I would much prefer to live in North Conway," Tanya said, "We'll think of something." Which we did. We decided we would have to have a horse and buggy and of course this meant we would have to get the builder to build a stable.

We finally decided we would aim to get married in March. Thus we had almost six months to make the necessary arrangements, at least when telling Anna and Joseph we jokingly said we would now have ample time to change our minds. As far as we knew then our friends had not made any commitments although they were regularly together.

The fall was certainly beautiful and our hotel was busy right through to the middle of October when many guests left. Those who stayed were retired people who had decided to spend Christmas with us. Several of the staff were at this time told they would not be needed any longer, however, we four were kept on, the only doubtful ones had been the two ladies, but I am sure the owners were well aware that they could easily lose Joseph and me if the girls were told they were not wanted. The summer chef left us at the end of

October, promising to return the next summer, and Martha once more was in sole control of the kitchen. I forgot to mention that the two strange men with the small attaché case had stayed on for a second week and in that time hired a buggy for one further day. When they signed off Joseph took them to North Conway where they caught a train going east. Before they left I had asked Joseph to find out where they were going, he said they were a bit evasive but after they had gone onto the platform he asked the station master who said their tickets were made out to New York.

We had our first snowfall in early November and Joseph had the job of preparing the wheel change to skis. The first fall did not last longer than two or three days but in the third week in that month it snowed heavily and wheels on carriages in the country became useless, Joseph had then to change all carriages to skis. All around was white and we all had to lend a hand at snow clearing, it was then we fully understood why the Jackson bridge had been covered, such a weight of snow would certainly have played havoc with the wooden bridge.

I well remember my first Thanksgiving Day in November, which Americans celebrate each year, when a number of people from Jackson were invited to join hotel guests and staff for the special meal and party held that evening. I also have good memories of our first Christmas and New Year Eve celebrations since leaving home.

Tanya and I in that time made as many visits as possible to see the progress on building our house; the builder had managed to spare men to build the foundations before the snow became too deep and just as soon as his carpenters were free from the other house he set them to work indoors at his depot preparing sections for ours so that construction would be speeded in the new year. Just before Christmas I had managed through my bank to send money to my mother and later in January I had a letter to say she had received it but that it was quite unnecessary to send money as I should know she had more than enough to live on, nevertheless she thanked me and was thrilled to know I had found someone I wanted to marry.

Chapter 18

THE WEDDING

The winter months passed quicker than I imagined they would, a few people attempted skiing but as yet the hotel had not gained a position on the growing ski market in the Washington Valley. Now it was March and thoughts of the wedding came much to the fore. Tanya and I were not churchgoers but thought however that we ought to get married in church and although both coming from Catholic families we were not concerned what denomination church we went to so long as the man in charge – priest, parson, or vicar – was prepared to marry us. We were introduced to the Episcopalian minister in North Conway by Mrs Donald and he agreed to marry us at the end of the month. Joseph was to be my best man and Anna would be bridesmaid to Tanya. Martha knew a lady in the village who was a dressmaker and it was she who made the beautiful dresses worn by Tanya and Anna. For my part I went along to town and ordered a new suit for the occasion, it arriving just in time for the wedding.

The house and stable were duly completed a week before the wedding and we had a little furniture delivered a few days later so that we could effectively move into the house after the wedding. Joseph had arranged the purchase of a horse and buggy and he drove this round on the morning of the wedding, then staying in town and coming back with the wedding guests. Those staff who could be spared from the hotel attended the church being driven there by Adam in the big four-wheeler. Afterwards we all returned to the hotel where Mr Donald and his wife had got Martha to prepare an excellent wedding breakfast which was attended by the few remaining hotel guests and of course our work colleagues. Tanya and I had decided to return to work the day after the wedding without taking further time off for a honeymoon, agreeing we would like to go away together later, when the weather improved.

"You haven't told us much about the wedding. I was waiting to hear what it was like," Mrs Davis interrupted.

Yes, I realise that, but of course it was a long time ago and strangely although I can recall a great deal of what happened in those first few years in America, even remembering what people said and did, there are some things that are not so clear at all. Maybe there is a reason, I just don't know. But I am pleased you are so interested. I had begun to wonder if I had been going into too much detail.

"No I am sure we are all interested and there doesn't seem to be any sign of the train moving. Do carry on."

Well I do remember the priest, or whatever he was called, was most kind and there was a pianist who played two hymns on an old out-of-tune piano, and of course Tanya looked exquisite in her dress as indeed did Anna in hers.

The day after the wedding and for a further few days we journeyed to the hotel from North Conway in our buggy but soon found that in inclement weather it was not very pleasant. Then when Mr Donald asked how we were getting along and I mentioned the buggy ride he said we could use one of the guest rooms and perhaps only go home once or twice in a week, "at least until the season picks up and all rooms are needed for guests," he said. So Joseph was given permission from Mr Donald to stable our horse and buggy and in return I said the hotel could use it for guests at any time.

The summer soon came around and the hotel was once again very busy, Tanya and I visiting our home only rarely as there generally seemed to be one room free in the hotel most nights. We knew that both of us had become very important to the owners, I because I had taken over many of the tasks previously carried out by Mr Donald, and Tanya because she had now taken over much of Mrs Donald's work. As you can imagine the holiday we had promised ourselves did not materialise that summer, but we both enjoyed our work and were very happy together.

At the end of summer young Adam announced he had got a place at a university in Portland, Maine, and would be leaving Jackson at the end of September. It seemed that his mother had been born in Maine and as the New Hampshire University in Durham was further away and more difficult to get to than USM situated in a place called Gorham outside Portland, with easy access from North Conway by train, he was able to get a place. I know he had ambitions to go to Harvard outside Boston but it seemed it was not to be, and he had done very well in any case to get as far as this in his education. "The faculty at my school had told me that a place at Harvard was a little too ambitious for me and that to get a place at a university was an achievement in itself and the University of Southern Maine, relatively new, was making a name for itself," he said.

We of course all missed Adam at the hotel, particularly Joseph who would now need someone to help him out on routine stable work and on the runs to North Conway. Luckily a young lad in the village, recommended by Adam, agreed to fill in while not at school. Adam also agreed to help out if needed when he was home during holidays.

At the end of summer the chef had returned to Boston and once again Martha ruled in her own kitchen. Only a few guests remained through September, being joined at the end of the month by a few others, all anxious to witness the spectacular 'fall'. Tanya and I had still not taken a holiday and resolved to take a few days break by visiting New York at the end of October and so we did.

The journey to New York was very tiring and we began to wonder if we had chosen our holiday break unwisely. However, we thoroughly enjoyed staying in a good hotel and visiting two or three theatres, Tanya particularly enjoying her shopping expeditions. For the return journey I managed to book sleeping berths after finding a through train to North Conway. We arrived there just after breakfast and were soon back home walking the short distance from the station.

Chapter 19

WE START A FAMILY AND PLAN THE FUTURE

Our first child was born in 1895, Tanya having the baby in our house with the help of a Mrs Walters, a respected midwife from Conway. We called the baby Edward. Tanya of course had given up her work at the hotel a few weeks before Edward was born and although I managed to get home most nights in the week I did occasionally have to stay at the hotel, especially when winter and the snow arrived. We had very good neighbours and everyone went out of their way to make sure Tanya was well looked after, particularly making sure when the weather got colder that she had adequate logs in the house brought in from the stock I had had delivered and deposited in the outhouse.

Joseph and Anna were regular visitors when they could be spared from the hotel and we had many fine evenings and meals through the next several months. As far as we could see although Joseph and Anna seemed to be constant companions there was no indication whether they had decided to take the plunge and marry. Joseph was now fluent in his new language and had acquired much of the local dialect which somehow missed me; in fact he began to sound much more like an American than any of us. I don't know why this could have been, I have often wondered and came to the conclusion it must be something due to working on the land, being close to the soil, maybe that is why in some countries a person from the country can always be recognised by his accent which somehow remains much the same irrespective of the differing local town dialects.

"I know what you mean, sir, I have an uncle who lives in a village outside Chelmsford, you know the town we passed

not long ago, and he talks like a man I heard on the wireless the other day who they told us came from a village miles away in the west country," John said.

Well, whatever the reason, Joseph had acquired the local accent.

Our third Christmas and New Year in the new country passed and we were now in 1896. Mr and Mrs Donald indicated to me that they were seriously thinking of retiring in the not too distant future and that perhaps next year they would put the hotel on the market for sale. They asked that I did not tell the staff as they did not wish to worry anyone but they felt that I might like to consider the possibility of taking over and that in the next year I would have the opportunity to consider how I could possibly arrange finance sufficient to cover the cost. I certainly had not in my wildest dreams contemplated owning an hotel, and such a hotel as Wentworth. I of course told Tanya and warned her that this had to be confidential. She approved of the idea but at this stage we really had no idea what such a scheme would cost, the Donalds had not indicated how much they would be expecting for the sale and I did not like to ask. However, I knew I would have to try to find out how much such properties could command before I could even consider it a possibility. It was true that as a result of selling the jewellery I had some finance, but how far what remained after buying our house would go towards buying a stake in what seemed to me to be a successful hotel, I did not know. All I knew was there was no urgency as I am sure they were being honest when they had said they were thinking that in a year or so they might be retiring, time was on my side. I resolved to go to a real estate agent as soon as possible and talk about investing in the hotel market, letting them think I was contemplating a small investment in the hotel business which was obviously thriving in the White Mountains area, with owners of reasonably substantial properties converting part into hotel accommodation. Also rumours were persisting that big money from New York were contemplating a huge investment in a very substantial hotel near Mount Washington itself, the land it was understood had already been acquired. As for the Wentworth, we were getting busier and often we were having to tell would-be customers that we were full; this was happening for a large part of the year but particularly in the fall and in winter now that skiing was becoming more popular and some ski lifts had been built and runs prepared.

Young Edward was doing well and had taken a few first steps; he could also say a few words in English and Polish. We would naturally make sure he knew he was an American and speak English but we also would ensure he could speak Polish and German, as at home we often talked to each other in German or Polish. There is really only one way to stay fluent in a language and that is to use it. Remember that John, as I am sure when you leave school that you will soon forget any language you have learnt unless you practise it from time to time.

"We learn French and Latin but I am afraid I am not very good."

I am sure it is the way it is taught, John, it is a great advantage to be around people who speak the language you are learning, but don't give up it could be of help to you when seeking a job. Anyway back to my story.

Tanya and I visited the one real estate agent in North Conway and began to learn the probable cost of investing in small hotels but nothing as big as the Wentworth and we did not like to ask as we knew it would become too obvious what we were talking about. I knew we would be well advised to go further afield to discover what we were after.

Spring came early that year and with the hotel half empty, it being the slackest time of the year, we arranged with our employers to take a short break.

"We are going to Portland," I told Mr Donald.

"Yes, I think that is a good idea. You will get better advice there, I assume that is why you are going?"

"I thought you would understand. We are, as you guess, taking what you said seriously; we are not wasting our time, are we?"

"Not at all, we do mean to retire as I told you."

With this double assurance Tanya, Edward and I caught a train to Portland where we found a small hotel which we booked for two nights. It certainly was not of the standard we had become accustomed to at the Wentworth but it was adequate and the manager was most helpful in advising the best agents in the city. So the next morning after breakfast we walked to the first agent whose offices were quite close to the hotel and near the town centre. Portland at this time was a very busy city and we did not find it easy crossing the roads with horses and carriages hurrying around. We could see that much of the traffic was heading towards the sea where in the distance we could see above buildings the masts of many vessels. Portland we had learnt was the most important seaport along the New England coast, with vessels from all over the world loading and unloading cargo in the deep water harbour.

The offices of Knight and Friend, the agent, were very elegantly furnished with comfortable seats for visitors covered in red velvet while staff desks in this outer office were all in highly polished walnut. The walls had a red patterned wallpaper broken up by gilded framed pictures of houses and offices we assumed the agent was there to sell or rent. The clerk nearest the door got up from his chair and asked how he could help. He was dressed in a smart finely striped suit with a white shirt and stiff collar which sported a brightly coloured patterned cravat, which we gathered was the height of men's fashion of the time. After I had told him what we wanted, he bade us be seated while he went to speak to one of his seniors. On his return he directed us into another well furnished office at the rear of the building where we were greeted by an older man with mutton chop whiskers, seated in an ornate green armchair. We shook hands.

"How can I help you?"

I told him we might be interested in making an investment in the hotel market, perhaps in the Mount Washington Valley, or in the countryside close to that area, and that we had come along to get some advice as to what funds might be needed.

"Of course our main interest is in Portland," he said, "but we have managed to agree sales of some properties in the area to which you refer. The hotel business at this time is certainly a booming market and we have had a number of enquiries about the availability of land west of Portland. Are you looking to build?"

I told him we were experienced in working in hotels and that I had virtually managed one for some time and we had just thought that it was time we worked for ourselves rather than always working for someone else.

"Very sensible, if you know how to go about it, have ambition, and the means of acquiring capital," he said. "Have you any capital?"

"Yes, we have. But I don't think it is enough for what we have in mind."

"And what have you in mind?"

I had given some thought as what to say and I reckoned that if we did not at this stage tell him exactly where we worked we could nevertheless tell him we were hoping to invest in the same hotel.

"We believe that in the not too distant future our employers are going to retire and as we know they have no children or close relatives, when they do decide to leave they will want to sell the hotel, and as we know all about the running of the place, and have a little capital, we thought we should put ourselves in the position to make an offer. We are very friendly with them."

He then asked us what size the hotel was, how many staff employed, what ground belongs to the hotel, what number of clients and had we any idea of the turnover. Also were there any other hotels close by that might take trade away at some time. We were quite able to answer all his questions as both Tanya and I had access to all the books since Mrs Donald had been only too pleased to hand over her work to someone else.

"From what you say it would seem the hotel has little competition at present but that it probably has peaked as far as visitors to your village are concerned. I mean it perhaps is not worth contemplating expanding the hotel at this time."

I agreed that that was the picture as I saw it, a well run hotel with, it would seem, guaranteed clientele whilst standards were maintained.

"Have the owners indicated to you that they may retire soon?"

I told him they had and had even indicated that they would be willing to consider an investment from us.

"I take it therefore they have no wish for other parties to be involved at this stage."

"That is so, although I am sure they would want the proper market price for the business."

Mr Knight, for we gathered that was his name, had been taking copious notes with a pencil, looked up from his writing.

"I have a good idea of what you need from me and I will do my best to give you my assessment of the situation. To be fair I would have to see the property and make the necessary enquiries as to rightful ownership etc. In other words I would want to be your agent, then depending on a preliminary valuation I could give you an indication of my fee, only payable if the sale goes through in your favour."

"Is it not possible for you to give us some idea of the amount of money we might need to conclude such a transaction?"

"It would be difficult to give you a figure of any accuracy, but based on what you have told me I think we could be talking of figures close to fifteen thousand dollars, but that is purely a guess. How does that seem to you?"

I told him it was better than I had imagined and he asked how much capital we would be prepared to invest. I told him I could invest five thousand and that we had a house fully paid for which could be added as further collateral. He said it would not be too difficult to raise the remainder on the basis of say a ten-year loan and if we were interested in employing him as our agent he would make sure we got a fair deal. On the basis of a sale of say fifteen thousand his fee would be say five per cent of the sale price plus some expenses amounting to say some $200.00 which would cover costs of train, bus and taxi fares to say somewhere in the Washington Valley.

I thanked him for his information and said I would talk it over with my wife and perhaps come and see him before we returned in two days' time. Edward, who had been asleep on Tanya's lap all through our interview with Mr Knight, had just started to stir and I took him from her as we left the offices.

We both said we were pleased with what we had heard and believed we would have a good chance of making a winning offer for our hotel when the time came. We thought Knight seemed an honest man and that we would be happy to have him as our agent. However, since we had been given the name of another agent by the hotel manager we thought we would see what he had to offer. As directed we soon found the other, Flower and Wise. The office was not as sumptuous as the previous one visited and the reception we got when we told the first person we saw what we wanted was not very favourable. The senior we met following this was not as helpful as Mr Knight had been and we did not stay long but made some excuse to get away.

Later that day we returned to the offices of Knight and Friend and told them we would be happy to use them as agents when the time arrived. We still did not give them the name and address of the hotel but instead gave them our home address in North Conway. Mr Knight did not press us for the name and address of the hotel but did say we should give him details as soon as there was any indication that the owners were definitely contemplating a sale.

We had concluded our business in Portland in the first morning and now had the rest of that day and one other day in which to explore the city and its harbour. During our stay Edward seemed quite content as he was being carried all the time, I suppose if we had been staying longer we would have tried to hire a baby carriage but that would certainly have restricted us from using the trolley cars that ran in the city. We returned by train to North Conway on the third day.

When I arrived back at the hotel I was surprised to learn from Joseph that the two men who in the previous year had so mysteriously taken up residence for a while, had returned and once again I was told they appeared to have little luggage but amongst this was a small attaché case. Later that day I passed them in reception and I spoke to them, saying we were pleased to see they had returned. One nodded his head in recognition but said nothing. The next day Joseph said he had to arrange the hire of a horse and buggy for them. I watched them go and could not help noticing they had the attaché case with them.

On this occasion our mystery men stayed for one week and made two more day trips in a buggy. They left on a train with tickets to New York minus a small attaché case.

Chapter 20

MUNROE HELPS AGAIN

That Spring and Summer was a very busy one for the hotel and for all the staff, once again we were joined by the chef from Boston and many of the guests were people we had got to know including my good friend Cyrus Munroe, the railway enthusiast, and his wife. Mr Munroe was keen to know how I was and whether I had made good use of my money. I thought it not unwise to tell him of the possibility of investing in the hotel at some time in the future and he was most interested.

"You say you have seen an agent in Portland – would you mind giving me his name and I will make a check on him to be sure he is genuine."

I did as he had said and two days later he came back and said the man had a very good reputation and would no doubt do his very best for us if and when the occasion arose.

The year seemed to fly by and before we knew it the days got shorter and winter was upon us.

Chapter 21

The winter proved to be the best season the hotel had had for skiing guests and the carriages and buggies were in constant use taking guests to and from the ski slopes.

Another Christmas and New Year passed and in this year, 1897, Anna and Joseph told us that they were going to get married and that they would rent a small cottage in Jackson that had become vacant when the previous lone tenant died. The wedding took place in the little Congregational church in Jackson and all the staff who could be spared attended. The married couple did not take a honeymoon which was just as well as far as the hotel was concerned as Joseph would have been missed terribly; he really had become an important member of staff.

I do not remember much more of what happened in that year, probably because everything went as in previous years. However, towards the end Mr Donald took me aside one day and told me that he and his wife were going to retire in the Spring. He asked if I was still interested in making an investment and of course I told him I had not changed my mind.

"It now comes down to the price and whether you have the finance to cover it. I intend getting a valuation and if what you are prepared to offer meets this then we will have a deal. I remember you told me you had talked to a real estate agent in Portland and I now suggest you contact him again."

I did as he had said and a week later Mr Knight came to the hotel and stayed with his wife for two nights. In that time he talked to Mr Donald who allowed him to look at his books and introduced him to the persons valuing the business on his behalf. It was all a very friendly atmosphere and Tanya and I had high hopes that a deal would be arranged for the following Spring.

"Did you get the hotel?" John asked.

"You shouldn't interrupt our friend, although I must say we are all anxious to know."

Mrs Davis said, "Your story is so interesting, I am sure we have all been living it with you. I had quite forgotten we were stuck on a broken down train. Please continue."

To answer your question, yes we did get the hotel for a price not too different from that Mr Knight had indicated to us in Portland the previous year. We took over the hotel officially in April 1898.

"What happened to Mr and Mrs Donald?"

They moved north into Maine, to a place called Bangor. It was where they had spent their honeymoon just before Mr Donald went to fight for the Union army in the War Between the States. We heard from them from time to time until in the early nineteen hundreds correspondence ceased and we learnt they had died.

1898 I remember was the year America went to war with Spain. Cuba wanted her independence from Spain and Cubans rose up but were suppressed. The reasons for America wanting to help the Cubans could go back to their own desire to be free from Britain but it was much more complicated than that. However, Congress asked for 125,000 volunteers for the armed services and I heard of men from the Washington valley volunteering. The president at the time was McKinley. Anyway apart from reading about the fighting that went on in Cuba and the fact that America sent troops and battleships to the Philippines to help the revolution there, it in no way had any affect on the numbers booking and coming to the hotel. The war in Cuba was over in a matter of months and Cuba was given her independence. It was here that a later president of the United States,

Theodore Roosevelt, made his name by leading his rough riders to capture a hill from the Spaniards. Fighting in the Philippines, however, carried on for two further years, with considerable loss of life in the American army. By the way, did you know the common teddy bear, I was told, gets its name from Theodore Roosevelt who was a keen hunter of bears in American forests.

Chapter 22

CENTURY ENDS

Our first year as owners proved to be a success and we were able to repay some of the loan and put a reasonable sum of money into our savings and loan account. Our little boy was making good progress and he was later that year joined by a little girl whom we named Caroline.

The end of the century saw the hotel still doing good business and, to greet the new millennium, we arranged a very special party, in which we invited as many guests from the village as we could accommodate. In such a short time we had been lucky enough to have achieved so much, we were the same people but living so differently from the four Polish immigrants who had left the steamer *Dresden* less than seven years before. It indeed was true, as was said – America was the land of opportunity.

Although we in the Washington Valley lived our own lives we were not totally unaware of what was happening elsewhere in the country. We of course had contact with the many guests who came from the big cities and they brought with them magazines, newspapers etc. and together with the usual local papers, conversations both with and overheard, we reckoned we knew a good deal. News from Europe, however, was spasmodic. America we knew was growing fast, many immigrants were entering the country and more people were moving west and New York the melting pot of immigrants was becoming one of the great cities of the world and many of its wealthy citizens wanted to spend holidays in our valley. The rumours we had heard long ago of big money coming to the area was coming true, for further up the valley we learnt of the plans for building a vast hotel bigger than any in New England. We could not help but wonder whether this would seriously affect our own business but we guessed it would be at least two years before it could be opened.

Our business continued to prosper and we frequently found we had to turn people away. But for the fact that we knew a new hotel was coming to the valley we would seriously have thought of building an extension to accommodate more people; we were, we believed, doing the right thing by being cautious. By the time the new hotel would be completed we knew our bank balance would be healthy and our loan well on the way to being cleared.

Young Edward had started school in North Conway and it seemed he was doing well. Caroline was walking and getting up to mischief as most young ones do. A few more houses had been built in our street and most neighbours were very friendly, many being immigrant sons and daughters from Scandinavia and consequently Caroline's blonde hair matching well with other children.

Anna and Joseph continued to live in their cottage in Jackson but were frequent visitors to our home, they had no children. I had made sure that Joseph was well looked after, not only because he was my friend but because he was just as valuable an employee to me as he had been to the previous owners. I made sure he had adequate help in his work throughout the year.

Adam had been helping out in breaks from university but nearing the end of his time there the help became less frequent. It was soon after the turn of the century that Adam came back to Jackson one day to tell us he was a fully qualified architect and that he was involved in the designing of the new hotel up the valley. It was from him we learnt how vast the complex would be. He said the owners were bringing to the valley over 200 Italian craftsmen as well as employing scores of workers of all trades. I never quite understood when he said the hotel was being designed in the Spanish

Renaissance style why they did not bring over Spanish craftsmen; I guess they thought the Italians superior or cheaper.

When completed it would have hundreds of bedrooms and suites, a majestic ballroom, restaurants and conference rooms. There would be a golf course, putting green, tennis courts, riding, and beauty and massage facilities. The hotel would be run as a holiday resort and all kinds of activities would be available for guests.

It was early in the New Year that the valley featured prominently in the news in New York, Boston and local papers when they were full of write-ups and pictures of a series of robberies over the past few years that had taken place in Atlantic City, New York, and Philadelphia, by the same gang who had regularly used a village in the White Mountains as a hideaway for vast sums of money. One member of the gang was captured, after a tip-off, in a raid on a house in the small New Jersey town of Ocean Grove, the home of a religious community next to the busy seaside resort of Asbury Park The raid, the papers said, had led to the discovery that the gang had also used a cabin in the White Mountains of New Hampshire as a hideaway for the proceeds of their robberies. The old log cabin was situated some quarter of a mile off the road leading to a place called Bretton Woods. The cabin, it said, dated back to the period in the late 1700s when a man called Abel Crawford built a rest house used by travellers in an area now known as Crawford Notch, Notch being the local word for valley. The paper went on to say that large sums had been recovered but that this amounted to only a small part of the money taken from banks and other businesses over a long period – the gang were believed to be Italians from New York but as yet no others had been apprehended.

We thought we should tell the police of the two men who had used our hotel and found when we did so that other hotels in the valley had also had what the police believed were members of the same gang staying with them.

Chapter 23

I had regularly corresponded with my mother since I first came to America, and in recent times I had asked her if she would like to come over to live or to see us but she said she was quite happy to live where she was as she had many friends and relations whom she met regularly. She had said she hoped Tanya, the children and I would one day find time to visit her. Sadly in June 1900 I had a letter from a cousin to say my mother had suddenly died of a heart attack. One feels so helpless when receiving such news and the sadness just doesn't go away quickly. I wondered whether my coming to America had been selfish, perhaps I should have stayed at home. I was at this time extra grateful to have Tanya with whom to share my grief and guilt.

Chapter 24

THE AGE OF THE MOTOR CAR

I cannot remember exactly when but it was around this time that I saw my first automobile – a young man drove one into North Conway, and he had driven his new vehicle all the way from Portland where it had been delivered to him. He said it came by ship from Montreal having been delivered there by train and ferry from Detroit, a growing town in the state of Michigan, where he said many automobiles were being built. He knew all about cars as he called them, he told me his had been made by a company called General Motors who were the first to build a factory for the manufacture of automobiles. He told me he would be driving back to Portland but had so far failed to get fuel to make the return journey. A supply of gas, the term used for the new fuel, was to be sent to him by train, ordered by the station master of North Conway. The journey from Portland may not sound so remarkable today but in the early nineteen hundreds the roads before the automobile were simply dirt roads often heavily rutted by the wheels of wagons etc, unlike in your country today where virtually all roads have hard McAdamed surfaces. Our part of North America, as far as roads were concerned, was no different from most other areas outside towns, in fact I was up on the mid Canadian provinces last year and even today in the thirties there was only one road between towns with a hard surface and that was the trans Canada highway, on all other roads in dry weather a cloud of dust followed every moving vehicle. However, the roads up there, since the automobile, had been graded at bends, and were generally well looked after and mostly devoid of ruts.

But, I digress…

"I suppose many of our roads were dirt roads at that time but I don't know any now," John still listening intently said.

Of course distances in England are never very great compared to those in America.

However, back to my story; I remember telling Joseph later that day what I had seen in North Conway and he being a man of vision said right away, although somewhat jokingly, he would have to look into this automobile business or he would soon find himself out of a job.

Chapter 25

Over the next two years there was much activity in the Washington Valley, scores of workers and much plant and equipment delivered to the site where the new hotel was being built. I went along on horseback several times to watch how the work was progressing and was taken round the site by Adam. Most of the workers, architects, engineers, and the imported Italian craftsmen lived on the site sleeping in one of the many huts built to house them. As was the case, I understand, when the railways were being built many of the workers were Irish to whom it seems building work comes naturally.

The new grand hotel was called The Mount Washington and it opened in 1902.

Edward was growing into a big lad and his little sister was soon joining her brother at the school in North Conway. I taught both of them to ride and Edward could confidently harness and drive the horse and buggy, and for his seventh birthday we bought him a pony. However, apart from taking the odd day off, I spent most of my time at the hotel where I was needed throughout the year. I did manage time to teach Tanya and the children to ski and we all learnt to skate on the rink that had been built in town. At school children were being encouraged to take part in sport and Edward was introduced to baseball and to football.

"I play football for my school, we have four teams and I have played in the third team," John interrupted proudly.

American football is not like your football, it is very complicated and played with a ball something like the ball used in your game called rugby. Frankly I have never understood the finer points even though I watched him play a few times.

At the hotel Martha still ruled in the kitchen except when our summer chef was there. Unfortunately the day came when he told us he would not be coming back the next year as he was going to retire. I now had the problem of getting a new chef as although Martha was an excellent cook she was not able to add that extra touch and variety to meals that customers wanted and trained chefs could bring. I advertised in many papers in the east including, as Mr Donald had done, the New York paper in which we had found the advertisement for the work we obtained in Jackson. Replies were, however, few and far between and it became necessary for me to make the offer of work much more attractive and finally I succeeded in getting a man from New York interested who agreed to come on a trial basis for one month in the off-season period. Martha always accepted that the special help of a chef was necessary and she was quite capable of knowing if a new chef would be adequately able to fill the vacancy. The new man arrived in February, it turned out that he was a recent immigrant from Italy who had previously spent time working as an under chef in a big hotel in Paris. His name was Enrico Minelli, and fortunately Martha took an instant liking to him and approved of what he was able to produce.

We still had most of the regular customers each year although we did notice one or two had not returned. However, our permanent residents, Mrs Brunel and her sister Miss Haverford were still living with us. Jenny who for some years had helped Martha in the kitchen had grown into a fine young lady and as she had become familiar with much of the work carried out by female staff and when Maggie Braithwaite left to get married and moved from the district, I offered Jenny that job which she had taken and had fitted in well. Why not Anna for the job, you may ask; well Anna was not so keen to do it she still had the urge to work in a store and now she was fluent in the language there was really nothing to stop her except there were not that many shops in North Conway and only the general store in Jackson. She liked clothes and one evening when Anna and Joseph were at our house for dinner Anna mentioned this again and I said, "Why don't you open a small ladies clothes store in town?"

She said it would be great but not that easy, first they would have to find an empty shop and then the money to fit the shop out and buy stock. I told them I would put up the money for a fifty per cent stake in the store; I would not interfere in the running but of course would help when it was needed. Anna was thrilled with the idea and the search began for suitable premises.

Chapter 26

By this time I had many contacts in town and I suppose had become a respected citizen. Many ladies who somehow heard of the proposal were keen to help as the only ladies clothes were presently sold in a general store in town, and certain of these ladies badgered their husbands to help find premises. In the end, we were offered a small piece of land next to a shop in town where it was possible to build. I managed to see Adam and in his spare time he drew up plans for the new premises, and the man who built our house put his men to work. In a very short time the store was completed.

Since Anna would now be required to spend time getting the store ready for business I found it necessary to take on another employee to fill in for Anna's absence; I managed to get a young school leaver from the village skilled in needlework to take over.

Since I was keen to see my money had not been wasted I was determined that the store would be a success and I was sensible enough to know that although I had complete faith in Anna I knew it was necessary for her to become familiar with what a good ladies dress store of the day looked like. I therefore sent her to Portland to spend time looking at stores, asking questions and seeing if there were any fashion houses and store fitters in that city.

When she returned she said she had seen one ladies dress store and had been to a department store that had one whole floor devoted to ladies garments. She had studied the fittings used and was told by the owner of the single store the name and address of her fitters. With respect to stock this lady relied on salesmen calling and she promised to see if any

155

when they called would be interested in a small store in North Conway.

"I left the lady the address but whether she will tell any salesmen I don't know."

I told her we could hardly rely on word of mouth and if we wanted to start business soon that we would have to try to make direct contact with a fashion house, even if it meant going to Boston or New York.

As a first step we wrote to the fitters in Portland giving the measurements of the selling space and a simple plan of the store, asking them if they would quote for fitting out as an up-to-date ladies fashion store. A week later we received the quote which listed all the equipment, cost of labour and travel expenses for two employees. They also stated when they could be available to carry out the fitting.

I talked it over with Anna and Joseph and we agreed to accept. So far, including the store fitting, I had committed myself to fifteen hundred dollars and knew that we would have to sell a lot of dresses to recover this and we still had to buy stock for the store. I placed a small advertisement in a Boston paper requesting fashion houses to get in touch with our store. At first we heard nothing, but in the middle of fitting out a salesman called having been sent by the store in Portland. As it happened Anna was on the premises when the salesman came. He told her he represented four companies and proceeded to show her one or two samples he carried in a large attaché case as well as handing to her brochures of the four makers in New York. I had suggested to her how much she might order and, guided by the salesman, she bought sufficient stock to start business. He promised her he would get it to her within a week which happened to be the time when the fitters said they would be finished. He told her that the stock he was providing was what was left over from the season's stock that had recently been cleared, but that it would be necessary for her to order stock for the season to come. This of course would be a further cash commitment

156

although not due for payment until a month after delivery in two months' time. My cash commitment was mounting and as yet we had not sold a garment. I must admit I began to wonder if I had acted wisely.

The stock promised by the salesman was duly delivered and we decided to have a grand opening of the store. We announced it in the local paper and had one or two notices put up around North Conway and in Conway itself. Anna and Tanya would both be present in the store on opening day and a glass of wine would be offered to all customers. The first day proved to be a great success with the three changing rooms being full nearly all day and the stock fast going down. Sales were being made not only to local ladies but to many holiday people staying in hotels in the valley. However, after the first day we realised that stock was dangerously low and we hurriedly sent a telegram to the salesman's address asking him if he could possibly get us some more stock in a hurry. Within three days the store was notified that stock had arrived at the railway station and would we collect. Anna had to make one more desperate request for more before the new season's stock arrived almost two months after the store had been opened and when it arrived we had very little left in the store to show customers. Our takings up to the arrival of the new stock had covered the cost of all the stock we had ordered including that for the new season. Although we were a long way from recovering my initial outlay I could now see there was every possibility that the investment would prove to be a success. I now owned a hotel and a fifty per cent stake in a ladies fashion store and I had been able to share some of my success with my good friend Joseph who, if Anna made a success of the store, would be the joint owner with me and his wife of an ongoing and hopefully prosperous business.

One day whilst looking at a magazine I saw a few pages devoted to a ladies fashion show held in a New York hotel and I thought 'I own a hotel, why not a fashion show there.' I talked it over with Tanya and Anna and they both thought it a good idea, that is until Anna said, 'Where do we get the models?' I obviously had not given the show enough thought. There were, we guessed, no models in North Conway or Jackson and to get anyone to come from Boston or New York would cost us far too much.

"We could of course just show the dresses on rails etc. just as in a store – or perhaps you Anna and Tanya could put one of the best dresses and hats on and parade around."

They both laughed out loud at this suggestion but it gave food for thought; "Why not get certain of the hotel staff to model clothes?" Tanya said. So we sat down to think of girls who might fit the bill and having worked out who we believed would look good in certain dresses we asked them to come along to my office to talk to Anna.

Anyway we managed to persuade all our possible models to agree. One or two were most apprehensive about parading in front of an audience but Jenny and Matilda jumped at the opportunity to put on the beautiful gowns they had seen in Anna's store and show them in the hotel.

We told customers who came into Anna's store and our guests in the hotel about our little fashion show but made sure to tell them that we were not able to engage professional models. We thought about advertising in the local paper but decided against it, fearing people would expect too much. I said we must look upon it as an experiment. Anyway the show proved to be a success with the girls showing off the gowns as best they could and a number of orders being taken. We resolved we would try another show the following season.

We thought about opening a store in the hotel but decided against it as we did not think the money generated from it would be worth the investment as the hotel was just not big enough.

Chapter 27

In I think 1900 the then president of the United States, McKinley, to whom I referred earlier, was assassinated and the hero of the war in Cuba, Theodore Roosevelt, became president. Although his time in office, as indeed with most presidents, had little affect on us in Jackson, we were told in the papers that he did some good things – breaking up Trusts which were rife in the country and taking decisions for the public good without seeking Congress approval. He also was the one who first put forward the idea of building a canal to join the Atlantic with the Pacific Ocean. He came from a wealthy family and the present president, Franklin Delano Roosevelt, is his nephew, although he is a Democrat, and cast as the 'black sheep of the family', whilst Theodore was a Republican.

Things were moving fast in the world in what I understand you in England later called the Edwardian age after your king Edward VII. The Wright brothers first successfully flew an aeroplane at the end of 1903 and telephones were spreading to many houses occupied by people with money and of course the automobile or motor car, as you know it, was making great strides. But not so good was what was happening in Europe and I was glad I had decided to emigrate. Germany under the rule of Kaiser Wilhelm was flexing its muscles, being envious of the empire that had been built by your country. The Kaiser gave orders for the German navy to grow in order to match the British navy who had the largest fleet of warships in the world. All this was happening in these first years of the century when for the ordinary citizens in America and in Britain life went on blissfully unaware of what was happening in the corridors of power which in the end was to cause such havoc in the world.

In spite of all this, my hotel through all the first decade of the century managed to attract customers so that for the most part we were full. Anna's store prospered and in 1908 we decided to open another store in nearby Conway, employing local staff to run it. Stock was ordered, delivered and checked to the North Conway store and then transported to Conway in the new truck I had bought the previous year for use by the hotel. We had also bought two automobiles for the hotel but many customers still preferred to be met and transported from the station by carriage, particularly in the winter when skis on carriages were used, so Joseph kept the horses and carriages. I also bought a small ten-seat bus for guests to be taken on tours of the valley and trips to the Cog Railway; this proved to be very popular with guests. I should mention that garages had appeared in the valley and North Conway was among the first to get one.

Mr Munroe, the gentleman who had been so generous to me when my jewellery was sold, had continued to come regularly until in 1903 he had paid a visit to the Mount Washington Hotel and was very impressed. I knew of this because whilst staying there he visited us at our hotel. Although we missed him and his wife, who I looked upon as friends, I was able to tell him our hotel was generally full in the seasons and that the Mount Washington had had little, if any, effect on profits although we knew that we had lost one or two of our more wealthy regulars. He of course could not resist talking about trains and he told me that due to the opening of the new hotel railway companies had been forced to put on many extra through trains from New York and Boston, at certain times in the year as many as one each hour arrived at Fabyan the station for the Mount Washington and other hotels in the area.

I remember I mentioned to him that I was going to put money up to open a ladies dress shop for my friend Anna. He was keen to know more and thought it was gamble but admired why I was doing it.

"Just make sure you get a solicitor involved in drawing up an agreement, even the best of friends sometimes do not agree and trouble can result."

I did take his advice when implementing the arrangement with Joseph and Anna.

Having just told you that, I realise my story is not always in sequence but I am sure you understand the things that occur to me whilst I am talking do not necessarily follow one after the other.

"Don't worry, Mr Livinski, I for one am following what you say with the greatest interest and I know John here is listening to every word. I am learning a lot about America and of things I have never thought of before. I know I should not say it but I selfishly rather hope the train stays broken down for a little longer, I want to hear more," Mrs Davis said.

Thank you for your kind words, I enjoy talking to you all, but please tell me if I go on too much.

Chapter 28

INDECISION AND SUFFRAGETTES

I told you that towards the end of the decade we opened a new store for Anna in Conway and as this prospered beyond our belief I thought about expanding further. I had recovered my original investment, and the fifty per cent share in store profits was now beginning to match those for the hotel. The problem was where to open this third store; we realised ideally it had to be in a large town or in a town in which visitors stayed for long periods, as we knew that a considerable part of the stores' income came from visitors to the Washington Valley. Since the advent of the automobile a favourite ride had been along the Kancamagus Highway to Lincoln and I seriously considered the latter to be a possible venue for the new store. I probably should mention why this highway was so popular with tourists. It is truly a very picturesque route and on it there has been built a number of stopping points at which visitors can enjoy views of mountains or take special walks to delightful waterfalls, all made safe by the authorities fitting barriers at dangerous points along the way.

I also considered Portland but reckoned the competition would be greater and in the end I decided it was too great a gamble. Nevertheless, the storekeeping bug had bitten and we, that is the four of us originals, started looking to other possible retail outlets. There were so many to choose from and since we were all in one way or another very well occupied already we had to be sure we would have time to give any new venture proper attention.

By the end of the decade we still had not risked another ladies fashion store or gambled on a new venture. Edward had finished high school and had no ambition to go on to university but helped me in the hotel and I could see it would not be long before he was quite capable of running things on his own. Caroline was still at school but she wanted to go to university and then perhaps open a library in North Conway.

She was all for the advancement of women and had avidly watched what was happening in your country with women fighting for the right to vote. Many times the papers from Boston and New York had given details of what the English suffragettes were up to in England. I expect you have heard about the suffragette movement, John, if not ask your mother – she will tell I am sure. That is right isn't it, Mrs Davis?

"Yes I remember it quite well, I was still at school but I remember hearing my mother and father talk about it and at school we had fights with boys over it. The fight went on for a good many years. My mother said it started at the turn of the century but really got going when Emily Pankhurst came on the scene two or three years later and for years women battled against the police and government. They chained themselves to government buildings, smashed windows and generally caused mayhem. Many were imprisoned, some went on hunger strike and were forced fed. Then in, I think it was just before the war a lady threw herself in front of the King's horse in the Derby and was killed. However, they stopped their action when war was declared and because of the work carried out by women in the war the government gave limited voting rights to women not long after the war ended."

When was it you got full voting rights, Mrs Davis?

"I'm not sure, but I seem to remember it was just after the first talking pictures came along – perhaps 1928."

"What about America, sir?"

I do know we gave full rights to women before that but exactly when I can't remember, probably just after the war. However, I do know that almost since America became independent a woman was allowed to be elected to

163

government – I seem to remember reading it somewhere and 1788 sticks in my mind."

Yes we were quite well informed of what was happening in the world. We learnt of the death of your king and his accession by George V and we read of the new battleships being launched by Germany and how big the German army was becoming. As far as we knew our army was quite modest but then we were confident that we would not get involved in conflicts which appeared to be brewing in Europe.

We in America were it seemed intent on industrial growth and from what we in the country away from big cities gathered advancement was very considerable. In New Hampshire the town of Manchester was leading the way as far as industry was concerned, taking shape, someone remarked to me after the city of the same name in England.

We had little industry in Washington Valley, we were in fact dependent on visitors for our growth and without these we knew we would lose population and probably we would have joined the trek to the West. I should mention that New Hampshire if necessary could have been self-sufficient in food as the original residents were farmers and many farms remained, we at Wentworth taking full advantage of local produce.

I think I mentioned earlier that Martha looked after much of the ordering of food and she certainly did this using local farm produce whenever possible, but sadly she became ill one day soon after Christmas 1910. She had been for many years in excellent health but as so often happens illness suddenly struck and she became so bad that she had to stop work. I was thus forced to look around for someone to fill her place, it was not easy as she had such a wealth of experience and worked all hours without question. Happily, after a few weeks and care from the good local doctor she recovered but decided at 70 years of age she had had enough of work. I found her accommodation in a small cottage in Jackson that I rented on her behalf and she lived to 90. Her replacement was a widow from North Conway whose husband had only recently died leaving her with a little girl called Laura. I arranged for this lady to have the accommodation vacated by Martha and agreed the little girl could stay with her in the hotel. Susanne, for that was her name, was a good cook and soon fell into the ways of the hotel and Laura became everyone's favourite little girl with both staff and guests alike.

Apart from the State Fair that many residents tried to attend each year I well remember the Buffalo Bill circus that came to town on more than one occasion. It only stayed for a few days but I think every boy and girl in town managed to get along to see it. It was also popular with adults from the town as well as many visitors. We saw shooting, lassoing, and plenty of excitement with Indians riding into the ring, whilst everyone marvelled at the aerobatics performed by men and women far above the audience on trapezes, and laughed at the antics of the clowns. I understand Buffalo Bill and the circus had previously crossed over to England and given shows there. Is that not right, Mr Davis?

"Yes that is very true, it is one of my earliest memories seeing Buffalo Bill. I didn't actually go to the circus but my dad took me along to the High street to see the parade and I saw him then."

Of course film shows were beginning to take over from the circus and picture houses were being built in towns all over. We had our own in North Conway and it proved most popular.

Into the second decade of the century everything was moving so fast. Airplanes were apparently being seen all over the place, although up until then I had not myself seen one. We read in the paper that a Frenchman, Louis Bleriot had flown a plane across the English Channel and there seemed to be nothing that could not be achieved. The year following a vast new liner built in Belfast, Ireland, reputed to be unsinkable, sailed to America and struck an iceberg with terrible loss of life. This as you know was the *Titanic*, the year was 1912.

Chapter 29

WORLD WAR I

It was soon after this that the daily papers from the big cities reported that the son of our old Emperor in Austria had been assassinated in a place called Serajevo. It was this that later gave the excuse for Germany to start a war. It was so remote from our quiet world of Washington Valley that we never dreamt it would one day involve us. The Germans with their mighty army attacked Russia and when the French entered having a treaty with Russia, the Germans entered Belgium – an easy way they thought of attacking France – and pushed across the border into France further south. As you no doubt know, John, Britain joined in the war because you had a treaty with Belgium. The British, with a big empire but a relatively small standing army as compared to the Germans, entered Belgium but after some fierce battles were driven back into France where the French were desperately hanging on trying to stop the Germans entering Paris as the Prussians had done in 1871. Were you old enough to get involved in the war, Mr Davis?

"Oh yes," John almost shouted, "My dad was mentioned in despatches."

"Let your dad speak. I'm sorry, Mr Livinski, John is so proud of his dad."

So he should be Mrs Davis. What were you in, Mr Davis?"

Mr Davis was not used to talking to strangers about his war effort, particularly knowing most men of his age in his country had been involved. "I was in the infantry," was all he said.

Since I am telling you my story I hope you won't mind if I ask that you tell me a little about your experiences. I have a particular reason for asking – my son was in the war too.

"Well I volunteered with my friends immediately war was declared and sent to training camp where we were kitted out. After some weeks of training I was made a sergeant in the 11th Royal Fusiliers. On a seven-day leave before going to France I married my sweetheart in a small country church. In France we were first sent to the front in Belgium around a town called Ypres, which the troops knew as Wipers. Eventually we were forced back and for some year or so fought in trench warfare, neither side gaining advantage. Then those up top decided they had a plan to drive the Germans back and built up hundreds of thousands of men ready for a big attack. This became the Battle of the Somme and on the first day the British and Empire troops had 50,000 casualties and gained a few yards only. On my father's request when my younger brother later volunteered to join my regiment, I managed to get him in my company. He was killed soon after. My youngest brother, mad on horses, joined the artillery and one day when I was returning to base from the front line on my own and the shellfire was getting very heavy, four horses with a single rider pulling a gun carriage came tearing up and the driver yelled, "Jump up, mate." It was then I recognised it was my brother – he was barely sixteen! He was later taken prisoner after being wounded. A couple of years later I was sent back to England to Officers Training School and the war ended at the time I received my commission.

That was most interesting, Mr Davis, how can I possibly follow that? But you have not told the whole story, how did you get mentioned in despatches as John here said.

"Oh that was nothing really, I simply carried rations up to the front line under heavy shellfire, that's all."

"We have a certificate signed after the war by Winston Churchill confirming Dad's action," John said and added, "My Mother saw a Zeppelin shot down, didn't you, Mum?"

"Oh yes, my friend and I coming home from work in the dark were told to lay down on the ground as it went sailing by almost overhead and then we saw a small plane diving about and then the Zeppelin burst into flames. The young man who shot it down got the VC." She paused as if again reliving the incident, and then, "But please go on with your story, Mr Livinski, you can't end here."

I was telling you how the war in Europe started, at least how we in America understood it from the newspapers, but I should have known you would know more about it than me, you were in it – although thankfully not you, John. We in Washington Valley carried on with our lives and the war in Europe was in another world. The two stores we owned continued to prosper as did the hotel with my son playing a big part in its continual success. Caroline had just finished university and Tanya and I decided we would open a small bookstore for her in town. It soon became a success as she not only sold books but loaned them out for a small fee.

As you know all the time you, Mr Davis, were fighting in France and Zeppelins bombed London, shipping was being sunk in the North Atlantic by German U-boats. It seemed these boats sunk any ship leaving or heading for Britain and of course often there were American passengers on board. In 1915 the liner *Lusitania* had been sunk with the loss of many lives including over 100 Americans. President Wilson protested to Germany and for some time U-boats did not attack passenger liners. However, in January 1917 the U-boats reverted to unrestricted sinking of vessels and in particular three American ships were sunk and in April something we never expected to happen occurred – we entered the European war and, as I understand happened in Britain, thousands of young men seeking adventure joined the armed forces, among these was my son. He was sent to a training camp not too far from home and we saw him in his uniform when he was given leave. Towards the end of the year he came home and told us he was going overseas and was shipped off to New York. We had a number of letters from him saying how he was getting on and how lovely the country was where he was stationed, then in the following letter he said he had met an English girl and he was getting married. It naturally came as a big surprise but we wrote back and said we were pleased. We had one further short letter to say he was on his way to France and no more. The next we had was a telegram saying he had been killed in action. It had happened all so quickly that it was difficult to believe that it was true, but of course sadly it was.

"Did you hear from the wife?"

Yes we did, we had no address to contact her but she wrote to us a few months later to say she was going to have my son's child and then not long before the war ended she wrote to say she had had a baby girl who she had named Davina. We wrote several letters to the address she had given but we had no reply and later our letters were returned 'Gone Away'.

"So you don't know what happened or where your grandchild is?"

We tried through the army to see if they could help but only found where the couple had been married. We were told we would be wasting our time looking further as the American Embassy in London had carried out a comprehensive search and found nothing. The address the girl had given did not exist. Several times we thought we would go over and see what we could find but we never did, knowing it would take us about three weeks travelling alone and time was precious as, having lost Edward, I was back again to taking the full weight of work in the hotel.

"Do you remember where the church was?"

Yes, I have the name of the village and I intended finding it today, although I knew in my heart that it would likely be a fruitless visit. I knew it was in the county of Essex and I was told to go to Liverpool Street station which served all railway stations in that county. I asked at a ticket booth but the man issuing tickets did not know it and said I should go to a library and they would soon tell me, but they would be closed today. That was when I saw the advert for this excursion and decided I could find the village another day and go to a library as had been suggested to me. After all it was almost twenty years ago since the marriage took place; it could wait another day, I thought.

"There are scores of villages in Essex but it should not be too difficult to find it. What was the name?"

Little Warley.

"My goodness, that is a village not far from where we are now. How strange, because the nearest station would be the one we just passed before the train broke down. It would be Brentwood."

How did you know that?

"I used to cycle a lot when I was young and I cycled out into the country this way and I remember Warley, quite close to Brentwood, and the pretty little village of Little Warley further on. It's a small world as they say. Mind you it could have changed in all these years."

I think I will try and go there tomorrow, *he paused deep in thought,* but what good it will do me I do not know, however, perhaps I can trace relatives of the young lady. The child, if she is still alive, would now be nearing the end of her teens – I wonder if she has any idea who her grandparents are, I guess not or I am sure she would have contacted us.

"You were telling us about your son and the war. What happened to you all when the war ended? I hope you don't mind going on but we have become so involved in your story, at least I know I have, that I feel I must know what happened next."

Well really I have never gone over my life in my mind the way I have today. I did not know I could remember so much and I am very grateful to you for listening, I have enjoyed going back remembering the happy times, the worrying times and the sad times. Tanya would have enjoyed listening too, I know, she often said, "You can tell a good tale, you should write a book."

If you want more of my story then I will go on.

"Yes we do," came in almost a chorus.

There were of course great celebrations in all towns and villages when the war finally ended. Of course we had only been in it for eighteen months or so, unlike you who had been fighting for over four years, but I am sure the relief that it was all over was no less in America than it was in your country. There was, however, in our household much sadness as the war end hit home and we suffered the full realisation that Edward would not be there again. Tanya was particularly sad and frequently burst into tears.

Chapter 30

POST WAR

Anna and Joseph were still living in Jackson and not having a family planned to adopt a child but it never happened. They were always very close to our daughter Caroline and I think in their minds they adopted her as they frequently visited her in her library and often invited her round to a special tea or dinner. The bookstore was doing very well and she had to employ an assistant instead of keep closing the store when she had other matters to attend to, such as going to book fairs in other towns both in and out of state.

During the period of the war we had lost some business in the hotel as perhaps people thought it unpatriotic to have expensive holidays when their boys were fighting thousands of miles away. However, 1919 saw people returning, and our mostly older clientele regaled us from time to time with stories of what their grandsons did in the war without at first knowing our own son had been lost to us. Mrs Munroe came back that year and told us that my benefactor had died peacefully the year before in their home on Long Island. So the great train man would be with us no more and remembering him I wonder what he would have made of our present situation on a broken down train. I am sure he would have had a story to tell us.

The town of North Conway was still small but it was growing with people buying homes for summer and autumn vacations. Business in the stores prospered even though some of the big money people were taking holidays further afield in the now busy Florida coast, in particular Miami. The crack trans-continental trains through Chicago we were told by our 'new' stationmaster were nearly always full as people flocked to Los Angeles and Hollywood, growing fast as the film capital of the world. The previous stationmaster who had become a good friend and who was there when we first arrived had retired some years earlier when he reached the age of seventy-five and thought it was time he left and, as he said, sat back on the veranda and watch the world go by. I always remember how proud he was to tell us his family was one of the first to settle in the valley and that his grandfather had fought in the War of Independence.

The more recent war had hastened the advance of the airplane and it was now often possible to fly to many destinations in North America. Women's clothes had changed dramatically since the war and instead of dresses made up with yards of material, they were each year designed to use less and less. Skirts became shorter and shorter and as for the large hats we sold when Anna's first store was opened, they disappeared and were being replaced by hats that fitted tight to the head like a crown, or else the ladies wore bands around their heads often sparkling with diamanté.

Due to the prohibition law that came into force in 1920, the making of alcoholic drinks for consumption at home or in the speakeasies that sprung up throughout the country fast became the province of men not afraid of the law and as gangs of men saw the vast amount of money that could be made we had the growth of gangsterism so vividly displayed in films. I am sure you have seen New York and Chicago gangsters featured in films fighting each other and the law, and the weapons they used was not only the small handgun but a new weapon that could fire many rounds at a very rapid rate. This was the Thompson Machine Gun, known in the business as the Tommy gun. Fortunately this lawlessness never came to the Washington Valley although I am pretty certain money gained in the big cities from liquor sales was often spent with us. I was told that there were at one time over 100,000 speakeasies in New York and this being so you can imagine that we in the Washington Valley had a few too, although Tanya and I never visited one.

As I understand is the case in this country every populated area had its own theatre where films were shown, but at this time films were all silent and to add atmosphere to that shown on the screen each playhouse had to have a piano and a pianist. However, in spite of there being hundreds of cinemas there did not appear to be any shortage of good pianists no doubt due to the fact that for many years the main form of entertainment in the home had been music and singing, and the piano had become a most popular instrument. We did not have a piano at home but in a spare room at the back of the hotel Mr Donald had kept a second piano just in case there was some unfortunate accident to the one in the main part of the hotel. He said we could use it any time and when I took over and the children were old enough Tanya, who had learnt to play in the old country, taught them, but neither Edward nor Caroline proved to be very musical.

In spite of prohibition and the gangster culture that followed in Chicago and New York, there was an air of prosperity in the country and most people lived well, but all this came to a sudden end in 1929 when there was disaster in the financial centre of New York and therefore the country. This became known as the Wall Street Crash and caused thousands to lose all their money which had a knock-on effect all over the country, it was the beginning of one of the worst periods in American history known as the great depression. It was probably peculiar to America that so many, what I believe you call, white collar and blue collar workers, invested their savings in shares on the Stock Exchange, so that most average Americans all over the country were directly affected by the crash and their losses put even more pressure on the under privileged. Factories and offices closed and very soon many citizens were forced to seek some assistance from the state in order to live. The depression lasted right through the early years of the thirties and had its affect on other industrialised countries in the world, including Britain. Many stories have been written on this period where in parts of America people were forced to move far away to try to start a new life; John Steinbeck conjures up the period well in *The Grapes of Wrath* and *Of Mice and Men*. I feel strongly about this period as it affected so many people, but I am pleased to say I and my family were lucky to survive, almost untouched, although bookings in the hotel and sales in our stores were well down.

"I know how you must feel, the situation was bad over here too, many people had a very hard time trying to find work and survive. In fact it has only recently begun to get better with some help perhaps by the government spending something on rearmament of the armed forces," Mr Davis interrupted. *"Sorry, Mr Livinski, please carry on,"* he added.

I don't know about you, Mr Davis, but talking about this sad period in America reminds me strangely of a sport I have not mentioned whilst talking to you, that sport is boxing and I am reminded of what we were told lifted the spirits of many people in our country suffering at that time. No, it was not that we were told we had the best boxers in the world but simply due to one of the 'no hopers' in the depression making it to the top. As I think is the case in this country, no one who listens to the radio or reads a newspaper in the twenties and to date in the thirties could miss knowing who were the big names in boxing, whether one was in the least interested or not. Everyone knew the names of Jack Dempsey, Gene Tunney etc but, this mostly out-of-work docker rising to the top is supposed to have inspired and given hope to millions at one of the lowest points in their lives. The man was James J. Braddock who took the World Heavyweight championship title from the holder, Max Baer. You probably remember it too. In fact I only read yesterday about your own man, Welshman Tommy Farr, being due to fight Joe Louis for the title at the end of this month.

Chapter 31

WORLD CHANGES AND GREAT SADNESS

As I am sure you know, John, the map of Europe has been changed following the war. The old Austro-Hungarian Empire has been broken up and once more Polish people have a country they could call their own. I have relatives of course in the new Poland but there was only one cousin with whom I had any contact and she wrote once or twice to tell me what post-war living was like. There was a great deal of unemployment all over central Europe, particularly in Germany which was suffering the after effects of starting a war and losing. My cousin said that travelling around as she did for the new Polish government, she had seen unrest almost everywhere and influenced by what happened in Russia many were agitating for change, some heading for communism and others going in the almost opposite direction to join parties who were generally known as fascists. Particularly in Italy where a man called Mussolini took control with his fascist party, and then in Germany a far-right party claiming to be National Socialists was growing fast and because it was adopting a disciplined approach and preaching the superiority and destiny of the German people it was gaining more support than those who wanted communism to take over. This party as you know is known as the Nazi party and is led by a man called Adolph Hitler. And then as you know there is now a war going on in Spain where the fascists are fighting the socialist or communist government.

"Yes I know quite a lot about that war and have good reason to remember it," John said.

Go ahead and tell us, young man.

"Only briefly, John, I want to hear more from Mr Livinski," Mrs Davis *added who knew her son liked telling everyone about the Spanish Civil War. John, happy to tell his story, started.*

"My school had joined the Secondary Schools Travel Trust and each year the trust organises a cruise, one year to the Baltic and the next south to Madeira etc. I never expected to go but when I brought the papers on it from school, much to my surprise Mum and Dad asked me if I would like to go, and, of course, I said yes. It was to be six guineas for the two weeks. A guinea, Mr Livinski, in case you don't know, is one pound plus one shilling."

"Get on with it, John," urged Mrs Davis.

"Well our party from school of about fifteen boys met hundreds of other boys at Waterloo station and we all caught the Boat Train to Southampton. When settled in on board we were all given cards to send home before the boat sailed, the card stating that the itinerary of the cruise had been changed. We should have been going to Lisbon, Gibraltar, Ceuta, Casablanca and Madeira, but now we were telling our parents that the ship would not be calling at Gibraltar or Ceuta. We learnt later that this was because a Spanish general called Franco had gathered an army in Spanish Morocco and was crossing the Straits of Gibraltar and landing troops in southern Spain, at a port called Algeciras. The British Navy in Gibraltar had closed the Straits to all shipping to avoid any international incident and hence we would not be able to call in at Gibraltar or Ceuta, in Spanish Morocco. So as you see I have good cause to remember the war in Spain which I have followed in the papers ever since, having I suppose more of a personal interest than most in this country."

That was most interesting, John, I imagine you will always have good cause to remember the terrible war still going on in Spain.

"Do carry on, Mr Livinski."

As I remember I was talking about how the map of Europe had changed since the war and that there was a great deal of unrest and poverty over there. This caused more massive immigration to America, among which were many Italians, mostly settling initially in New York where I was told recently that one in eight people in that city are Italian; at present New York has a population of over six million.

Many things changed in the twenties – wireless broadcasting started in most countries, feats of man as always were of interest and with the new, now more advanced methods of propulsion, newspapers fed us from time to time with stories of, how fast or far someone had travelled in the air, on land or on water. Countries vied, or so it seemed from the newspapers, with one another to see who had the fastest, automobile, boat or airplane. We in Washington Valley could not boast of any such connection with speed, although we did have I believe the oldest cog railway in the world.

We were now getting better roads and better automobiles but as today the cost of having an automobile was too much for the average person.

"That is the same over here. I don't know anyone who has a motor car and yet there seem to be plenty on the roads in London."

One day I don't doubt we will all have automobiles but I can't see it in my lifetime. Anyway in America, and I believe in Europe, a great deal was made of a man called Lindbergh flying solo across the Atlantic from New England to France in a single-engine aircraft. The ocean having previously only been crossed at a narrower point by a twin-engine plane, first with, I believe, two Englishman on board.

"That's right, Alcock and Brown."

Thank you I thought I was right.

But I should get back to my story in Jackson, or else I will not finish before this train manages to get going.

We had now had the hotel for twenty years and I was beginning to feel it was time Tanya and I had a holiday. Many times we intended to go away but something always came up to stop us. In order to take a holiday I knew I would have to get a man in to gradually take over from me in the way Mr Donald had done with me shortly after we first came to Jackson. So I advertised for an experienced man and had one reply from a man who had for the past several years worked in the Mount Washington Hotel as one of the many assistant managers. I interviewed him and he seemed to have all the right qualities and so I took him on. He was single and simply changed his living accommodation from one hotel to another. He was tall and had a shock of red hair, I think you would call him ginger, and of course he was known to everyone as Red, his real name was Robert McGregor and his family had emigrated from Scotland at the turn of the century. Although living in America practically all his life he still had a little of his Scottish accent which he had obviously acquired from his parents who were now living not far away in Lincoln. The guests took to him right away and I heard they liked to hear him speak. He came to us in 1924 and the following year both Tanya and I felt secure enough to let him run the hotel while we took a holiday, which apart from our short break in New York many years before would be our first. Where to go that was our problem. We could have gone south but as it was getting near to summer and neither of us liking it too warm we decided to go north to Canada. Tanya said she would like to see the Rockies and so, remembering the colourful Canadian Pacific brochure, that had helped us all those years ago in New York, we wrote for their latest and booked to join the trans-continental express in Montreal going all the way to Vancouver and stopping over in various places of interest on the way. We were away for a month and when we returned we found all had gone well. We also found the two stores had had a good month and in talking to Anna she let slip that Caroline had taken a liking to our new manager. They were both of a similar age and I expressed to Tanya that they seemed well suited for each other.

A week or two later Caroline told us of her friendship with Robert McGregor and asked what we thought of the young man. We both of course said we thought him a very good man, which we could see pleased her, and a few months later she came to us in great excitement telling us he had asked her to marry him.

The wedding took place in August 1925 and they now have two children – one a little boy just 10, Daniel, and a little girl, almost 6 called Abigail, known as Abby. So you see I have two grandchildren in America and one I hope to find over here. Tanya lived long enough to see Daniel but sadly died at the end of 1928 after catching pneumonia, so never saw young Abigail. We all miss her terribly.

As he said this a slight choke came into his voice and at the same time the guard of the train who Mr Davis had spoken to earlier came along and interrupted.

Chapter 32

MORE ROMANS?

"It looks as if we should be able to get going soon Bert, They reckon in about half an hour. The fire brigade are clearing up."

"Clearing up what?" Mr Davis asked.

"Well I can't tell you much as everyone seems to be cagey. I don't reckon we will ever know for sure – something about Romans, if you ask me they are all potty," he said.

Those in the compartment looked at each other somewhat in astonishment, as the guard walked further down the corridor, but nothing was said until Eileen piped up.

"I thought you told me the Romans left here hundreds of years ago."

"Yes, they did. I think someone is pulling our legs."

"Bit of a coincidence though," Mrs Davis added. "However, since we might soon be on the move I want to hear the rest of our friend's story."

"Yes, please go on, sir, you were telling us about your daughter marrying and having two children," John said.

"Yes you did not say much about them and as I have a picture of most of the people you have told us about I need to fill the gap by you telling us where they went to live after they were married," Mrs Davis added.

Oh I helped them with some money to buy a house not far from where Tanya and I lived, I did not give them all the money they needed so they had to take a loan out from the good old Savings and Loan.

"I assume they are still there? The children must be growing up now."

Yes they are.

Chapter 33

PROGRESS IN THE AIR AND ON THE GROUND?

We talked earlier about airships, in particular the Zeppelin used in the war against London. Then earlier this year we read and saw on newsreels the dreadful crash of the Hindenburg when it was landing in New Jersey. It is amazing when one sees the pictures that so many people survived but I imagine this will be the end of this form of travel in which the Germans had invested so much. England appears to have already given up after one of your airships crashed.

John excitedly butted in, "Yes I saw it fly over my house in London in the evening on its way I think to India but it crashed in France. It was the R101. I was about eight at the time."

You have beaten me, John, I have never seen an airship except at the cinema, I am sure none ever came to Washington Valley.

I of course jumped ahead a little mentioning the crash of the Hindenburg which only happened a few months ago, but apart from that I think I have brought you up to the end of the twenties. Let me see what else of interest happened. *Our story teller paused and his eyes said he had become sad, but with the others looking at him he fought hard to carry on.*

You don't need me to tell you that in the late twenties we had the first talking pictures when an entertainer named Al Jolsen starred in a film in which he sang. I think the year was 1927 and very soon all film companies were forced to change to talkies. Many of the silent film stars were unable to make the change however, as their voices did not match the roles they were used to playing, instead new stars arose.

"I saw one of the early talkies, it was called Weary River, Mum and Dad took me."

Yes the cinema and talkies in particular, have become an important part of many people's lives throughout the world. Picture houses have opened up everywhere.

"We have three in our town and in less than a mile or so there are four or five others," John said.

It is certainly the same in the populated areas of the States. One of the benefits, apart from general entertainment, the talkies have brought I suppose is the news bulletin giving people a better knowledge of what is going on around them and in the world today.

"Some of course might say it is better not to know as most news is often bad," Mr Davis said.

Yes, that is very true, particularly what seems to be happening in Germany with the ill treatment of Jews. Of course those fortunate enough to have money did have a brief opportunity in the early years of this decade to emigrate, mostly to America.

"We have a German Jew in our class at school, he said his parents were driven out some three years ago."

So I guess many have come to your country as well as mine.

Chapter 34

THE EXCURSION ENDS

While speaking, Mr Livinski had sat with his back to the window away from the corridor but when he finished the last sentence he stood up and as he did so he was thrown sideways as the train moved.

"We're off at last."

The train quickly gathered speed as Leon Livinski seated himself once again.

"It won't be long now," Mr Davis remarked as the train flashed through a station called Harold Wood, "Fifteen minutes at the most."

"That was a fascinating story, Mr Livinski, I thoroughly enjoyed listening, I am sure we all did. Thank you so much."

The train was now passing another station but it was going so fast the name could not be read.

"What station was that, Dad?"

"Gidea Park. She must be up to eighty now, she'll have to start slowing soon as we have fourteen coaches fully laden."

Livinski looked at Mr Davis and said, "You would have enjoyed talking to my friend Mr Munroe I told you about."

"Well I've driven trains on this line for years and my father and brother have too."

"Your brother?"

"Yes, the young lad who picked me up in France on the gun carriage during the war. He doesn't drive here now, he went out to Nigeria to drive engines there and earn a lot of money."

"How did that come about?"

"A few years back the government in Nigeria advertised in England for drivers. My brother decided to go and tried to persuade me but I decided against it. He goes over for eighteen months and then gets six months leave and travels first class on ships. The journey to Lagos takes two weeks and he earns three or four times what I earn and has been able to buy his family a house and move away from the East End. The engines he drives are great big things and he has two black firemen and, as he says, he hardly gets his hands dirty. He lives the life of Riley."

"Sounds as if you regret not going."

"Well certainly I envy his lifestyle when he comes home but he misses the children growing up being away so much, I wouldn't like that."

Mr Davis had hardly finished talking when the train started to slow and began rattling through suburban stations at a much slower speed until it passed Bethnal Green Junction where the driver put the brakes on much harder and a minute or two later they glided into platform 16 of Liverpool Street station It was nearly half past ten.

"I am afraid it is much too late to go anywhere but back to our abodes, I had planned to take you out for a meal. Would you let me take you out some other time? I have enjoyed your company."

By this time the train had stopped and people were getting out onto the platform.

Mrs Davis answered as they left the compartment and walked along the corridor to the nearest door.

"Thank you but we seldom come up to London and Bert doesn't get much free time. Perhaps you could come and see us, we only live at Stratford just a couple of stops up the line. You are on nights this week aren't you, Bert?" Bert nodded agreement. "Next Sunday would be fine – about one o'clock, that would give Bert time to have a little sleep before you come."

Livinski really had no desire to go to their home and certainly did not want them to prepare a meal for him, however, he did not wish to offend so he said yes but only on the understanding they allowed him to take them out for a meal.

"There is nowhere I know of near us where you can eat other than rough workmen's cafes," Mrs Davis said.

"Don't you worry I'll take care of it, I'll come by cab and the cab driver can take us somewhere. Let me write your address down." He took out a pencil and scribbled the address on a piece of paper as Mrs Davis gave it him. At the ticket barrier he shook hands with them and said goodbye. "I'll be there at one o'clock on Sunday next."

He walked out of the station and caught a cab back to his hotel.

Part Two
The Granddaughter

Chapter 1

The following morning after breakfast he again made his way to Liverpool Street station and bought a return ticket to Brentwood. A porter directed him to platform 15 and at the barrier he checked with the ticket collector that the train on the platform stopped at Brentwood.

The train stopped just once before pulling into Brentwood where he alighted. Outside the station he looked for a cab but there were none to be seen. He asked at the booking office and the clerk said there was one cab usually at the station and he guessed it would be back shortly.

Brentwood, about eighteen miles from the London terminus, was in the thirties quite a country town and there were not many people about near the station, just a few more than North Conway. Livinski found a seat outside and waited. Some ten minutes later the cab arrived.

"Could you take me to Little Warley, I want to go to the church there."

The driver told him to get inside and started off up the steep hill outside the station.

"I may be a little while at the church, how do I get you to come and pick me up?"

"Ring this number and you might get me, it's the call box outside the station, if not you will have to catch a bus, they should run every hour."

It was only a short ride through Warley to the pretty little village and the driver dropped his passenger outside the church.

Livinski walked up the short path to the church and opened the door which was unlocked, no one was about. He walked up the knave and looked at the old oak pews on either side. He knew the church register of births and marriages would likely be in a room at the back of the church but the door was locked. Outside the church he went over to the nearest house which he thought might be the vicarage and knocked at the door. It was opened by an elderly lady.

"Yes, can I help you?"

"I would like to look at the parish register as I am trying to trace the whereabouts of someone."

"The vicar has gone out for the morning but I may be able to help you. Just a moment while I get the key." She returned a minute later and beckoned Livinski to follow.

She went into the church and opened the door at the end and there on a table was a very big book.

"This is our register. What is the name and what year are we talking about?"

"As perhaps you have already guessed, I am an American and I am trying to trace my grandchild whose mother married my son during the war in 1918. My name is Livinski and I believe the young lady might have come from this village but I don't know her maiden name."

The lady opened the book and started turning pages until she came to a page where dates were 1918. "Here it is, your name shows easily as we have never had any name like that. There you are – 30th August 1918 your son married a Margaret French."

"Does that name mean anything to you?"

"There have been a number of people in this area with that name but I can't say I know anyone living in the village today."

"Was the present vicar around at that time?"

"Yes he would have been, he has been vicar here for just over twenty years so he would have been the one who married them."

"Would you mind if I wait until he comes back?"

"Not at all, come over to the house and I will make you a cup of tea."

They went over to the house and the lady gave him a comfortable chair near the fire and brought him a cup of tea.

"How is it you have lost your grandchild?"

"Shortly after they were married my son went to France and was killed, his wife wrote to us later and told us she had given birth to my son's child, a girl. We wrote back but got no reply and later letters were returned 'gone away'. We tried to trace her through the army who said although the embassy in London had searched they had had no success."

"Well I do not know what to suggest but perhaps the vicar will be able to help when he returns."

It was about an hour and a half later when he did return.

They were introduced and the lady told the vicar the story almost word for word as she had been told.

"Yes, I remember the young man. You can't forget a name like Livinski in this country. But I cannot remember the name of the young lady, although I do have a picture of her being quite dark."

"Have you any idea how I might trace her?"

"I gather you have already looked at the register and got her maiden name, all I can suggest is that you perhaps call at houses in the village and perhaps there is someone who may remember her."

"I suppose I could do that but some people might wonder who on earth I am and not even open the door, particularly older people who might be just the ones who may have information."

"Let me come with you, many of them know me even if they don't come to church."

"That is most kind of you, Reverend."

"Give me a chance to have a bite to eat and I will join you. By the way have you eaten?"

"I'm really not hungry."

"Well at least have a piece of cake or something, Mrs Lovett will get you something."

The vicar left the room and Mrs Lovett duly brought more tea and a slice of home-made cake for Livinski.

"The vicar is eating the food I prepared for him in the kitchen, he won't be long."

And he was not long.

"Where are you from, I gather from your accent that you must be from America?"

"Yes you are right, I am from a small town in New Hampshire in New England."

"Sounds quite romantic, I'm afraid I have hardly been anywhere. Do I detect a very slight foreign accent too?"

"Yes, I have never quite lost it, I was born in the old Austro-Hungarian Empire in what is now Poland – I am Polish or at least my parents were Polish."

"Well that is interesting, I would like to talk to you more but I think we ought to get going on our round, it could take some time."

They called at six houses in the village and no one who answered had anything to offer, but at the seventh cottage a man and his wife said they remembered the American soldier coming to the village.

"A few American soldiers did some training for a short while on the common – you know, vicar, Warley Common. But I think the one who got married over at the church was the only one I saw in the village a couple of times, except of course on the day of the wedding when I saw one or two others come out of the church."

"Did you know the young lady?" the vicar asked.

"No, but I remember she was a very dark lass, not at all like the local girls. I remember saying to Bessie here that perhaps she came from the gypsy camp up the road, they come there pretty much every year. I know nothing more, as I told another American who called many years ago."

"Thank you, Mr Simmons, that is most helpful."

They said goodbye to the friendly old people in the cottage and as they walked back up the garden path Livinski spoke. "I think we would be wasting our time calling elsewhere, I am almost convinced that my son married a gypsy girl – I guess they move around all over, and unless I can find an encampment, who happens to be the same ones who camp near here, I doubt I have any chance of finding what I am looking for."

"You are probably right but you mustn't give up, you now have a clue."

Livinski walked back to the vicarage and was given another cup of tea.

"Might I suggest you find who owns the land the gypsies camp on around here. If they are there regularly they have probably got permission to camp, or else I am sure there would be trouble. They probably come when there is harvest time on the farms, or fruit picking for the farmers."

"What a good idea, could you show me where the land is where they camp and perhaps we could ask around and find out who owns it."

Mrs Lovett was in the room clearing cups and saucers and heard what was said.

"I know where they camp and I know who owns the land. It is Lady Winthrop who lives up at the manor – you know, vicar, she has been once or twice to our church."

"Yes I know. Good thinking, Mrs Lovett. I tell you what, I'll drive you up there, we might be lucky and find her in."

"That's great – thank you so much, both of you."

The vicar led the way to his little car, a Standard Eight.

"I haven't ever been up to the manor house but I know where it is, not far from here."

They drove for about a mile and then turned off the road and up an unmade road which led to an old house a few hundred yards off the road. The vicar stopped his car in front of the main entrance and they both climbed up the six stairs to the front door. The vicar pulled the chain by the side of the door and they heard the bell sound within. They waited a few minutes and were just about to give the bell another pull when the big door opened. A smartly dressed grey-haired man appeared at the door

"What can I do for you?" he said and then obviously noticing the vicar's collar added, "Reverend."

"May we speak to the lady of the house? We are not selling anything we just wonder if she is able to tell us about the gypsies who use her land each year."

"Madam is out at present, but I know they always ask her permission."

"When will the lady be back or perhaps you know when they will be likely to come again?"

"Well, sir, I do know the lady was talking about it the other day. She told me to expect them in two or three weeks' time. But one can never be sure except I know our farm has plenty of work for them."

"It is now August 10th do you think they will be here before the end of the month?"

"It is quite possible, sir."

"Well thank you for your information, no doubt you will tell her ladyship we called and if she knows a more definite time perhaps you would ask her to let me know at the vicarage, we have had a telephone installed so she will find our number in the book."

"I will do that, sir."

They thanked the man for his help and went back to the car.

"I expect you have got to get back to the station, I'll take you."

"That's most kind it does not seem too easy to get a cab."

On the way back Livinski answered a score of questions and when he left the vicar told him he could telephone at any

time and that if he came back to Little Warley to make sure
he called in.

Chapter 2

RETURNING THE FAVOUR

Livinski had an uneventful journey back to London and spent the next few days seeing the sights of London, visiting the Tower, Houses of Parliament, Madam Tussauds, the Monument, St Paul's and Westminster Abbey. He even went along to Lords for a short time to see whether he could understand a game of cricket, but although Middlesex were on top form that day and scoring heavily, he only stayed to watch through the morning.

On the following Sunday he rang the vicarage at Little Warley and spoke to Mrs Lovett, the vicar taking a service at that time, she said she had been told to expect a call at some time from him and to tell him there was no further news. He then booked a table for five people at the Savoy and at 12.30 ordered a cab to take him to the address he had been given in Stratford, arriving at his destination just before one o'clock. He told the cabby to wait and opened the iron gate, only two paces from the door, and reached for the knocker that had a thick cloth tied around it. The sound the knocker made was muffled. However, the door was opened.

"Oh I had forgotten to take off the cloth, I put it on to soften the noise and hopefully avoid waking my husband when he is on nights. I am so pleased to see you, we are ready but in all honesty we did wonder if you would come. John was sure you would."

"I have the cab outside."

Mrs Davis went back into the house and was followed by the family all smartly dressed in their Sunday best as the previous week. Livinski ushered them into the cab and told the driver to go.

"Have you had any luck with your search?" Mrs Davis asked.

Livinski told them what had happened.

"This is the first time I have been in a taxi," Eileen said.

"It is my first too," Mrs Davis added.

"I've been in one haven't I, Dad?" John said.

"Oh yes when I brought you back from the hospital some years ago."

"Where are we going?" John asked.

"To a hotel in London near the river," Livinski said, but he did not enlarge.

The taxi made its way up through the City and on towards the West End. For those who do not know much about London, which applies to many who live in and around London also, the City is the original area, the 'square mile', of the old city within the walls once there. People who live in metropolitan London, even when quite close in, still say they are going up to London when they go up to the City or West End.

Passing Temple Bar and the Aldwych the taxi entered the Strand and almost immediately turned into the short drive to the Savoy entrance.

"Phew! The Savoy!" Mrs Davis uttered. "I never dreamed I would ever come here."

"Is it a posh place, Mum?" the little girl said.

"Yes very!"

They all got out onto the forecourt and Livinski paid the cabby. The doorkeeper, in a smart colourful uniform with peak cap, opened the hotel door and ushered them in. Livinski directed them to the restaurant, where they were met at the entrance by the Head Waiter who, after Livinski gave his name, took them to their reserved table. They were seated and menus handed to each one.

"Now choose what you like and if there is anything you don't understand I will try to help," Livinski said. "I will order some wine and soft drinks for the young ones."

"It's a long while since I was in a restaurant like this," Mr Davis said.

"When was that, Dad?"

"Just after the war."

"Your dad was an officer in the army and I went to one or two high class restaurants with him, but never the Savoy."

The meal was a great success.

"That was an excellent meal, Mr Livinski. I know we all enjoyed it.

"My pleasure."

"I'll be able to tell my friends at school about this. Is your hotel like this one?" John asked.

"Oh no, my hotel is nowhere near as big but I am proud to say our restaurant, although much smaller, is of a similar standard, it is so important in an hotel to keep a high standard where people eat."

They now left the hotel and picked up one of the many taxis that were in and out of the Savoy every few minutes. Livinski told the driver that he wanted to go to Stratford but that first he would like him to give them a sightseeing tour of some of the places of interest in the West End and City, "Mainly for the sake of the children," he added.

"I expect you have seen it all before," he said, addressing the parents.

"Yes I think we have seen most, but never in a taxi, we'll love it I'm sure," Mrs Davis said.

After the tour and on their way back through east London to Stratford, Livinski asked Mr Davis, who surprisingly to him, had seemed to be most at home in the restaurant, "Why after being an officer in the army did you choose to do manual work as a railway engineer – sorry, I mean engine driver?"

"I was offered a job in one of the railway offices but the pay to start with was very poor so I went back to what I had been doing before the war."

"Do you regret it?"

"No not really, I suppose I would by now have been in a better position but apart from the awkward hours I enjoy my work, I like driving engines."

They were soon back to the Davis's and Livinski declined the invitation to stay for a while and instead said he would go off back to town.

"Don't forget to keep in touch and if we can be of any help in your search let us know."

The taxi drove off with the family waving and curious neighbours moving curtains to see the taxi, a rare vehicle in the street, leave.

Chapter 3

FOUND?

Back at his hotel Livinski wrote a letter to Joseph telling him he might be over in England longer than he had previously anticipated since he now had a clue but had to wait a week or so before he could take any further action. He said he would explain later and hoped everything was going well at the hotel and stores.

He rang the vicarage twice in the week that followed but still had no good news. However, on the Monday of the week following, 19th August, having left his hotel and room number with the vicar, he had a call just before going to lunch to the effect that Lady Winthrop had telephoned to say the gypsies would be making camp at the end of the week. She also said that she had warned the chief man, one Louis Zola, that an American might call to speak to them shortly on a matter concerning his grandchild who he was trying to trace.

Livinski could hardly wait for the weekend to come and on the Saturday morning he again took a train from Liverpool Street to Brentwood. This time he was lucky and got the one taxi from outside the station. He had earlier warned the vicar that he would be coming to Little Warley that day and would call in first to get directions to the camp site.

Knocking at the house he was greeted by Mrs Lovett who said the vicar would only be a few minutes as he had had to go over to see a parishioner in the village. Livinski had hardly sat down when the vicar came back.

"Very good to see you again, if you are ready I can take you along to the camp – seeing a man with a dog collar might make them more friendly."

"I was hoping you might say you would come along."

They drove off in the little Standard Eight and at the cross roads turned left and a short way along they saw the caravans parked on a cutting in the forest. The vicar drove the car to the edge of the cutting and as they got out of the car they were met by two or three dogs, children and much shouting. Bending down to speak to the biggest girl the vicar said, "Could you take me to Mr Zola."

The little girl said nothing but beckoned them to follow. She went up the steps of one of the smartest caravans and knocked on the door which was answered by an elderly man.

"Mr Zola?"

"Yes, what is it?"

"I have brought along Mr Livinski, an American, who would like to speak to you, can you spare him a minute?"

"I'll come down and we can sit over there, he pointed to a small table surrounded by four chairs."

Seating themselves at the table the gypsy spoke first. "I was told you wanted to speak to me about your grandchild, what's this all about?"

Livinski proceeded to tell him the whole story of how his son met a young lady and married her in the nearby village and that she later had a daughter, after his son had been killed in France.

"We were unable to trace the daughter once she had written and our letters were all returned 'gone away', the army told us the address she had given did not exist."

"What made you come to see us?"

"Well we looked at the parish register and found the young lady's maiden name, but no one in the village we have spoken to knew her and older residents were sure she had never lived there. However, the vicar here and one of the villagers said they had seen her when she was married and they both said she was very dark, indeed one villager suggested she could have been a gypsy from a nearby encampment."

"What was her name?"

"The name in the register was shown as Margaret French."

"Never heard of a gypsy with that name, I happen to know there are families living around here with that name – one I know is a farmer, lives in Warley and has a farm. I have done some work for him – might be worth calling there. But if she was a gypsy she could have simply borrowed the name French, maybe to fool your son. I don't think I can help you. I suggest you see the farmer French who lives in Woodman Road in Warley. I will put the word around among our people and see if anyone remembers anything. That is the best I can do."

"I would not wish to offend, but I am so keen to make contact with someone who knew or knows the whereabouts of my daughter-in-law or her child that I will reimburse any expense they may incur in getting the information and, if it should lead to direct contact, reward them accordingly. Thank you for your time, Mr Zola, I will next do as you suggest and go and see the farmer."

With that they left. "If you like I will take you along to see farmer French, I know Woodman Road and someone will soon tell us the house, it is not far from here. But I must say I am not at all hopeful."

"Yes I feel the same but I must try."

They found the house and Mr French, a big man wearing a typical gentleman's farmer wear, listened with interest but said he knew nothing that would help them.

"It could well have been a gypsy girl, I know one or two of them used to go up to dances at the barracks."

"The barracks?" Livinski queried.

"Yes, Warley Barracks, home of the Essex regiment and usually one of the guards regiments. It's just up the road."

They thanked the farmer and left.

"Where do you want to go now?" the vicar asked.

"I think I might as well go back to London. I feel I am hitting a brick wall."

"What do you think you will do? Look any further or go back to America?"

"I always knew in my heart that I was on a wasted journey, so I guess I'll book a passage back to the States. Depending on the sailings I will try to go back on your fast liner the *Queen Mary*. I'll let you know when I am due to sail, just in case any news comes from that man Zola. Anyway thank you so much for your help, if you ever get away for long enough you would be very welcome in North Conway, New Hampshire, New England," Livinski said with a twinkle in his eye.

Back at his hotel he rang Cunard and was told the *Queen Mary* was at present in New York and that the next crossing would be one week from today. Livinski booked a berth, warning them he might have to delay sailing.

On Thursday whilst at lunch in his hotel the waiter told him there was a telephone call for him in reception. Livinski left his meal and went to reception. The call was from the vicar.

"You will be interested to hear that Lady Winthrop telephoned me this morning as she had had a message from Zola in the camp. He told her that he did now have some information that the American might be interested in hearing, he said no more."

"Thank you for letting me know, vicar, I'll catch a train down this afternoon. Is it all right if I come to you first?"

"Of course, come along and I will take you to the camp myself."

It was three o'clock on a sunny afternoon that Livinski finally arrived at the vicarage. Mrs Lovett opened the door.

"Welcome back again, I do hope the gypsy has some good news for you. The vicar won't be long he just went out. Can I get you a cup of tea?"

"No thank you, Mrs Lovett, I had a cup on the train, it was a mainline train and had a restaurant car, first stop Brentwood – a good service."

The vicar was back some ten minutes later.

"You are here earlier than I expected."

"Yes I was lucky to catch a fast train and even got a cup of tea on it, but I only just had time to drink it and we arrived."

"Yes it is a very quick run on the express. Shall we go?"

As they left the house a black cloud passed over the sun and it started to rain heavily and by the time they arrived at the encampment there were puddles everywhere. They got out of the car, it had almost stopped raining, and gingerly stepped over puddles and made their way to Zola's caravan. He opened the door before they reached it and asked them to come inside. Livinski said afterwards that he could not help noticing how well furnished the van was, every piece of furniture looking expensive.

"I understand you have something to tell me, Mr Zola?"

"Yes, I put the word out and had a reply from friends I know who at present are near Rugby. They tell me they have someone on camp who says he knew the lady."

"That is good news and did your friend say any more?"

"No that is all I know, whether it is worth a visit I can't say but I thought I ought to tell you."

"Thank you very much, I will follow up the lead right away. I have no idea where Rugby is but I will find it. Do you know if these people will still be there and in any case whereabouts in this town are they?"

"I think they are there until the middle of next month. They are just outside the town at Hillmorton, get there and anyone will tell you where they are."

"Thank you again, I will be in touch."

On the way back to the vicarage Livinski asked the vicar if he knew where Rugby was.

"I only know it is the town with a famous public school after which the game of rugby is named. It is somewhere in the Midlands, up near Birmingham I think. We'll have a look on my atlas back at the house."

Yes Rugby was indeed in the Midlands and the vicar said he knew that much of the Midlands was covered by the LMS (London Midland and Scottish) railway which had two stations in London, Euston and St Pancras. He was sure a train from one of those would take him there.

Livinski was taken to Brentwood station by the vicar and after promising to keep him informed he returned to his hotel. He straightway rang Euston who confirmed that many trains ran to Rugby from there or he could also go from St Pancras. He checked the times and decided he would catch the ten o'clock from Euston the following morning.

Arriving in Rugby at just after eleven he got a taxi to take him to Hillmorton and the driver who happened to know the gypsy encampment took him straight there. Livinski paid the man and walked over to the site and meeting a man inside the camp asked for Terry O'Neil.

"That's me, what is it you want?"

"I am told you knew a lady who married an American soldier in Essex during the war."

"Yes, that's right."

"Do you remember her name and where she is now?"

"Yeah, she was Maggie Francisco."

"Are you sure?"

"Sure, I knew her well."

"Where did this marriage take place?"

"Back where Louis Zola is now. She had a little girl, kept her with her at first and then got her adopted."

"Where was this, do you remember?"

"Why sure it was near Bedford, we were outside a village called Silsoe when she told me she had got the girl adopted."

"How would she have done this?"

"I don't know, except she was splashing a lot of money about soon afterwards. She said her husband's parents had sent the money."

"What happened to her?"

"Shortly after she got tied up with a fellah from Luton, a lorry driver who had given her a lift to town, so she told me. He used to pick her up from the camp, finally she left altogether. Then later I heard she had been killed in a lorry accident outside Peterborough on the Great North Road."

"When was this?"

"Oh, I don't know for sure, I know we were near Ely at the time when we heard. I think it must have been about ten or twelve years ago."

"What did this lady look like?"

"Oh she was a right beauty. Very dark, her family must have come from middle Europe somewhere. I remember they used to have a 'roll your penny' stall at some fairs, they joined us for a while and then left."

"What was the name of that place where you think she got the baby 'adopted'?"

"I said we were camped near Silsoe but I don't know if that was where she got the girl adopted."

"And Silsoe is somewhere near Bedford, is that right?"

"Yes, it's about ten miles to the south."

"Thank you, Mr O'Neil, I think the lady you have told me about must be the person my son married, it all fits, only the name she gave when she got married was Margaret French, but the same initials as Maggie Francisco. I think I will have to go to this place Silsoe and see if anyone there knows of an adopted child."

"Louis said there would be a reward for information, is that right?"

"Yes that is quite right, I believe what you have given me is as much as I am going to get about my daughter-in-law so I will give you the reward which I decided would be one hundred pounds."

"Begorrah, it's my lucky day, that it is."

"How do I get back to Rugby?"

"You can take a bus, or better still I'll take you meself."

O'Neil drove Livinski in an old Ford to the station in Rugby.

Back at his hotel he decided to ring the vicar to let him know what he had found out and told him he would be making a trip to this village called Silsoe.

He then spent some time finding out how to get to this village and the next day he got a train from St Pancras to Luton where he had been told he would get a bus to Silsoe. He arrived in the village at near midday. Apart from a pub, a few houses and a big gate leading, he imagined, to a big house there was not much there. He decided to go to the pub first and see if anyone had any information. Inside there were three men sitting at a table drinking and two smartly dressed men at the bar who casually looked at Livinski as he entered.

"What is it, sir?" the barman asked.

"I'll have a half a pint of your ale and a sandwich if you have one."

"I'll make you one, that'll be one and three pence. You're American aren't you? Recognise your accent from the films. And what would you be doing in our small village, if you don't mind me asking?"

"I am searching for my granddaughter."

"Oh we ain't got any Americans round here, never seen one afore."

Livinski smiled and the two men at the bar turned and smiled also.

"Where are you from?" one of the two men asked.

"I am from New England."

"I heard you say you were searching for your granddaughter, has she been lost long?"

"It's a long story, I have never seen her. My son was in the American army in the war and married an English girl and she had his baby but he was killed and the girl disappeared. I have been searching and I have had some information that leads me to believe she might have been here. She would be about nineteen now."

The barman, obviously a local, came forward again having listened to what Livinski had said.

"What makes you think you might find her here? I've lived here many years, I know nearly everyone in the village."

"I am looking for a child who was adopted some eighteen or nineteen years ago and I have been told that the mother of this child had her adopted whilst in this area, that is all I know. I realise it may not have been in this village but I have to start somewhere."

"What about the mother, haven't you found her?" one of the strangers asked.

"As far as I know the mother is dead, killed many years ago in a road accident. You say you know nearly everyone in the village, exactly when did you come here?" Livinski asked the barman.

"Well it was in 1923, but I'm a local anyway, born just up the road at Barton, lived here all my life."

"I think my granddaughter may have been adopted two or three years before you came to the village so there is a chance that someone who was living here then might know. You say you know all these people, do you know a family who were here before you arrived and had a little girl?"

"Now let me see. No I can't rightly remember, but I tell you who might know, and that's old Charlie Stokes – lives at the house next to Pear Tree Cottage."

"Where is that?"

The barman explained and Livinski finished his drink and sandwich and left.

He found Pear Tree Cottage, which had a little notice outside announcing 'Teas', and since there was only one house to the side he walked up the path and knocked at the door which was opened by a young lady.

"Is Mr Charlie Stokes in, if so may I have a word with him?"

"Dad, someone here to see you."

"What's he want?"

"I dunno, he talks funny though."

Charlie Stokes made his way to the door.

"Yes, what is it?"

"The barman at The George says you might be able to help me. I am looking for my granddaughter who was I believe adopted by someone in this area some eighteen or nineteen years ago. My son in the American army married a girl who gave birth to my son's daughter, but my son was killed in France and we were unable to trace the mother, who I have since learnt is dead."

"You lot didn't come into the war until near the end so I think the littleun would likely only be a baby when the mother gave her up."

"Yes that is what I believe."

"So I reckon she would probably only be a few months old when you say she was adopted and that would make her eighteen or nineteen now. I only know one village girl about that age, works over at the Park."

"Would you tell me her name?"

"The name is Reeve. Her mother is a widow, Sarah – lives at a house just down the road, you can't miss it, it has a red tiled roof. I don't know the number."

"Thank you so much, I'll go along and see what I can find out."

Chapter 4

SAMANTHA

Livinski walked down the road and found the small house with the red tiled roof. He walked up the short path and knocked on the door which was opened by a lady who looked to be in her fifties.

"I don't want anything today thank you," she said quite abruptly.

"Sorry, madam, I am not selling anything. I only want to ask you a few questions. I am an American over here to try to find my granddaughter. I am wondering if you could help, Charlie Stokes sent me over to see you."

Mrs Reeve at first did not answer and Livinski sensed a change in her manner.

"You better come in then," she said somewhat nervously "How can I help you?"

Livinski told her how a gypsy up in the Midlands had known a lady who had her child adopted somewhere in this area and as he talked he noticed the lady was seeming to become tense with her hands twisting nervously. He knew then that he had almost certainly found his granddaughter. However, he did not wish to worry the lady, he after all wanted simply to find the girl not drag her away from her home. He continued, "Mrs Reeve, I want you to know that if I do find my granddaughter I have no intention of trying to take her away from her home or bother about how she came to be there, I would simply love to see her and tell her who I am. I may be able to help her as although not wealthy I do have money, in fact I own an hotel in the States."

At this Mrs Reeve relaxed somewhat.

"Can I get you a cup of tea, you have probably travelled a long way?"

"Yes, that would be very nice."

She left the room and came back a few minutes later with a tray and two cups of tea and a sugar basin. "Help yourself to sugar and please sit down. What led you to the gypsy up there?"

Livinski went on to tell how he had started his search at the church where his son was married and how it led to the gypsy in Rugby.

"My daughter will be home soon. I would like to break the news to her myself, she does know she was adopted, we told her when she was sixteen, just before my husband died. I think you guessed you had found her, it is very difficult to hide one's feelings. I must admit I was at first very worried and wished Thomas had still been here with me."

"I am so relieved you have told me. Please do not worry, I repeat I will not take her from you, you are mother to her and always will be. What is her name?"

"Samantha, people in the village and at work know her as Sam."

"That's a nice name."

"Can I get you something to eat?"

"No thank you, I had a sandwich over at the George."

"Samantha comes in for lunch about this time."

She had hardly said this when they heard a key in the door and into the room walked the lost granddaughter.

"Oh hullo, I didn't know Mum had a visitor."

Livinski had stood up when Samantha had entered.

"I have something to tell you," her mother said, "This gentleman we believe is your grandfather."

"Grandfather? How suddenly do I have a grandfather, where have you been all my life and why have you come now?" Samantha looked a little angry. Livinski hesitated a moment and was about to speak when Mrs Reeve interrupted.

"This gentleman has been searching for you. His son was killed in the war and his wife, your mother, never replied to letters and disappeared without trace. The gentleman comes from America, he'll tell you about it."

Livinski knew directly she had entered the room that this indeed was his granddaughter, she had his son's eyes and chin and the way she held herself was just the same as Edward would have done. He, still standing, briefly told her how he had traced her and how the American army and embassy had failed to find her mother, and how at the time all he could do was accept what they had said as it was not possible for him to take time to search further.

Samantha listened intently and appeared to soften towards the American.

"So my real father was a soldier, how old was he when he was killed?"

"Only twenty-three."

"What did he do before the war?"

"He was managing my hotel."

"You have a hotel?"

At this point her mother interrupted, "Your dinner is in the oven, I'll get it. I expect you have got to go back to work."

"Thanks, Mum. Yes I have got to go back, even though it is Saturday, we have to get a particular bed ready for planting. Will you still be here when I come back this evening?" she asked Livinski.

"Yes I most certainly will, if you want me to be here."

"Of course I do, I want to know more about any relations I may have, but I'm not leaving Mum."

Mrs Reeve brought in her daughter's dinner and put it on the table by the window.

"Of course you are not leaving your mother, I have not come to try to take you away."

Samantha sat down at the table to eat.

"I don't even know your name?" she said between mouthfuls.

"It's Livinski, Leon Livinski."

"My goodness, are you Russian or something?"

"No, not Russian, Polish. I was born in Europe and emigrated to America as a young man. I am an American."

"Wait till I tell them at work."

Samantha finished eating and said she was going. She kissed her mother and called out laughing as she left, "Make sure you are here when I get back, Leon Livinski."

They both went to the door and watched her as she cycled off up the road.

"She's a lovely young lady, you must be very proud of her. What work does she do?"

"She has always wanted to work in horticulture and she managed to get work in the Wrest Park estate. She works with the head gardener. She would like to have gone to a horticulture college but it was not possible."

"If I can be of any help with money I would be glad to provide it."

"She'll be excited about that. Anyway, Mr Livinski, how long do you intend to stay over here and are you staying over tonight?"

"I can go back to the States when I like, although I did tentatively book a berth on a liner for the end of this week. As for staying in the village I think I will go over to the George and see if they take guests. I might be able to stay there for a couple of nights if you would not mind me being around."

"I will be very pleased for you to stay in the village, and I know the George take in guests, I would ask you to stay here but we only have two bedrooms."

"Don't worry about it I shall be fine over the road. In fact I think I will go over there now to make sure they have a room. I'll come back later if that is all right with you."

"Come back when you like and have tea with us, Samantha will be back soon after five."

"I will, I'll get my room settled and then catch a bus back to Luton. I have brought nothing with me and I need a few things for tonight and a razor. I'll enjoy a little shopping in a new town, especially now I can relax. I also have a few telephone calls I must make."

Chapter 5

GETTING TO KNOW HER

He left the cottage and went back to the George. The bar was closed but he rang the bell and the door was opened by a lady.

"I understand you take in guests. Have you a room for tonight?"

"Yes, we have, I'll show you it if you like. You can bring your bag in now I am sure you will find it satisfactory."

"I have nothing with me, I did not know I would be staying out tonight. I intend going back to Luton to get a few things. You no doubt can tell me the time of the buses."

She led the way up some stairs and showed him into a room at the front of the building. It was very well furnished and the bed looked very comfortable.

"This is fine. Now about the buses?"

"Oh yes, well they are every hour, on the half hour here. Let me see it is now a quarter past two – there should be one along in about fifteen minutes. The room and breakfast will be seven and six. Breakfast is from eight and dinner, should you want it, is from seven."

Livinski fished in his pocket for some money and handed the lady a pound note. "Take for two nights please, I shall probably want to stay over. I want to make some telephone calls – where is the telephone?"

"There is one on the landing, it has a pay box, you'll need some change."

With the help of the lady, Livinski acquired change and successfully made his first call through the operator as it was a trunk call. He told the vicar of his success in finding his granddaughter, thanked him and said he would be sending some money for the church funds, asking him to give something from it to Louis Zola for his help.

He had no time to make any further call as he knew it was time for the bus. Outside he found the bus stop right opposite the George and close to half past the bus arrived.

He completed his shopping in Luton and at the bus station caught the four o'clock bus back, unloaded his shopping, made a call to Cunard delaying his booking, and walked towards the red tiled cottage. It was a little after five o'clock and as he walked along he heard a bicycle bell and turning saw the smiling face of his granddaughter.

"So you are still here, Grandfather Livinski. What have you been up to?"

"I have been in to Luton and I have booked to stay at the George."

"Oh that's good; I was hoping you would stay overnight."

By this time they were at the cottage and Mrs Reeve hearing the talking opened the door.

"Come along in. Did you get your shopping done?"

"Yes, and I have booked in at the George."

Samantha said she was going upstairs for a wash.

"I've made tea, Mr Livinski, when Samantha comes down we can have it. I hope you like salmon, I opened a tin."

"Yes, that'll be fine, you should not have bothered I can eat over at the George, in fact I could have taken you both over there tonight – ah well, maybe tomorrow night."

Samantha was not long before she appeared and they all sat down at the table to the tea her mother had prepared.

For the next hour or so Livinski fielded questions from both females that came at him thick and fast, and he himself began to learn something of his granddaughter and what he learnt he liked.

"You must stop calling me Mr Livinski, Mrs Reeve – I'm Leon and you, Samantha, can call me what you like."

"I think I'll call you Granddad Leon – no I won't, it'll be granddad Livinski, sounds more impressive."

"That's a bit of a mouthful, you'll soon get fed up with that."

"The people at the Park were very interested to hear about you. Would you mind if my friend Julia came along tomorrow to meet you, she has never met an American before, come to think of it neither had I."

It was still broad daylight at nine and they were still talking, having moved to chairs placed around the empty fireplace. Earlier whilst she and her mother were washing up Samantha had put a twelve-inch record on the small wind-up gramophone in the corner of the room. It was a melody of music from the operas. Livinski learnt that Samantha had got to like some opera and classical music from listening to the wireless but she had never been to a concert. "The only ones I have heard of happening near here have been in Bedford. It's a long way to go on your own at night and expensive too."

Livinski had said he would like to take her some day although neither he or her father had been very musically minded.

Just after nine he said he would leave them and go over to the George.

"I'll come and see you tomorrow and we'll talk some more. I won't come over early as it is Sunday, you might like a lie in after being at work all the week."

"You come over when you like and by the way I asked my boss if I could take Monday afternoon off to see you since you had come such a long way, and I wasn't sure you would be around tomorrow." She paused, "and guess what, he said I could, so I shall be able to stay after I come home to dinner on Monday."

On Sunday he went over to the cottage about eleven and he and Samantha went out for a walk around the village and when they returned her mother had dinner ready for them. In the afternoon there was a lot of talking. Samantha talked about her one remaining grandfather who lived in Norwich who had been a butcher but who she had only seen once or twice and then she talked about her father who had worked on a nearby farm most of his life. Livinski was of course questioned a great deal about America and how he got there. He was also able to give them a potted version of the long story he had told the Davis family on the train, particularly as it was still fresh in his mind. He left them later that evening.

The following morning he was up early and had breakfast in time to catch a bus to Bedford. The bus was fairly full with, he supposed, people going to work and he had to go upstairs where he could enjoy the view of the countryside but had to suffer the smoke for most of the men appeared to be smoking. He resolved when he returned that unless the bus was empty he would find a seat downstairs.

Another new town to explore, he really felt he was now on holiday and he wished Tanya had been with him to enjoy it. He noted that there was a concert advertised at a place called the Corn Exchange but it did not take place until later in September when he expected he would be back home. After doing a little shopping he returned so that after a drink and a sandwich in the George he would be in time to meet Samantha.

He made his way over to the red tiled cottage and found Samantha was already home and eating her dinner.

"I began to wonder if you weren't coming after all," she said.

"Now how could I do that? Actually I did not want to worry your mother over food again so I had a quick sandwich at the hotel. I went to Bedford this morning and haven't been back long. Would you like to go out somewhere this afternoon, your mother can come too if she would like to?"

Mrs Reeve heard what Livinski said. "No you two go out, I have some ironing to see to. You can get to know each other better."

"Where would you like to go? We could go to the stores on the bus to Luton or Bedford, or go for a walk – you choose, perhaps you have other ideas."

"I haven't been to Luton for some time, I would like to look at the shops."

"OK, then that is where we will go." And then addressing her mother, "Would you mind if we were back a little later, we might find a good place for tea?"

"I don't mind at all, but you'll have to hurry if you are going to Luton as it is almost half past the hour."

They hurried out of the house and on to the bus stop and could see the bus coming in the distance as they reached it.

The afternoon was bright and sunny and Samantha made her grandfather climb the stairs and walk to the front of the bus.

"You'll be able to see everything from up here, it is a pretty ride over the first few miles, but I suppose it doesn't compare with the country you were telling us about near your hotel."

"The countryside is not too different but of course my hotel is amidst mountains, not mountains as in Switzerland but lower forested mountains. Your countryside is just as beautiful and some of your villages with their small cottages are really picturesque – no, English countryside takes some beating."

Samantha chatted all the way to the bus terminus and carried on talking for most of the afternoon. They looked at the windows of many shops and Livinski managed to persuade her to let him buy her something, although she was reluctant at first. In the end she let him get her a smart jacket she had seen on a model in the window. They ended the afternoon in a teashop near the bus station where they had tea, scones, jam and cream. Livinski had thoroughly enjoyed himself in spite of having to answer hundreds of questions put to him at great speed. Sam, as he started calling her, was obviously so excited. She told him she had two grandparents but she hardly ever saw them as they lived a long way from her home, "But not as far as you do," she added.

"When are you going back?" she finally asked.

"I haven't yet decided, soon I expect as I have been away so long."

"Oh dear, I will lose you so soon."

"How would you like to come over and see me with your mother?"

"Oh how exciting, do you really mean it?"

"Yes of course I do."

"That would be lovely, but what about my work, I only get one week's holiday a year, apart from Bank Holidays of course, and you tell me it takes about a week to get there. No I don't think it is possible."

"Of course it is possible. Do they think you are any good at what you do at work?"

"I think so, but they would have to employ someone else to take over while I was away and I am sure they would not wish to do that. No I think I would have to leave."

"Well then you will leave."

"Just like that? I have to work, Mum needs my money and there are no other jobs in the village I would want to do. I love working with plants, trees and flowers, not ordinary farming, and I certainly don't want to be a waitress at the George!"

"We will work something out. I'll give it some thought, I am staying over at the George tonight."

Back at the cottage Samantha told her mother about the afternoon and showed her the jacket Livinski had bought for her. She then told her that he had asked whether she would like to go over to America and see him, "You would have to come too, Mum," she added. "I did tell him it would be impossible because of my job but he said he would give it some thought tonight. It is nice to be asked though, isn't it, Mum?"

It was lunch time, or dinner as working-class people called it at that time, when Livinski made his way over to the red tiled cottage to see Samantha. Her bicycle was leaning against the fence so he knew she was in. He knocked at the door.

"Come in," Mrs Reeve hesitated and then added, "Leon. We were expecting you, did you have a good night?"

"Yes, it was fine. Did a lot of thinking."

"Samantha told me you had asked her to come over and see you."

"Yes, I did and I may have the answer." He turned to Samantha, "You say you like working with plants and flowers, well I have been busy this morning telephoning various places and have found where one of the top places is in England to learn all about plants and flowers. I have spoken to them and you could start with them at any time if you so wish. It doesn't have to be now or even next month or next year, but I have found out what it costs and you could go there because I will pay. So you can quit your job and you and your mother can come back with me to the States. How about that?"

There was a stunned silence, no one at first said a word.

"Oh you certainly have been busy, I don't know what to say, you have taken us by surprise as you can see, it hasn't sunk in yet."

Mrs Reeve said nothing but looked almost in shock.

"I couldn't go, I have the rent to pay," she said.

Livinski waited, he could see he had sprung this on them, they were after all country folk who generally never went any where far, and this must be frightening to them, especially the mother.

"I'll tell you what I will do, I will go away and leave you two to talk it over between yourselves and I will come back this evening. You, Sam, might like to talk to some of your friends at work, it might help straighten out your mind. There is no pressure, you can say no and you can still go to the horticultural place at any time." He said goodbye and left.

There was less than half an hour left for Samantha and her mother to discuss the matter before the daughter had to return to work. At work there were two girl friends and she told them what her grandfather had suggested.

"It sounds a wonderful opportunity, Sam. I wish it were me," Julie said, "Surely you are going to go?"

Sam said she was worried about her mother. "Mum's never been many places and she is not so young, I think it might worry her a lot."

"Your grandfather is no doubt older than her and look what he has done."

Samantha told them that her grandfather had travelled a lot in his life so he was used to it. They carried on talking whilst they worked and gradually Samantha could see there was much sense in what they said, it was a good opportunity and something that many people would jump at. By the time she left for home with Julie who wanted to meet Livinski, her mind was more or less set that she would try to talk her mother round to taking up the offer.

At home she told her mother what the girls had said, backed up by Julie who repeated she would jump at the chance. Julie stayed for tea and by the time they had consumed the last cup of tea and eaten most of the cake Mrs Reeve had baked, it looked as if the lady was beginning to think it may not be such a bad thing to go with Samantha to America.

Livinski arrived at the cottage at six o'clock, and was introduced to Julie who said, "I've never met an American before, you talk just like on the films – something like Paul Lucas, but I suppose you don't know who I am talking about, he has a different accent to most others."

"That is because I was not born there."

Julie asked Livinski a few questions and then said she had to leave or her mother would start to get worried.

Chapter 6

PREPARING TO GO

When she had gone Livinski did not immediately raise the matter he had left with them to think about, instead he waited to let them say something first.

"We have thought over what you have said and we are almost of a mind to accept your kind invitation. There are one or two things we want you to advise on, and all being well Mum and I would love to come back with you."

"What sort of things can I help you with?"

Samantha asked about what clothes they should take, how long did he think they might be away, what should they do about leaving the house, and many other small matters that had come to mind while considering going with him.

"We haven't got anything to pack our clothes in so we will have to buy a case, and Mum will have to pay the rent or we will lose the house, also don't we have to have passports or something?"

"Yes you will have to get passports. I'll take you up to London to make sure we don't have to wait too long for them. We will need your birth certificates."

"Oh dear, Samantha hasn't got one."

"So her mother never left it with you?"

"Thomas dealt with it all, and he said the lady said she had not registered the birth of the baby. I never thought it that important at the time nor did Thomas."

"Did she say when she was born?"

"Yes, she told Thomas the baby was born in Market Harborough on May 20th 1919. He wrote it down on a piece of paper that I have upstairs and he got the lady to sign it, but her writing is almost unreadable – Thomas said he didn't think she could write properly."

"That is no doubt why our letters were never replied to, the ones we did receive must have been written by someone she knew. Thomas said many gypsies were unable to write as they often did not go to school and the authorities could not be bothered to chase them up."

"I'll have to think up some way of overcoming the difficulty. I think I will get in touch with the American embassy in London, I am sure they will help. I'll go up to London tonight and see what I can arrange. I expect you have a birth certificate Mrs Reeve don't you?" Mrs Reeve nodded yes.

"That's good. Don't worry I am sure we will get Samantha a passport somehow."

Chapter 7

PASSPORTS

Livinski left the cottage to catch the bus to Luton at seven thirty and was back in his hotel before ten. The following morning he found the American embassy and asked to speak to someone who could help him get a birth certificate for his granddaughter in order to get a British passport. He was able to speak to someone who having listened to his story was most sympathetic.

"I believe what you have told me but I will have to get confirmation from at least one independent person who can verify as much of what you have said as possible."

"I suggest you telephone the vicar of the church in the village of Little Warley in Essex, the Reverend Brown. He can give you the details of my son's marriage and if you check with army records they will be able to confirm when my son was killed in France. I also had an interesting journey with an English family some weeks ago and because the train broke down they listened to me talk about my life in America and they know why I came to England – they could confirm this if you want to get in touch with them."

The embassy man said he would get in touch with the vicar but although he took the address of the Davis family he did not think he would find it necessary to contact them. Livinski also gave him the piece of paper that Mrs Reeve had given him which purported to confirm the date and location of birth and signed by the mother.

"Give me your hotel and when I have something to tell you I will call. I hope we will be able to do something which will give the British authorities sufficient information to issue a passport."

"I will probably be going to the village where my granddaughter lives for a few days so I had better give you the number of the hotel there. If I don't hear by the beginning of next week I will give you a ring anyway to see if you are having any luck."

Livinski returned to his hotel and again rang Cunard, this time making a booking for three people on the next sailing of the *Queen Mary* to New York at the end of September. He stayed there overnight and next morning went back to Silsoe, booked in at the George and went round to see Mrs Reeve, it was near the time he knew Samantha would be coming home for her dinner.

"I have set the wheels in motion to get Samantha her passport and hope to have some news in the next few days. I will then take you both up to London, to visit the passport office, as I want to avoid as much delay as possible as I have booked us on a sailing at the end of the month."

"Oh dear, that is soon," Mrs Reeve looked a little worried.

"There is nothing to worry about, everything will be fine."

"Yes I know, but you see I have hardly ever been away from here, it will all be so strange."

At that the front door opened and Samantha walked in.

"Oh good you are here, how did you get on, any news?"

"I was just telling your mother, I have been to the American embassy in London and they are, I hope, taking some action to get a certificate or at least persuade the British authorities to issue a passport. I have also booked us to sail to New York at the end of the month."

"That's exciting isn't it, Mum?"

"Your mother's a little worried at it happening so quickly, I have told her she will be all right."

Samantha had her dinner and as she left for work said, "I'll tell the girls and the boss I will be leaving – I should give in my notice, I only have to give one week. I do hope you get the passport for me. The girls are going to want to know all about it. Do you know what ship we are sailing on?"

"The *Queen Mary*."

"Oh mother!"

Samantha rode off on her bicycle and Livinski returned to the George to have a meal and to write a couple of letters. His first letter was to Joseph to tell him he had found his granddaughter and that he was bringing her and her widowed mother over to the States for a holiday. He told him they would be back on about the seventh, and of course hoped all was well in Jackson and North Conway. His second letter was one to the Davis family telling them of his good fortune and that he would be returning to the States at the end of the month. He gave them his address in Jackson just in case they wanted to keep in touch.

He went over to the cottage just before Samantha was due back and asked Mrs Reeve if she would like to come over to the George with Samantha to have an evening meal. "We have both had our dinner, I don't know if I will be able to eat much more."

"Come over anyway."

"That would be nice, I have never had a meal there although I have been told they serve a good one. People from the village don't go there except for a drink, it's mostly business people, salesmen and the like who do something up at the Park. I'll tell Samantha when she comes home. What time should we come over?"

"Let's say seven, I'll be waiting for you."

They enjoyed the meal and, as Samantha said, "a first taste of perhaps what it's going to be like – it's wonderful going to posh places."

The following day was Saturday so Livinski arranged to take the ladies to Bedford to buy cases and things they might need for their holiday. He would not let them spend any of their money until they insisted on buying him a tie he had looked at in a shop where they had bought the cases.

There was no call for him from the embassy on Monday, so on Tuesday he rang.

He was told that the official he had spoken to had called in sick that day and that his work was being handled by a Janet Johnson. He asked to speak to her and was relieved to find that she knew about the problem and had not long before heard from the military authorities confirming the death in action of his son in 1918.

"I understand my colleague has spoken to the Reverend Brown and we have studied the document you handed us giving the date and place of birth. Leave it with me and I will follow it through, you will appreciate this is a most unusual situation and no one here is quite sure what to do. I will ring the British passport office and talk to them. Give me a call tomorrow."

Livinski was disappointed, but being an optimist he was convinced he would get Samantha her passport.

On Wednesday before calling the embassy again he walked over to the entrance to the Park and walked through the gate. Samantha had said he could walk up the drive and see the big house from the outside, she would be working around the side and would tell her boss that her American grandfather might be along. It was quite a long drive and on either side there were well manicured lawns and to the right he could see a lake and an ornamental bridge over a stream close to the lake. It was a very pleasant place to work and as he walked along he could not help wondering if he was right in taking her away, knowing she would not be returning to work there. He dismissed it from his mind as he saw three young ladies and a man working around the side of the mansion. He went over to speak to them and for five minutes or so work stopped as introductions took place with Livinski then required to answer questions, the boss man in particular being interested to know what the countryside was like where the American lived.

"As I expect you know we are here coming to the end of the growing season and shortly the leaves will fall and it will be Autumn."

"Where I come from we call it the Fall, and in my part of the country we have a spectacular Fall, the colours have to be seen to be believed and people come long distances, I mean hundreds of miles, just to see the brilliant colours. Of course not too long after we get snow, particularly on the higher ground, you see I live amongst mountains."

"Sounds wonderful, Samantha is a lucky young lady to be able to go back with you." They continued talking until he looked at his watch, "Well I suppose I had better get on or we won't get this area cleared. Nice to have met you, and look after her, she's a good lass."

"I will."

Livinski returned to the George and straightway rang the embassy.

"I have good news for you, Mr Livinski, I have talked to the British passport office and they are prepared to accept what we have told them. I suggest you bring the young lady, if it is possible, and visit their office and ask to speak to Mr Robinson, he knows all about it and I am sure he will soon see that the passport is ready."

"Thank you so much, Miss Johnson, that is indeed good news, I'll get the young lady to come with me to London as soon as it can be arranged with her work. Thank you."

When Samantha came home for her dinner Livinski was there to tell her the good news.

"I want you to ask your boss if you can take tomorrow off as you have to go to London to get a passport. Say you don't expect to be paid for the day or you'll work an extra day but that you have to be present up there as your birth certificate has been lost."

Samantha duly told her boss and he allowed her the day off. So the next day Samantha and her mother, the latter armed with her birth certificate, were taken off by Livinski to London and the passport office. They saw Mr Robinson who, after requiring signatures from Samantha, issued her with a passport almost immediately. They had to wait a while for one for Mrs Reeve as she had to complete a lengthy form of application, somehow not required for Samantha.

Afterwards Livinski took them for a meal in his hotel and then to St Pancras station where he gave them their return tickets to Luton and the bus fare up to Silsoe. He said he would see them at the end of the week as he had several things he wanted to do. He wrote down the telephone number of his hotel, in case they wanted him before he came back to Silsoe, and left.

Chapter 8

THE DAVIS FAMILY AND WARLEY CHURCH

Over the next few days Samantha and her mother did those things they thought necessary for being away for a long holiday. The next-door neighbour said she would keep an eye on the cottage and when the rent collector called Mrs Reeve did as Livinski had told her and paid him eight pounds for twenty weeks' rent in advance, the money given to her by Livinski and, as he had said, 'make sure you get him to correctly mark up your rent book.' Mrs Reeve had been a little unsure when Livinski had said twenty weeks but he explained it would be better to make sure rent had been paid a long way ahead in case something happened to delay their return, 'it will avoid you worrying about whether the house would be let to somebody else while you are away.'

Samantha had given in her notice and worked the extra day as promised so that she left work on 25th September, just four days before her grandfather had said they should go up to London. Livinski had in the meantime made a special call late one afternoon to the Davis household in Stratford. He had gone there by taxi but knew he would have to find his own way back. Mrs Davis and Eileen were at home and she said John would be back from school shortly, Eileen went to school locally whilst John had to travel by train. She made a cup of tea and said she was so pleased to see him and to receive his letter, she would she said never forget that train journey and his wonderful story. John arrived home at five and had many questions to ask and much to talk about what had happened at school since the excursion. Livinski was not able to see Mr Davis but told his wife he wished to be remembered to him. John walked with him to the railway station where he caught a train up to Liverpool Street.

Back at Silsoe he said he was going to make one last visit to the church where his son had got married and, as he was hoping, Samantha asked if she could go with him.

"It's quite a long way, so don't expect us back for some time. We have to go up to London then out again on a different line," he explained to her mother.

They caught the half past nine bus to Luton and got to St Pancras an hour later, then across on the underground to Liverpool St and out to Brentwood. Again Livinski was lucky with the taxi.

"I can guess where you want to go," the cabby said.

"That's right, only this time there are two of us."

They were dropped off at the vicarage gate and walked up the path to the house, but as they walked they saw the vicar coming across the grass from the church.

"How nice to see you, so this must be your young granddaughter."

"Yes this is Samantha, we have come along to have a last look at the register and to show where her father was married."

"Right let us go over to the church now and then when we come back Mrs Lovett will make us some tea."

They walked over to the side entrance to the church and Reverend Brown opened the door which was level with the altar, to the side of which was the door to the vestry in which was kept the register. The vicar turned the pages to 1918 and there prominent on that page was the line they had come to see.

"Oh, I see my mother was a Margaret French. Perhaps one day I should look up the French family."

"We have already done this," her grandfather said, "but we were unable to trace anyone, I think it would be a waste of time." Livinski hoped this would settle things in

Samantha's mind as he did not want her to know what he had found out about her mother.

They had a final look around the church and then went over to the vicarage where Mrs Lovett, who had seen them arrive through the window, had tea ready for them. Before they left the Reverend thanked Livinski again for the money sent to the church and he confirmed he had given Louis Zola a share as requested. He drove them down to the station and saw them off to London.

Chapter 9

Two days later with their cases packed and in a hired car from Barton they were driven to Luton where they caught the train and went to Livinski's hotel to stay overnight.

The next morning after breakfast they took a taxi to Waterloo station. Neither Mrs Reeve or Samantha had ever been to this station and they marvelled at the impressive entrance. Livinski called over one of the porters waiting for taxis and got him to take the luggage and take the ladies to a seat whilst he went over to the booking office to get the tickets. The porter found a seat close to the booking office hall.

"Off on your holidays?" he asked.

"Yes, we're going to America."

"Then you'll be wanting the Boat Train, let me see that's off platform 10. It's not in yet, I reckon you've got time for a cup of tea, doesn't leave until eleven."

Livinski returned with the tickets.

"The porter says the train doesn't leave until eleven and it is not in the station yet."

"That's right, guvnor, platform 10, you got over half an hour yet. You can take your bags to the left luggage office or I'll look after them if you want to go to the tea room here. I'll come and pick you up in time to get it. Have you got reserved seats?"

"Yes I have."

"Give the numbers to me and I'll get your bags on as soon as the train comes in, it's usually in about twenty minutes before it is due to leave."

Livinski gave the porter the coach and seat numbers and being a little hesitant about leaving their luggage with an unknown porter, and perhaps showing it in his face, the porter added.

"Fred Potter is my name, everyone knows me round here," he called over to a passing uniformed man, "What's my name, Charlie?"

"Blimey forgotten it again, Fred?" and went on his way laughing.

"Don't let us miss it, we'll be in this tea room."

"I won't."

They had something to drink and Samantha the cream cake displayed on the counter and some twenty minutes later, true to his word, the porter returned and took them to the train and directed them to their seats where their luggage was on the racks; they had the compartment to themselves. As the porter had hoped, Livinski gave him a good tip and five minutes later the train slowly glided out of the station.

It soon picked up speed and stations flashed by with Samantha eagerly looking out of the window trying to read some of the names. She read Clapham Junction, Wimbledon and Surbiton but thereafter the train rattled through stations too quickly for her to see and she gave up. There was a restaurant car on the train but as they had already had some morning refreshment they decided not to go along.

At about 12.30 the train slowed and entered a platform not many yards from the towering side of the liner they would soon board, the *Queen Mary*. Porters were waiting to collect baggage and our three travellers walked behind the one Livinski beckoned over to help. They were taken to one of the gangways leading up to the side of the ship where a member of the crew took the bags after an officer checked their names and a second official looked at their passports. They were given a card showing their cabin numbers and then climbed the steps and boarded the ship. The crewman took them to their cabins which were on A deck, Livinski having a single and the ladies a double close by.

"When you have settled in, give a knock on my cabin door – number seven just along from you – and we can go and find the restaurant to have some lunch or have a look around the ship before that. She is not due to sail, so I was told, until five this evening."

The food on board ship is nearly always good and the first meal they had in the first class restaurant was no exception.

"This must be a little different from when you first sailed to America?" Mrs Reeve commented.

"It certainly is, a whole lot different. We had to fend for ourselves, no restaurants for us below decks and the crossing time was three times as long as that this ship will take."

"How long did you say it will take us?"

"About four days, possibly a few hours less. This ship travels at over 30 knots all the way. Very often we call at Le Havre but as we are going to be full we are making a straight crossing, at least that is what they told me when I booked."

After lunch they had a walk around part of the ship. They went up to the Sun Deck, down to the Promenade Deck and then the Main Deck by way of a grand central stairway which continued down to the cabin decks below, right down to E deck but they did not venture below their own deck A.

People were boarding the ship all afternoon and close to five the gangways were removed and ropes began to be loosened and finally untied. The ship moved slowly away from the dockside at exactly five o'clock. It sailed out into the Spithead and round the Isle of Wight and then headed up the channel to the Atlantic. The sea was quite calm in the channel but later that evening as they were passing the Scillies the ship began to roll as the sea had built up. The following morning Samantha said she felt a little unwell and did not want any breakfast but later in the day she was better and had a good evening meal. On the third day out Livinski came to tell Samantha and her mother that one of the officers had come to his cabin to say he and his companions were invited to join the Captain at his table for dinner. Samantha was excited but her mother was very nervous and said she would rather not come. However, when Livinski told her there would be a number of other guests and officers at the table and that she would have no need to sit near the Captain, she agreed to go along. After the dinner the orchestra played music for dancing and the captain came straight round and asked Mrs Reeve for a dance. She said afterwards that she thought she would collapse but in fact carried off the dance, a waltz, very well. Dinner at the Captain's table had indeed gone well, particularly as Samantha's mother had been seated next to a man of her own age who happened to come from the village of Ampthill, not far from Silsoe, where as a young lass she had learnt to dance.

The remainder of the voyage was uneventful but in the late afternoon of the fourth day the Captain announced over the tannoy that the ship would very shortly be entering the narrows leading to New York harbour. Following this there was general movement of passengers to the rails on various decks getting as close to the bows of the ship as possible. Once through the narrows there was the first glimpse of the New York skyline dominated by the Empire State and Chrysler buildings.

"That over there is Ellis Island where as an immigrant I first landed," Livinski pointed as they passed.

"What happened then?"

Livinski explained briefly the procedure as he had done when talking to the Davis family. He then went on to tell the ladies how he had then met the young lady who later became his wife.

"It was over there, a part known as the Battery."

The *Queen Mary* cruised slowly up the Hudson River and turned slowly to dock alongside one of the many piers that jutted out into the river at right angles to the shore. A band was playing on the quayside. Cranes began working right away to unload people's baggage that had been stowed in the hold. However, none of Livinski's or his companions' had been so stowed and thus they were able to make their way to the gangways and disembark. On the jetty Livinski engaged a porter who with the luggage on a trolley asked them to follow him. Passports were carefully examined at the end of the jetty and from there they took a taxi and were taken to the Waldorf Astoria – a rather grand hotel where they would stay for two nights so they could see a little of the big city. They were given rooms on the fourth floor.

Chapter 10

Livinski decided that for their evening meal, rather than eat in the hotel he would find something different and typical New York. He therefore asked at reception and was told that an unusual place to go would be Billy Rose's Diamond Horseshoe in the Paramount Hotel on 46th Street west of Broadway. So they collected a taxi and drove round. The chosen place on the top floor of the hotel was a great success with live entertainment and reasonably priced food and drink. Samantha kept her copy of the menu and marked what she had had. She had started with Cream of Tomato Soup, 60 cents followed by Chicken à la King in Sherry Wine, $3.00, and then Fresh Apple Pie à la Mode (i.e. with ice cream) 75 cents, and to drink she had a Champagne Cocktail, $1.28 – a total cost of $5.63.

"That was the most enjoyable meal I have ever had, I thought the entertainment was marvellous and to hear they had or were about to make a movie has made it even more memorable. Thank you so much for bringing us. It's the first time I have been to anywhere like this, I suppose it is really a night club – wow, wait until I get home and tell my friends and show them my menu. Have you been here before, Granddad?"

"No, I hardly know New York, I asked at reception before we came out. Yes I enjoyed it too."

That night Samantha decided she was going to write a diary about their visit to America, so taking some hotel paper in the desk in the room she wrote down what she had remembered of the day. The next morning before breakfast she found a shop near the hotel where she was able to buy a small diary in which she folded the notes she had made the night before.

Over the next two days they saw a good deal of the city, Livinski remembering the time he had been taken around by carriage arranged for him by one of the guests at the hotel, a Mr Cyrus Munroe, and tried to let them see all he had seen and more. They went to the top of the Empire State building and rode around Central Park in one of the popular horse-drawn carriages. Finally on the evening of the second day they collected their luggage and took a taxi to Grand Central Station, the station he, Tanya, Anna and Joseph had first caught the train to Boston and then up to North Conway; in those days it was simply known as Central Station.

The train they caught was a through train with sleeping berths and thus they would not have to change at Boston. Livinski telephoned the hotel and managed to speak to the manager who said he would arrange for an automobile to meet them at the station.

Chapter 11

JACKSON, I'M BACK!

The journey was uneventful and the train pulled in to North Conway at 8.30 in the morning which just gave them time to finish breakfast in the restaurant car. The conductor put his steps in place and our small party got off the train.

"It seems strange getting off a train this way, just the same as I have seen in the movies – makes me realise I am in America," Samantha said as she helped her mother down the steps, with Livinski following and the conductor handing him their luggage.

"We should have transport waiting for us outside, ah there he is," and coming towards them was an elderly man with a big grin on his face. Livinski moved forward to meet him and the two men embraced.

"It's so good to see you again, I did not expect it would be you to meet us."

"I could not let my old friend arrive back with his granddaughter after being away so long and be met by a stranger." He stopped and looked at the two ladies, "So this is the young lady, she's lovely – and you, madam, her mother," he greeted them both warmly.

"As you must have guessed this is my old friend Joseph who I have told you about. It's so good of you to come down to meet us. How is Anna?"

"She is well, Leon, and everything is well. Anyway I'll give you a hand with your luggage, the carriage awaits you." With that he and Leon took the two large cases and the two ladies the small ones and Joseph led them through the station booking office and outside where much to everyone's surprise Joseph had brought along the Surrey to take them back.

"I thought our guests would appreciate the ride in the Surrey rather than in an old automobile, most guests still enjoy the ride out to Jackson this way."

"How exciting, this is wonderful, not just the carriage but the old station and everything. Don't you agree, Mum?"

"Yes I know just what you mean, I was thinking the same."

The men having loaded the luggage on the rear platform followed the ladies up into the carriage and with Joseph taking the reins they were off. It was after the carriage had passed the buildings of North Conway that the ladies really first noticed the wonderful colours of the leaves on the many trees on either side of the road and up the high ground beyond. Unless one has seen these colours it is very hard to imagine.

"The colours are breathtaking, I have never seen anything like it in England and I have lived all my life in the country," Mrs Reeve said.

"Yes you have arrived back at the peak period for sightseeing in Washington Valley; this year I think this is going to be the best week. Sometimes it could be a week earlier or a week later but from what I have seen this, I am sure, will be the best."

Joseph said, "You must get Leon to take you out on a tour, it is something you must not miss."

"Oh, would you, Granddad?"

"Of course, I will just have to clear up a few things and then we can take one of the automobiles and go for a ride – of course it won't be as good as riding in a carriage but at least we should be able to go much further."

By this time they were approaching Jackson and the red of the covered bridge came into view.

"What is that, Granddad?"

"Oh that is our bridge, it is covered with a sloping roof to protect it when there is a heavy snowfall. I remember how proud an old friend of mine was when he first drove us from the station all those years ago. You remember how old Adam told us proudly that he reckoned his bridge was the best in the valley?"

"I sure do, a great young boy Adam."

Through the bridge and past a few neat cottages and then the hotel.

"He was proud too of the hotel wasn't he, Leon?"

"Yes he was and he did what you are doing – slowed so we could take it all in."

"Yes that's right and then he took us in to see Martha – my goodness how it comes back all those years ago."

"When was that, Granddad?"

"Oh the year was 1893, I'll have to tell you the story one day, Joseph and I and the two ladies we had met in New York came here to find work."

"And now you own the hotel, Granddad."

"Yes, I was lucky."

Joseph drove the Surrey into the yard and the party were soon in the kitchen sitting and having coffee, poured for them by Susanne, the lady who had taken over from Martha, Leon had mentioned just a while ago.

"How are you, Susanne, how long is it now since you joined us?"

"It's twenty-seven years."

"Oh dear, how the years go by, you'll be thinking of retiring soon I guess."

"I would like to keep going a couple more years, like you Mr Livinski and Joseph here, you both keep going."

Samantha and her mother enjoyed the chat they had in the kitchen where Mrs Reeve felt more at home, and they were then taken to a room with twin beds on the first floor of the hotel which had been made ready for them.

"You will no doubt like to settle in, feel free to take as long as you like and when you are ready go down into the lounge and I will join you later. I must see my daughter if she is home and have a word with her husband, my manager, and see if everything is all right." He turned to Joseph, "I asked you about Anna and you said she was well and everything was well, I take it the shops are still doing good business?"

"Yes they are, we have had one of our best seasons even though we now have competition in both towns."

"That's good, I'll come and talk to you later, must go and talk to our Scottish manager and then see if Caroline is around."

"I don't think you will find her, she stayed at home last night."

Livinski found Robert McGregor in the restaurant.

"How is everything?"

"It's fine, Leon, we are as you can imagine at this time of the year quite full, in fact we could have done with one or two extra rooms. Did you have a good trip, I know it was successful, you must be very pleased?"

"Yes I am, she is a lovely girl. She and her mother have just gone up to the room you arranged for them. I said I would see them in the lounge when they have settled in. You must meet them. How's the family?"

"Caroline is well and so are the children. She's been staying at home with the children as we are so full here. I think you'll find her at the bookstore, the kids are at school."

"I'll talk to you later." He hurried to reception and picked up the telephone and dialled the bookstore." Caroline answered.

"Dad, it's so good to hear your voice, did you enjoy your trip?"

"Yes I did, Robert says you are all well. Anyway if you are going to be there today I will come over and see you and bring your new niece with me. See you later."

Livinski met Samantha and her mother in the lounge and asked them if they would like to go with him to North Conway to see his daughter and if they were not too tired of travelling go on for a short tour to see the leaves of the forests in their full glory .

"We would love to come with you," Mrs Reeve said.

"I'll wait for you in reception; the weather is quite mild so you won't need a coat."

The car Joseph provided was a Buick the hotel had bought a year or two earlier.

The bookstore/library was quite close to the train station and when they arrived Caroline was serving a customer who had just bought two books. The customer left and Livinski made the introductions.

"This is your new aunt, Samantha – Aunt Caroline," the two embraced, Samantha clearly overcome had to wipe a small tear from her eye but managed to say, "and this lady is my mum."

"What do we call you?" Caroline asked Mrs Reeve.

"Your father calls me Mrs Reeve but I hope you will all call me Sarah."

"There you are, Granddad, meet Sarah."

"I know how formal you are in England so I felt I should address you in the way I was introduced, but from now on it's Sarah, such a nice name."

"I gather I have two young cousins to meet, I shall look forward to that."

"Yes they are both at school today. Daniel is eleven and Abigail is nearly ten. You'll have to come over at the weekend. I expect someone will bring you over."

"I would like that. Now may I have a look at your shop?"

"Of course, do you read much?"

"I can't say I am a big reader but I do like to read books on horticulture, have you any?"

"Yes, you'll find them on that back shelf over there. Help yourself to one."

Before leaving the store Samantha did choose a book to read.

Chapter 12

As promised Livinski took the Samantha and Sarah on their first tour around the White Mountains. He drove first to Conway where they popped into Anna's second store which was being looked after by a local man who greeted Livinski as an old friend.

From there they turned onto the Kancamagus Highway and drove steadily along between the forests on either side all with colourful leaves

"What was the strange name you called this road?"

"Kancamagus Highway."

"Is that some old Indian name?"

"Yes, it is. Kancamagus was the name of an Indian chief who many years ago tried to keep peace between the Indians and the new white settlers. He formed some sort of confederacy of Indian tribes in his efforts to keep the peace but it seems repeated harassment by the English forced the tribes to move elsewhere."

"That's sad, it is such a beautiful place."

They carried on and stopped at nearly all the places on the highway which were designated as stopping places. Some simply to marvel at the scenic beauty and others where one could take marked trails to picturesque spots or to the site of a spectacular waterfall.

The highway was about thirty miles long and in the small town of Lincoln at the end of the highway he took them to lunch before taking, as he said, the northern return route to Jackson. On this route they drove in to see the magnificent

Mount Washington Hotel and went inside to take a look around. Livinski was known to one or two of the staff but in any event the hotel was quite happy for people to look around.

"This is a wonderful place, I expect it costs a lot to stay here."

"Yes one can pay a good deal but there are rooms that are no more expensive than some of ours in Jackson. Some people who come to our hotel say this hotel is too big for them and they like the intimacy and friendly atmosphere of the Wentworth better."

They drove on with Livinski telling the names of villages they passed and pointing out where it was best to ski. They were back at the hotel before three.

"That was a wonderful ride, Granddad, thank you so much. Is there anything I can do to help in the hotel, you seem so busy."

"Well, I'll have a word with Robert, he's the manager, and you haven't met him yet. But don't worry about working, you are on holiday."

"Yes I know but there must be something we can do to help."

Livinski introduced Robert to the new arrivals and on the following day he did find Samantha a small job to do in the office while her mother went to the kitchen and apart from having a good natter did give a little help to Susanne.

On Saturday Joseph, who was going to town to help with stocktaking in the store, gave Samantha and her mother a lift to Caroline's house.

"I'll pick you up after lunch."

Samantha met the two young cousins who were out playing with some other children in the garden. Daniel and Abigail proudly told the others that these ladies had come all the way from England and that the young one was their cousin.

"That is right, isn't it? Ma said you were coming."

"Yes that's right, I'm Samantha and this lady is my mother, Sarah."

All the children gathered round wanting to hear some more of the way they spoke.

"I thought they would speak like your dad, Daniel, but it is quite different," one of the older children said to him when the adults went into the house.

Caroline and Samantha seemed to get on well together and the three adults talked for some time until Caroline announced she was going to serve lunch, which she had already prepared, laid out on the table in the dining room.

Joseph came round soon after they had had coffee and drove them back to the hotel.

"What do you think of our valley?" he asked.

"I think it is wonderful and so does my mother. You are very lucky living here."

"I expect Leon has told you how we came to live here."

"No, he has not told us a great deal, he did say he did not think it fair to burden us with the whole story. He said something on the boat coming over that he had told the story to an English family he had met and he just did not feel like going all through it again as it made him so sad. But I would be interested to hear, I am sure it would be exciting."

"If you like I can tell you something about it. I have one or two things to do when we get back but if you go and sit in the lounge I will join you and tell you how we came to be here. My story could be a little different from Leon's, we often see the same things in a different way."

"Of course you do, everyone has their own personal memories."

Joseph met them in the lounge and proceeded to tell Samantha and her mother how they came to be in Jackson. Although Joseph had remarked that his story might be different from Leon's it seems they both emphasised the same points and any stranger listening to Leon telling the family on the train about his life would find that much of that would be like listening to the story that Joseph gave.

"As you see, Leon took most of the decisions, after all he was educated at a university and I was just a farm boy with little or no education."

"I'm sure you were equally responsible for what you both have done. You say Leon gave you a start in business but from what you have said he was given a start by his mother with her jewellery. I reckon if you had had the piece of jewellery you would have done the same. What was my father like?"

"Oh he was a great lad. Everyone liked him and he worked so hard when Leon made him the manager of the hotel. It was terrible when he left us to join the army and such a short time later to be killed. It nearly broke his mother's heart; she never really got over it. War is such a useless and terrible thing."

"Yes I am glad I am not a man. From what people were saying back home in the village we will have to watch out for more trouble in Europe where there seems to be so much unrest and all that fighting in Spain."

Joseph said they had better change the subject and remember they were on holiday and that Europe was a long way from Washington Valley.

The next few weeks flew by, they sampled their first Thanksgiving Day and shortly after Samantha and her mother said that they thought they ought to go home; in particular Mrs Reeve had in mind her cottage.

"Granddad, we cannot expect to live on here week after week at your expense. It is time we went home."

"But I don't want you to go, I enjoy having you around for company. Look it is nearly Christmas, you must stay at least a few more weeks."

"What about my house?"

"Don't worry about it, Sarah, if you remember we paid twenty weeks and I am sure that is not up yet. No you must stay."

So that was that, Leon insisted they stay. It was now the end of November and for several days the snow had fallen and everything around was white. The cars had to have chains on their wheels and Joseph and his help had to change to skis on the carriages. The Jackson Bridge covering was doing its job and piles of snow settled for a while on the sloping roof was regularly plunging into the partly frozen river below.

"I am taking you into town today and we are going to buy you winter clothes you will need if you venture out of the hotel. We will see what our store has to offer and if we cannot find suitable clothing there we will go to the general store in Conway where I know old Jacob White will be only too pleased to fit you out."

They bought one or two items in Anna's store but most were bought in the general store in Conway.

All dressed in their winter wear, they returned to the hotel.

"We look like real Americans now, Granddad. You are too good to us."

"It is my pleasure, Edward would have liked me to do it for you."

They agreed to stay for Christmas and the New Year and then to return home.

Several guests at the hotel were driven daily to the ski slopes and one day Robert asked Samantha if she would like to try her hand at skiing.

"Oh I don't think I could do it, but it does look fun."

"Of course you can do it, with the proper instruction, I'll take you. I'll have a word with Leon so that he is around and we will go, perhaps tomorrow. I'll see you are fixed up with the right gear."

"All right I'll try it, you don't mind, Mum?"

"Of course not; as long as you don't expect me to come with you."

The following day Robert collected Samantha and saw she was fitted out with all the gear necessary and off they went to the nearest beginners slope. He used a buggy fitted with skis to make the return trip. When back at the hotel some three hours later she told everyone who would listen, how exciting it was and that Robert said she did very well for a first time.

Skiing became part of her life at the Wentworth, going along with any of the guests who were venturing to the slopes and who were happy for her to go along with them.

To Mrs Reeve, sorry Sarah, hotel life was strange, she had spent her life in a small English village and everything that had happened to her over the past months seemed unreal. She spent a considerable amount of her time helping in the hotel kitchen where she felt much more at home and could talk to Susanne. She had enjoyed the holiday but clearly not as much as Samantha who was so full of life, always doing something hardly ever finding time to sit down. Sarah could see that her daughter was liking the life and people in America and she began to worry that she would not want to go home; certainly she believed that after all this high living Samantha would no longer be satisfied with a life in a cottage in the quiet little village of Silsoe. However, she knew that Livinski, when getting them to stay for Christmas and New Year, had recognised that they would then go home.

Chapter 13

To Return?

Christmas and New Year, when the rest of the family came to Jackson, and joined the many hotel guests and staff in lively parties, were a great success and Sarah in the company of some guests of her own age seemed more relaxed and admitted to Samantha that the parties were the best she had ever attended. Nevertheless, Samantha knew her mother was not completely at home in the hotel and she herself knew that this holiday would have to end and they would have to go home sometime.

One day when sitting with her grandfather on the veranda in front of the hotel Samantha made her mind up to say it was time they returned to England.

"We have so much enjoyed being here, Granddad, but we must go home. I have to find a job and as you know Mum is worried about losing her cottage. All holidays have to end and you have been so kind to allow us to stay as long as we have."

"I understand what you say; it has been great having you. Of course you will have to come back again some time. We will all miss you. I have your return tickets so I had better make a booking on a liner to take you home."

Samantha told her mother that they would be going home.

"Granddad is making the booking. He said we will have to come back some time."

The following day Livinski told Sarah and Samantha that he had booked them to sail on the French liner *Normandie*. It seemed there was an agreement between the French and English companies that in certain circumstances return tickets could be used on liners from either of the companies, The *Normandie* would be calling at Southampton.

"I thought you might like to sail on the *Normandie*, it is a similar ship to the *Queen Mary*, very fast and equally luxurious, and don't worry about the language – many of the people you will be in touch with will speak English, they have to, as Americans are using her to cross the Atlantic as much as they use the *Queen Mary*. She leaves New York on the 23rd, so you have five days to get there."

After her granddad had given her the date they would have to get to New York, Samantha went to her room and sat down. She felt sick inside as although she had told him they must return home she really did not want to leave, she had had such a good time and the realisation that it was all about to end made her quite unhappy. Her mother came into the room shortly afterwards and Samantha gradually became her old self and the sickness disappeared.

Over the next three days Samantha busied herself making sure she saw everyone she had met since being there, and nearly everyone said how sorry they were to see her go. On the fourth day, having packed their bags Sarah, Samantha and her grandfather were driven to the train station in a horse and carriage fitted with skis.

"You should get to New York at nine tomorrow morning. You have sleeping accommodation on the train and your evening meal and breakfast in the restaurant car are paid for. When you get out at Grand Central you should get a taxi to take you to pier 54 where the *Normandie* will be docked. Get a porter to carry your bags to the taxi. Here are your train tickets and the confirmation that you are booked to sail on the *Normandie* and I have included in this envelope money to cover the taxi fare and tips."

"Oh, Granddad, I don't know what to say, thank you so much. I wish you were coming with us."

The carriage pulled up outside North Conway station and the young driver, recently employed by Joseph, took the bags and carried them to the platform. Livinski got down from the carriage and helped the two ladies alight onto the hardened snow underfoot. He accompanied them through the booking office and into the empty waiting room to await the train. They seated themselves close to the fire in the grate whilst Livinski told his driver that he would be waiting to see the ladies on the train and suggested he too wait there as it was cold outside. The station master, who knew Livinski, came a few minutes later to say the train was approaching the station and suggested they went outside to meet it. It rolled into the station shortly after, the engine dwarfing them as it passed. A few people alighted and the conductor came down and along to pick up the baggage and told the ladies to follow. Livinski hugged Samantha and hurriedly kissed Sarah and the ladies climbed aboard.

"All Aboard" seemed superfluous when there were no others at the station, but it was nevertheless called by the stationmaster, and the train slowly pulled away and they were on their way. Livinski watched while the train disappeared and then went out to the carriage and was driven back to Jackson. He sat by himself in the carriage and stared out at the snow but said nothing to the young driver, his thoughts rapidly going through what had happened over the last few months since taking the decision to start a search for his granddaughter. It had been worthwhile he knew, but he now was sad and he so missed Tanya, he felt more alone now than he had done for a very long time. The carriage was soon at the hotel stopping outside the main entrance and thanking the driver Livinski walked in through the doors and into reception where he spoke briefly to Robert before climbing the stairs and going to his room.

He sat in an armchair and closed his eyes, just thinking, and soon he was asleep and dreaming. Some time later a child ran past his room and he awoke with a start. His mind was still in his dream, he would have to get Tanya to stop Edward running along the hotel corridors and disturbing guests. He came to almost immediately and knew exactly where he was, he must pull himself together, go down and see if he can find Joseph, Joseph was a down-to-earth man and would soon put him straight.

He got up out of the chair and walked across to the door, opened it and went down the stairs, through the kitchen and into the yard. It was snowing heavily again and as he stepped down his shoes sunk into the fresh snow and were covered. He walked towards the stables but it was so dark he could not see, he realised he had forgotten to switch the courtyard light on in the kitchen, but it did not matter Joseph would have a light on where he was working. Livinski carried on walking but instinctively knew he must be walking the wrong way as he did not come up to the stable door as expected. He turned about and started to retrace his steps but saw no light from the hotel kitchen, perhaps Susanne had gone into the storeroom and automatically switched off the light until she returned. He stepped a few more paces forward but suddenly realised he did not know where he was. This is silly, he thought, I have lived and worked here for over forty years how can I be lost?

He was getting cold now as he had not bothered to put on a coat in his hurry to speak to Joseph, the snow was blinding him and the wind had started to howl. He turned again, walked a few more paces into the wind and then suddenly slipped and fell hitting his head on a wall. He was dazed but conscious and tried to get to his feet but found he was unable to move his legs. He shouted as loud as he could but the wind was making such a noise that he doubted if anyone would hear. The snow began to cover him and he felt terribly cold but his brain was active. He tried to move and the best he could do was to roll over on to his side. He had been stupid not to think before he rushed downstairs and out into the cold. Joseph might not even be in the stables, it was after all evening time and he had probably gone home leaving the young lad to answer any calls for transport that might be required.

He thought hard as to what next to do, he was sensible enough to know that if he stayed there all night he might be dead by morning. 'What a ridiculous way to die,' he thought, 'outside the hotel I own, people might think I have lost my mind or have committed suicide.' I must get up. He tried again but nothing. He could move his arms and hands and managed to push the snow from his waistcoat and get hold of his pocket watch but could not read the time as it was too dark, however, the snow had now almost stopped and he could see the clouds moving across the sky as the full moon suddenly gave light. He could now see all around him and realised he was outside the yard and on what would be the grass verge at the end of the road. He looked at his watch, it was 11.15. There were lights now clearly seen in the hotel, if only he could pull himself along the verge to the end of the hotel proper he would have a chance of making someone on the veranda or leaving or entering the hotel hear his shout. He rolled sideways and over two or three times and was now in sight of the veranda but no one was on it, indeed why would anyone want to go on a veranda on a night like this, he thought. He rolled over again and again and was now in front of the hotel but feeling exhausted, and so cold. He called out loud again, "Help, Help, I am in front of the hotel." The wind had dropped and he felt sure someone would hear. He could clearly see the windows on the veranda and a light from one of the bedrooms above. This window suddenly opened and a face appeared. Livinski shouted again, "I'm down here, I have fallen and can't move." The face now became a body as a man leant forward to look. "Hold on I will get someone out to help."

A few minutes later the hotel door opened and three men appeared and ran over to Livinski. They lifted him and carried him into the hotel reception area and placed him on a couch.

"Thank you so much. I'm so sorry to bother you but I was getting desperate."

One of the men recognised who it was, "You're Mr Livinski, what on earth were you doing out there without a coat?"

"I will tell you, but please could someone get me a blanket I can't stop shivering."

A lady in a dressing gown had appeared carrying two blankets which she threw over him.

"Thank you, madam, I did a silly thing and went to go over to the stables without thinking about the weather and I fell over, I don't seem to be able to move my legs, at least when out there I couldn't."

"I think we better call the doctor."

"No please don't bother him, let me see if I can move my legs now. I shall be all right when I get warm. There you are my legs moved."

"You look as if you have cut your head," one man said, "It's only a small cut."

"Yes I hit my head against a wall, stupid of me. Now please leave me I'll go up to my room." Livinski staggered to his feet, the remainder of snow falling to the floor and then helped by one man and the lady made his way shakily up the stairs and to his room.

"You sure you will be all right? Let us help you off with some of those wet clothes."

They went into the room with him, unbuttoned his cardigan, pulled his braces over his shoulder and told him to sit on the bed. The man then removed his shoes and pulled off his trousers. The lady took the clothes and folded them on a chair.

"I would get under the blankets and get yourself warm before you try to wash up. Call out if you need any help, I'm in Room 22 along the corridor. Now do as I say."

"Yes, I will, thank you so much." The two helpers left the room.

Livinski was getting warm now and had stopped shivering. He stayed in bed until he felt comfortable and then undressed properly, washed and went to bed. He did not go to sleep immediately but went through the things that had happened to him that evening, he had been lucky, he thought, he could still be out there and then in the morning nothing. Yes he was getting old and stupid, he must take more care.

The following morning he bathed in a nice hot bath and went down to breakfast feeling more relaxed, he had had a good night's sleep. In the kitchen where they usually had breakfast he found Joseph had already finished his.

"What is all this about you falling over in the snow?"

"Oh I came over to speak to you without thinking of the time or bothering to switch the light on in the courtyard, or indeed putting a coat on."

"Why would you do such a crazy thing, it's years since I worked late at night in the stables? It must have been something important you wanted to say – now what was it?"

Livinski shuffled his feet, he felt slightly embarrassed as Susanne was in the kitchen and could hear.

"Well to be honest, having seen Samantha off home I came back and I suppose I was a little depressed and needed to speak to my old friend to put me straight, but I am better this morning, really."

Joseph put his arm on Livinski's shoulder, "Any time, I think I know what you must be feeling. We all need someone when we are down to share our worries, and I am just your man. What do you say Susanne, give the man an extra helping of bacon and eggs and a cup of your good coffee, we'll get him on his feet again, won't we."

"Joseph is right, we can't have you feeling down. The young lady had to go home and I don't doubt she will come to see you again some time. I know how you must feel, it is like losing someone even though you have known her for such a short time. You have still got your good friend Joseph, and Caroline and the children, and all of us here who have known you so long. You can talk to any of us at any time, you must know that."

Susanne had been busily cooking whilst she talked and as she finished talking she placed his breakfast in front of him.

"There you are Mr Livinski, that should help."

It was nice to know he had so many friends and he would of course do his best not to show what he felt within, but in spite of having so many friends he realised he was more lonely now than he had been for a very long time.

Chapter 14

BACK TO ENGLAND

Samantha and her mother found their way to pier 54 after arriving in New York and boarded the *Normandie*. The crossing to Le Havre and on to Southampton was uneventful, as was their journey by train to Waterloo. They took a taxi across to St Pancras and got a porter to help them with their luggage onto the train going to Luton. Strangely they both said they felt they had not been away, it was almost as if the few months had been a dream, it seemed so unreal. However, struggling with luggage from the rail to the bus station was real enough but they managed. The bus station was as busy as ever but it did not take them long to find the Bedford bus and a fellow traveller kindly helped them lift the luggage on board. It was a cold morning and there were traces of frost on the countryside outside of town.

"I wonder how much longer the snow will last in Jackson," Samantha remarked as the bus drove through Barton where, judging by one or two small piles of dirty snow at the side of the road, it had snowed a day or two before. Her mother did not reply.

Soon the bus was slowing and it stopped outside the George. The conductor helped lift the luggage off the bus and they were almost home.

"I'll go and get the old pram, Mum, it'll be easier than struggling, I've got my key."

Samantha was just about to walk away when an old school friend came out of the pub.

"Hullo, Samantha, haven't seen you for a long time. Looks as if you could do with some help. Here let me take them. Been away have you?"

"Yes we have been to America."

"America! How come?"

Samantha told him their story as the three walked back to the cottage.

"Are you going out there again?"

"Oh I don't know, one day perhaps."

Chapter 15

STORM CLOUDS OVER EUROPE

Returning to his room after the special breakfast prepared by Susanne, Livinski remembered that he had forgotten to give Samantha details of the horticultural college he had made arrangements for her to attend, if she so wished, when back home. He therefore sat at his desk and wrote a letter giving her all the information and enclosing a dollar cheque to cover the fee he had been quoted plus expenses she would need in travelling and accommodation and sufficient spending money and rent of her mother's cottage for a full year. At the same time he wrote to the Royal Horticultural Society in London to confirm what he had done, telling them that his granddaughter may well be in touch with them shortly to take up her promised place at RHS Wisley.

He posted the letters the following day and believed Samantha would get the letter soon after she was back home.

At the end of February he had a letter from Samantha thanking him for the cheque and offer, stating that she was going to take a day trip to RHS Wisley to see what it was like and find out how easy or difficult it would be to find accommodation. She confirmed she would not cash the cheque until she had made up her mind about taking up the offer. She would write again.

Three weeks later another letter was received in which she told her grandfather that she would be starting at Wisley at the end of March. She said she had found accommodation in the village of the same name close by and that she was going to take her bicycle with her as the village was very remote being a few miles from both the county town of Guildford and its neighbouring town of Woking.

Livinski was pleased Samantha would now be able to fulfil her ambition of pursuing a career in horticulture and asked her to keep him informed of how her work progressed.

So, apart from the good news that he had been able to get Samantha to what, he had been told, was the best place to learn horticulture in England, the year 1938 proved to be unremarkable, at least as far as those concerned in our story.

Caroline, on hearing from Robert of her father's depression, had immediately invited him round for Sunday lunch with the children and after playing games with the young ones he became more relaxed and when he was taken back to the hotel later in the day he told Joseph he was feeling much better.

Livinski, although still lonely, thus gradually overcame the deep depression that set in following the departure of his granddaughter, and to counteract this did what he could to help in the running of the hotel, although in truth his help was not really needed as Robert, Caroline's husband, had proved himself quite capable of looking after things by himself

Being a European immigrant Livinski had always taken an interest in what was happening on that continent and the news now was not good – the civil war was still raging in Spain, Mussolini was boasting of the military power of the Italians after taking Abyssinia, and Adolf Hitler was making claims for more land for the German people, having already annexed Austria he was now wanting the Sudeten Land of Czechoslovakia. In late summer the English Prime Minister, Neville Chamberlain, acted to appease Hitler after meeting him in Germany and the result was guaranteed non intervention if Hitler occupied the Sudeten Land. He of course did this but did not stop there; instead he occupied all of Czechoslovakia.

On the face of it Chamberlain's action had avoided war, and in any event troubles in Europe were felt to be very remote from America and certainly in the Washington Valley no person would have thought their country would be affected. In any event since the last war America had followed an isolationist policy at home and abroad and Europe was somewhere very remote to the average citizen. Livinski had lost touch many years ago with any relations or friends in Europe but now he had once again gained a personal interest in happenings over there as his granddaughter lived in England. He was thus pleased when he read in a New York daily of the British prime minister's action.

He had further letters from Samantha and she reported how she was so much enjoying working at Wisley. It seemed the village cottage she stayed in was not far from the village church which she described as being many hundreds of years old and very tiny. 'Edward the Black Prince who beat the French at the Battle of Crecy had connections with the village and church' she wrote. The lady who looked after her was a widow and provided her with breakfast and a meal in the evening. Samantha said she went home once a month and that she thought her mother had got used to her being away. She described the countryside around Wisley in some detail saying that she had cycled into the Surrey Hills which although not so high as those mountains in the Washington Valley nevertheless were just as beautiful.

"If you ever come over to England again, Granddad, I will show them to you," she wrote.

Thanksgiving, Christmas and New Year 1939 all passed and in February Caroline with the help of Joseph and, of course, Robert, organised a surprise party for Livinski's 70th birthday. Outside the snow was thick on the ground but, apart from hotel guests and relations, Caroline had seen to it that his many friends and acquaintances in Jackson, Conway and North Conway were all invited and Joseph had arranged transport for them to make sure they were all able to attend. Among the guests, other than relations and hotel guests, was the stationmaster at North Conway, the son of the jeweller who had helped Leon with the sale of the necklace, Jacob White the owner of the general store in Conway, and Adam and his wife Amanda. Young Adam, as Livinski and Joseph had always known him, was now 60 years of age and had a thriving architectural and engineering practice in Lincoln. The party was a great success and the local press gave it a write-up and included photos.

In was in 1939 that Joseph and Anna gave their North Conway store a facelift, in fact this was a second facelift, but this time they had managed to acquire the store next door which had become empty. With the approval of Livinski they made the two stores into one and had fitters in from Portland to reburbish throughout. The store was closed for just over a week and when it reopened in late August the new winter stock had just arrived. Sales of this stock was much better than they had expected and, as when they first opened the store all those years ago, they found they had to desperately get agents to send in as much additional stock as they could manage.

It was the week following the opening of the new store that the papers and radio announced that a war had started in Europe. Germany had invaded Poland and Britain and France had declared war on Germany. Livinski's country, Poland, was quickly defeated and once again was going to be occupied. In fact Russia and Germany divided it between themselves; this was the country that had only again gained independence following the First World War, long after Livinski and Joseph had left Europe. On the German western front nothing much at first happened with Germans staying behind a line of defence called the Seigfreid Line and the French behind the 'impregnable' Maginot Line. The British Expeditionary Force crossed into northern France near the border with Belgium. In the first months of the war, which in England became known as the phoney war, nothing happened to alter much the lives of people living there. Samantha wrote that everything was normal, except they were required to carry gas masks and had had a scare on the first day of the war when the air raid sirens sounded, but that was all. She was continuing to work at Wisley, although when war was declared she had at first thought of returning home. In April she had completed her first year and as she said she was doing well. However, everything changed in May when the Germans surprisingly advanced into Belgium and Holland, circumventing the Maginot Line, and with pressure further south, around Verdun, Paris was being threatened. The British at first went to meet the Germans in Belgium but were pushed back to the coast by superior forces and eventually had to evacuate its army from the beaches of a place called Dunkirk. Paris fell and the French surrendered. Britain was now alone in fighting. Hitler decided he would invade Britain but to do this he had to get command of the air. Goering, the commander of the German airforce, sent hundreds of bombers with fighter escorts to smash airports in Britain but was thwarted by the RAF fighters who, though outnumbered, managed to hold back the Germans and indeed win the air battle over England, aided by two famous fighter planes, the Spitfire and the Hurricane, but most of all by the courage and tenacity of the few brave pilots who flew them. This became known as the Battle of Britain.

Livinski followed the events avidly and thought it was time to try and get Samantha and her mother over to America. Having failed to beat the RAF the German airforce, the Luftwaffe, next concentrated on bombing London, in particular the London dock area of the East End. Samantha assured Livinski in letters that the bombing was away from where both she worked and where her mother lived but nevertheless he said he was going to try to get them away. He got in touch with the American Embassy in London and the British Embassy in Washington and with persistent pressure eventually managed to get two berths on a ship which would be sailing in convoy across the Atlantic hopefully some time in September. He gave all the details to Samantha and her mother and also money for their fares to the place from where the ship would sail. He told them to be ready at short notice and said the tickets had been arranged and paid for, he warned them that they would likely only get twenty-four hours notice of departure. As stated earlier, until the Germans invaded France and Belgium nothing much had happened in England but at sea it was different where U-boats and pocket battleships had been active ever since war was declared. The best way of getting across the oceans had been determined as in convoy with the Navy escorting them.

Chapter 16

RETURNING TO AMERICA

It was a hard decision for her mother to agree to going but for Samantha it was less so as she could not wait to get back over there. Thus Samantha and her mother packed their bags ready to go in August. Samantha carried on working at Wisley but arranged to leave there immediately a call came through from her mother to say they had notice to leave. On the first weekend in September whilst Samantha was at home they received a telegram stating they were to report to the American Embassy in London on a date and time which was less than two days away; they should bring the telegram with them. Samantha rang Wisley on the Monday to say she would not be coming back to complete her course, perhaps until after the war.

Thus on Tuesday they travelled to St Pancras in London and got a taxi to take them to the American Embassy. They presented their telegram when checked at the entrance to the building and were told to join others in a waiting room. Inside there were several people with cases, mostly Americans, all it was assumed waiting to sail to America. About an hour later they were told to leave and board a bus, each person being checked as they boarded, their baggage was stored under the bus and it drove off to Euston, the main rail terminus of the LMS (London Midland and Scottish Railway) where they were again checked before boarding a train with their baggage. The train was crowded but the party from the Embassy had four reserved compartments. They were given food and drinks and told the journey would be

272

about four hours, they had no idea to what port they were going.

It was early evening when the train came to a stop at a station they were told was Liverpool. Again there was a careful check of each person by a custom official against a list of names he had, each person being required to show their passport. They were then told to walk across to a ship waiting by the dockside. They were helped up a gangplank to the deck and their luggage followed carried by crew members. Samantha and Sarah were allocated two bunk beds in a cabin shared with two American ladies who introduced themselves.

After settling in Samantha suggested they go up on deck to look around. Their cabin was on the deck below the main deck and the stairs to it were no more than ten paces from the cabin. On deck they found a great deal of activity and were asked to stay where they were as further along a crane was lifting baggage into the hold. The crane and the men below looked almost unreal covered for a time in the brilliant red haze from a colourful sky as the sun slowly set to the west. They learnt from a crew member standing close by that the ship was likely to sail that evening and would join a convoy out at sea but before sailing there would be a boat drill. Each person had been allocated a lifejacket found on the bunks with a note telling them to which boat station they should report for roll-call scheduled for five o'clock. They returned below deck and at five o'clock an announcement over the tannoy told them the drill was about to take place and at the same time a klaxon was sounded to show what in future would be the call to boat stations.

Boat drill over, they returned to their cabins and shortly afterwards chains could be heard raising the anchor and the engines started. Many of the passengers, including Samantha and her mother, went up on deck to see the ship leave port. As the ship sailed up the Mersey they could see other ships ahead and others leaving their berths, all they expected to join the convoy to be formed at sea. When clear of the river they saw how vast the convoy of ships was to be and in the distance they saw a grey sleek vessel moving faster than the others and were told this was part of the escort to be with the ships for the first days of the crossing. Standing by the rails on the starboard side, one of the ship's officers came and stood near to Samantha and she asked him how long the crossing would take.

"It will be at least twelve days to sheltered waters."

"That seems a long while compared with the crossing I made two years ago."

"I expect you were on an Atlantic liner which is built for speed and although some of the ships in this convoy could no doubt get across in a much shorter time than in convoy, we have to move at the speed of the slowest ship. Twelve days is not too bad but it also depends what route has been planned, I have been on runs that have taken well over fourteen days."

"Do you know where we going?"

"No, only the captains know where we are heading, could be Halifax or even up the St Lawrence to Montreal, and possibly New York. This ship is the flagship of the convoy and on our own we could certainly go much faster, it was built as a cruise ship and can sail at 16 knots but in convoy we will probably be averaging 10 and change course many times."

"Why if it could travel much faster does it sail in convoy?"

"Well even at 16 knots it is too dangerous to sail on one's own, the big liners travel over 20 knots and some over 30 and even then they zigzag all the way. The convoy will be changing course several times too."

"Thank you for the information, I do think all you men are so brave to keep sailing across the ocean when it is so dangerous."

"Someone has to do it, for without shipping bringing food and other supplies into Britain we might as well give in."

With that he said he must go and left her standing by the rail thinking.

Chapter 17

DISASTER

The date was September 13th and the ship they were on was the SS *City of Benares*, a ship of 11,000 tons built as a cruise liner only three years before. On board were people like Samantha and her mother trying to escape the war, among these were ninety children who had been taken from what were considered vulnerable areas, to spend the war in Canada. The food they soon found, as on most ships, was excellent being quite different from what was available in England at that time and the first few days out had been a happy time for most, although some had succumbed initially to sea sickness.

It was now the evening of the fourth day, 17th September, and all the children had gone to their bunks some time before, many of the adults were up on deck or taking a quiet drink in the bar, when it happened. A sudden crash and the ship heaved and it became obvious to those who were awake that the ship had been hit. In fact it had been torpedoed by a German U-boat. Samantha later found it difficult to describe exactly what happened, she said had been going below when the ship lurched and she tumbled down the stairs and for a time must have been unconscious. She remembers the passageway past the cabins being full of people pushing to go up the stairs and she stumbled to her feet and pushed her way back along to her cabin; the door was open and the cabin empty, her mother must have gone with the crowd to get on deck, she thought, so Samantha followed. Both she and her mother knew where their boat station was and she headed for it but the ship was listing badly and she never quite got there before she was bundled by a crew member into a lifeboat that was just about to be launched, and suddenly they were on the sea and floating away from the side of the ship. She said afterwards that she saw other boats being lowered and many people in the sea and she prayed her mother was in one of the boats. The men aboard managed to drag one or two people out of the water and then they saw the ship go down. It was pitch dark except when a sailor who had a torch switched it on as the boat searched around for survivors.

They had some supplies in the lifeboat and at daylight they met other boats from the ship but Samantha searched in vain for her mother. They spent a whole day and one further night in the lifeboat before they were picked up by a destroyer which been escorting another convoy. They were told the ship would catch up their convoy and transfer those passengers wanting to continue their journey to another ship whilst others would be returned to England. Samantha was transferred to a cargo ship and some ten days later this ship, when apparently nearing Halifax, left the convoy and headed south keeping close to the coast and then entered a big sheltered harbour and anchored.

The passengers were taken ashore in tenders whilst the ship almost immediately started taking on cargo for a return voyage where Samantha was told they would join another convoy from Halifax and return to England. The place where they anchored she learnt was called Bar Harbor, a town in the northern New England state of Maine. On the tender she recognised two ladies she had seen in the American Embassy and she made herself known to them. The three and a few other survivors were taken to a hotel near the sea front where they were questioned; they explained they had lost all their luggage and money and the only article carried by the three of them was a passport that Samantha had carried in the pocket of the coat she was wearing. That night they stayed in the hotel and in the evening Samantha managed to get the telephone number of the Wentworth. She rang and Robert answered the phone, she asked to speak to her granddad

"Samantha, how nice to hear your voice, so you made it, where are you?"

"Have you heard anything from my mother?"

"No, didn't she come with you?"

"Yes she did. Oh dear, I hoped she might have rung you from somewhere," she sounded excited and spoke hurriedly. "Our ship was sunk and I am sure a lot of people were lost, I was bundled into a lifeboat by a sailor but I didn't see Mum. I am hoping that any other survivors might have been taken to a different place to where we are. She's not here, I've asked and looked." She sounded breathless.

"Now try and calm down, you haven't told me yet where you are?"

"I'm in a place called Bar Harbor, it's in Maine, we have been put in a hotel."

"I know Bar Harbor. Have you any money?"

"No, I lost everything except my passport and the clothes I was wearing."

"Oh I am so sorry, how terrible." He stopped talking and for a moment she thought they had been cut off, but then, "Now listen to me carefully. I will arrange to send money to you. Let me think, ah I know – give me the telephone number from where you are ringing and in the morning I will get my bank to advise the hotel that money is being transferred to them. I will call you, say at eleven to morrow, so stay around. I suggest you try and get a good night's sleep, we'll talk tomorrow."

The hotel provided the survivors with a meal and a shared room. Whilst they were eating a man came into the restaurant, spoke to a waiter and was directed to their table.

"Excuse me, ladies, I am from the local newspaper, all the town seems to know that survivors from a ship sunk in the Atlantic have been landed here. I know it may not be easy but would you mind telling me about what exactly happened to you?"

One of the American ladies answered first and she told what she remembered and then Samantha gave her version and said that so far she had not been able to find her mother. He asked each where they were from and when they expected to leave Bar Harbor.

"I have spoken to my grandfather on the telephone and he says he will arrange for money to be sent and will be in touch with me tomorrow morning. He has a hotel in New Hampshire at a place called Jackson." The other ladies told him what they expected to do. He questioned them further and said he would be passing some of this on to New York and Boston papers. He left and they finished their meal and returned to the room provided.

The following morning the reporter returned again whilst the three survivors were sitting in the lounge, this time he gave them each a paper in which he had written their story. He confirmed that a story would almost certainly appear in the main New York and Boston papers. At eleven o'clock the call Samantha expected came and she went to the telephone at reception. Her grandfather told her that money should be made available to her shortly if she asked for the manager.

"The bank have spoken to him and I also did a short while ago. You must get to Bangor – I would guess it is about forty miles from where you are, and there you should buy a ticket on the railroad to North Conway. You will have to change trains at Portland. The hotel manager will tell you how to get to Bangor, there will be enough money for a taxi if that is necessary. When you get to Portland telephone us and say what train you are catching from there and we will be at the rail station to meet you."

"Thank you so much, Granddad, I'll give you a call from Portland."

"Now look after yourself and ring if you have any more problems."

She went to reception and asked to see the manager. He confirmed what her grandfather had told her and gave her the money set aside for her.

"Tell your grandfather that the newspaper has said they will take care of the hotel bill so I have added this to the amount he credited us with. I understand he has told you to get to Bangor to catch a train to Portland."

"Yes he did, but how do I get there?"

"I was just about to tell you, you have nothing to worry about as the newspaper are arranging to take all three of you ladies there by their own car. They will call for you at 1.30 so you will have time to have some lunch. I will leave you to tell the other ladies."

"Oh thank you so much, everyone is being so kind."

The newspaper reporter arrived at the hotel and took them to his car.

"It'll take a little over an hour, some of the roads are not too good but we will get there. You are all going south I believe and I checked on train times. There is one due at 3.30, it goes right through to Boston."

"I have to go to Portland," Samantha said.

"Oh that is all right, the train will stop at Portland, I think it should get there by about six this evening. And you other ladies?"

"We will go all the way to Boston, we are both going on to New York."

The reporter got them to Bangor rail station at 2.45 having questioned and listened to more stories about the sinking of the *City of Benares* that he would no doubt use in his paper when he returned. The train to Boston arrived some ten minutes later than the reporter had told them but seemed to travel fast all the way down to Portland and arrived there at ten minutes to six.

Samantha said farewell to the two American ladies and went to find the time of the next train to North Conway.

"There is one due in from Boston in about half an hour," she was told.

"What time does it get into North Conway?"

"It should be in at 7.50 but that depends on how it is running from Boston."

She thanked him, telephoned the hotel and then made her way to the appropriate platform.

The train came in and left Portland on time, according to the conductor, and would with any luck be in North Conway at the time the booking office had told her. At the station she was met by Livinski in the Buick with a new man driving.

"I am so pleased to see you but am very sorry about your mother; I suppose you have had no news?"

"No, no news."

"There has been a lot in the New York papers about the sinking as it seems many young children were lost. There is a report that the British government are now stopping any further general evacuation of children to Canada, it is too risky."

Samantha said little on the short ride to Jackson. When she arrived she briefly met Robert who told her which room had been prepared for her.

She thanked him and then turning to her grandfather said, "I would like to get to bed now, if you don't mind, I am afraid I do not feel much like talking."

"Yes you go off, you look tired. I hope you have a good night and we will see you in the morning."

Chapter 18

WORK IN AMERICA

Samantha was up quite early for breakfast and went down into the kitchen where Susanne greeted her warmly and said how sorry she was to hear about Sarah.

"It must be terrible for you leaving your home to come to safety and then this happens. Let me see, it was about this time when you came out before because I remember how thrilled you both were at seeing the colours of the leaves, I think they are equally as good this year." Whilst talking she was busily preparing breakfast for the others who would join her in the kitchen before the later breakfasts in the dining room were prepared.

Joseph was the next to come into the kitchen and said much the same things to Samantha as Susanne had, and then seeing a look he had seen on Leon's face when people kept saying how sorry they were after Tanya died, he continued, "You will be getting quite a lot of people saying how sorry they are and wanting to know more about what happened, however, you don't have to say anything unless you want to. People are usually genuinely sorry but will also be interested to know what happened, particularly as most over here are hardly aware of a war going on in Europe and it takes something like this to jerk them into realising that the effects of this war can be far reaching." Joseph had made his mind up to say something like this but he had had no intention of blurting it out straight away but seeing the look on her face he had reacted.

"Oh that is all right, I know what might happen. I don't mind talking about it, in fact I suppose it will do me good to get it off my chest, as they say."

"Leon tells me you have been going to a Horticultural school in England."

"Yes, he fixed it up for me and I had only a few more months to go before I would be taking my examinations. I will have to see what, if any, work there is for me in horticulture while I am over here."

"There are such places over here so I believe. I seem to remember there is one in Worcester, Massachusetts, but there may be others nearer, perhaps even in New Hampshire. Anyway we will see."

"I don't know whether I ought to go to school again, I really ought to work."

"Oh well, we will have to see what Leon has to say."

The day following Samantha's arrival Livinski, who for many years had made a habit of staying in the hotel instead of going home, met her in reception.

"How are you today?"

"I am feeling much less tired than I was yesterday, thank you."

"And what do you want to do today?"

"I was saying to Joseph I ought to find myself a job."

"There will be plenty of time to do that. You have had a terrible experience and I recommend we take a ride out into the country, which as you know is particularly beautiful this time of the year, and relax. If, God willing, your mother is found she will know where to get in touch. I will phone the British Embassy perhaps tomorrow, but it may be too soon, and see if I can get hold of the names of the survivors. What do you say – will you accompany an old man and see what the White Mountains have to offer?"

She raised a smile and nodded her head gently. "I would love to come with you, Granddad."

Thus over the days that followed Livinski did his best to keep Samantha occupied, not allowing her to think too much about what had happened. He got in touch with the British Embassy and was told that there was no one among survivors who matched Sarah, it did seem as though the lady had been lost at sea.

Livinski's next action was to make enquiries concerning horticultural schools in New Hampshire and found that there was a department of the Thompson School in the University of New Hampshire which studied horticulture. The school was in Durham which was about 60 or 70 miles from Jackson. He telephoned them and they were going to send him information on entry etc. He told Samantha but she said she really wanted to work and that she already had acquired an excellent knowledge of horticulture and did not think she would learn an awful lot more by going back to school. No, she was adamant that she wanted to work and earn some money.

Livinski continued to make enquiries concerning work in horticulture and found the American Horticultural Society most helpful. However, there did not seem to be the possibility of getting Samantha involved until the following year and as winter would soon be upon them there was unlikely to be any work locally in horticulture from November through to say the end of March. So he had a word with Anna and she agreed to employ Samantha in the North Conway shop, ostensibly with the intention of gradually being able to give more time for Anna to get more involved in her charity work. Thus Samantha, in the middle of October, started to work for Anna. Livinski knew that Anna expected her staff to be smartly dressed and as Samantha had lost all her clothes, other than those she was wearing at the time the ship sank, he asked Anna to fit her out and pass the bill to him

Samantha did not know a great deal about smart women's clothes but soon learnt under the careful instruction of her boss who herself had entered the business as truly an amateur but had now gained vast experience. Much to her surprise Samantha found herself enjoying the job of a store assistant and therefore learnt quickly and at the end of her first week, with Anna or another member of staff, Julia, on hand all the time, she made her first sale.

She cycled back to Jackson that evening most excited.

"Granddad, I made my first sale – it was an expensive dress and Anna told me I had done very well. It is not so bad working in a shop, in fact I have quite enjoyed my first week."

"I am pleased, it is surprising that often the things we had never thought of doing turn out to be what we do and enjoy. Look at me, I was trained as an engineer but ended up working in a hotel. I doubt if I remember very much of what I learnt on engineering."

"Granddad, I want to start paying towards my upkeep and I don't want you to say I need not. I want to be able to stand on my two feet. As you know I will not be earning a great deal but I must give some of my earnings to you."

"If you insist, but do not leave yourself short and if possible put a little by. Who knows, if you continue to enjoy the work you may wish to set out on your own in this field."

"Oh I would never be able to do that."

"Why not? Think about it, Anna and Joseph are not getting younger and one day may want to retire, or perhaps sell the business, and who better to carry on that business than someone in the family. Anyway we shall see."

Chapter 19

New Year Party

Thanksgiving and Christmas 1940 passed and everyone in the hotel was preparing for the big party Robert had arranged for the New Year. There was little doubt that this was going to be the biggest party seen in Jackson and North Conway for many years as Robert had taken the unusual step, in fact a first, of advertising in both places and the response well before Christmas had been overwhelming and already he was having to tell people that he was sorry there were no more seats available. Undoubtedly the popularity of the twice weekly dances held in the ballroom since the twenties to which people not staying in the hotel could come, had prompted many outsiders to decide to book for this new addition to the local calendar.

Once it was known how many would be coming the task was to ensure adequate staff and above all food was available and that kitchen staff could cope with so much additional work. The winter chef from Boston managed to get two more assistants from that city to help in the kitchen and extra temporary staff were brought in from the surrounding villages. Livinski favoured what Robert had done but wondered whether financially the charge made would be enough to cover the undoubted additional expenditure. Food, party hats, crackers, fancy dress, cutlery, crockery, glasses and furniture began to arrive directly after Christmas and family, including Daniel and Abigail, and all staff, put in many hours to ensure everything was ready on the night. Even the orchestra, usually piano, saxophone, base and drums was boosted on Livinski's request by two trombones, a clarinet and another saxophone. It seemed the delivery vans over the four days before the great day never stopped calling and two extra giant refrigerators, brought in from Conway, were filled to the brim.

Fortunately on the night of the party the weather was kind and, although cold, people could arrive in open carriages if they so wished, and many did. The winter scene and sounds were perfect with many horses and carriages fitted with bells. Particularly spectacular were the big wagons on skis pulled sometimes by four horses bringing in guests from the surrounding villages. One enterprising photographer stationed himself on the Jackson side of the covered bridge and with flashlight took some remarkable pictures as carriages crossed; two of these were later shown in the local paper.

The ballroom, which was on the first floor, had tables of all shapes and sizes, some seating six and some eight, arranged in such a way that there was still a substantial part of the floor available for dancing. The orchestra occupied its usual position at one end of the ballroom. As guests arrived they were offered drinks in the reception area by three local young ladies employed for the evening. An extra cloakroom had been necessary and for this the manager's office had been taken. It had been decided that although it would have been nice to serve the meal in the ballroom, the fact that it would mean waiters carrying food from the kitchen up the main staircase was too much to ask and thus the restaurant would be used with guests making their way to the ballroom when the meal had been finished. The regular pianist would be playing on the baby grand in the restaurant.

How everyone was served and the food and plates kept hot was due to very good organisation by Susanne who later Livinski praised together with the chefs for making the meal such a success. It was gone ten o'clock when the last of the guests made their way to the ballroom, only a few having left for home directly after the meal. The orchestra playing tirelessly throughout the remainder of the evening made a valiant attempt to play in the style of the recently acclaimed Glenn Miller big band whose rendering of Tuxedo Junction and others had sold so many records earlier that year.

Samantha, who for most of the evening was helping in various capacities, working in the cloakroom, then handing out drinks and later doing what she could in the kitchen, went up to the ballroom about eleven o'clock. She had never danced before but had once seen over a balcony in a ballroom in Bedford other young people dancing, it all looked too difficult for her and she never ventured down on the floor in case someone asked her to dance. Entering this American ballroom she at first stood by the door and then was called over to a table where Joseph and Anna were seated. She had hardly been seated when a young man came to ask if she would dance. She embarrassingly told him she could not dance but he and the others on the table persuaded her to take to the floor and reluctantly she got up. In truth very few people on the floor were doing anything that could be recognised as a dance, just holding each other and shuffling round the floor. Ballroom dancing as she had seen practised in England appeared not to exist in this ballroom and she realised she did not have to worry. However, things changed when the orchestra played a fast rhythm some couples breaking loose from holding each other and danced simply holding hands and doing any number of steps in time to the music. Samantha and her partner left the floor to watch.

"This is the new dance craze," he said. "They call it jitter bugging!"

"Looks exciting but I don't think I could do it."

"Oh it is only practice, just follow the beat, come on have a go."

So Samantha had her first lesson in jitter bugging and returned to her seat exhausted but happy. The same young man came over again later and she danced with him again.

"You are not American, are you – where you from?"

She told him and that her uncle who owned the hotel had brought her over.

"I'm Kirk, what is your name?"

"Samantha."

"That's a lovely name, are you staying in the hotel?"

"Yes I am, at least for the time being. I hope one day to get a small place of my own. Do you live locally?"

"Not really, at least this is not my home, I come for the winter season, I'm a ski instructor. I am staying at small hotel in North Conway. My home is on the coast, a small town called Rockport."

They continued talking right through to the countdown to midnight when after the clock had sounded twelve he kissed her and wished her a happy new year. It was the first time she had been kissed by a boy since Willie Johnson had kissed her at the school party. But this kiss was nothing like that one and she was thrilled. After Auld Lang Syne as she was about to leave the ballroom with Joseph and Anna, Kirk came up to her and grabbing her arm asked, "Can I see you again?"

"Well I will be around; I work in Anna's store in North Conway. You may have seen it, it's a ladies dress store."

"Oh yes I have seen it. I'll come in and see you, it'll give you time to think if you would like to see me again. I hope you do."

Samantha wanted to say that she did want to see him again but thought it might be considered a bit unladylike so she just said, "I shall look out for you," and then said goodnight.

The party had been a great success and Livinski felt sure they had gained a lot of goodwill for the hotel and even when looking at the finances found they had practically broken even.

Samantha thought it right to warn Anna that the young man might come into the store one day to see her.

"If he comes in I'll leave you to talk to him. He looks a nice young man. Where is he from?"

"He's only here for the winter, he comes from a place called Rockfort or Rockport, I'm not too sure. He is a ski instructor."

As he had promised, Kirk duly came into the store a couple of days later and Samantha agreed to go with him to the cinema the following night where *Gone with the Wind* was showing. Samantha had earlier that day read in a paper in the store that as the film had been so costly to make and lasted four hours, having an interval halfway through, the price of seats had been more than doubled.

"We will have to get there early as I am sure everyone will want to see it," he had said, and early they were next evening and joined the line-up that had formed some time before. At the interval he bought Samantha an ice cream and held her hand in the second part of the film.

"I enjoyed this evening very much, thank you," she said as they came out of the cinema.

"What did you think of the film?"

"I thought it was wonderful and I thought Vivien Leigh played her part very well – she's English you know," she said proudly, "and so is Leslie Howard."

"I thought the scenes in Atlanta were terrific, didn't you?"

"Yes, it must have been terrible, especially as it was a civil war."

Kirk managed to get a taxi to take them back to Jackson and the driver waited while he said goodnight to Samantha and saw her safely back in the hotel. He kissed her before leaving.

Returning to her room Samantha, reminded of war, could not help but think of the war back home. For some weeks she had turned it away from her mind, unlike her grandfather who had been following closely what had been happening over in Europe.

Chapter 20

The Luftwaffe were continuing to bomb London and each day the American dailies and the various radio stations reported in detail what was happening, usually from an American in London, Ed Murrow, who watched while it happened. The papers reported that the bombing had started at the end of August and almost every night since then London had suffered – first the dock area in the East End and then the City, that is the old city, the financial centre of the country, and then the many industrial areas in the Lea Valley and elsewhere. In fact there were no parts of London, including the suburbs that escaped.

One day in January after listening to the radio, Livinski decided to write to the Davis family hoping they were safe and to tell them that many Americans were with them. He hardly expected to get a reply but at the beginning of March he got an Air Letter from Mrs Davis.

Dear Mr Livinski,
We were so pleased to have a letter from you. It is so nice to know you think of us. I am afraid we have had quite a time of it, the air raids happen every night and the bombing has been heavy all around. Much of our road has disappeared but we have been lucky and apart from broken windows and plaster falling off ceilings we have escaped. We have had to go down the shelter at the end of the road most nights and Dad has to go to work no matter what is happening. Trains continue to run and he is one who has to see they continue. John still travels by train to school and will shortly be leaving, he is in the sixth form having passed his matriculation and is simply

waiting until he is offered a job. Bert has told him not to take anything like he had to when he was young, get in an office job and one with a pension, he says.

Eileen is getting on well and becoming quite a young lady. We all hope the bombing will stop soon, they are killing so many people and smashing buildings everywhere, but we carry on in the day as if nothing had happened, it has become a way of life. I hope the war will end soon as John seems keen to join the RAF and I don't want him to go. The wireless tells us how many planes we lose every night trying to give the German people what they give us, so many young men die.

It was so nice to know you remember us and so pleased you found your granddaughter. I hope she is safe in the country.

Yours sincerely

Jean Davis

He read the letter several times to himself, to family and to one or two others in the hotel, he wanted as many Americans to know how the people of London were bravely carrying on with their lives.

The one piece of good news, as far as Britain was concerned, came from North Africa where the Italians, who had entered the war at the time of Dunkirk, had in October begun an advance to capture Egypt but the British Generals Wavell and O'Connor had swept forward with British and Commonwealth troops, although outnumbered four to one, and captured in a few months over 200,000 Italian prisoners and were poised to invade Tripolitania in February when the Germans under General Rommel were sent to save the Italians. Livinski made sure that his friends knew of these victories in North Africa even though it did not rate much of a mention in some of the papers.

Over the next few weeks Samantha became very friendly with Kirk and saw him frequently and when she was free often accompanied him to the ski slopes. In April he left the area and returned home to Rockport in Maine where he had a summer job in Camden, guiding tourists over the hiking trails of the Camden State Park. They continued to correspond and he said he would be returning to North Conway at the end of October. For Samantha the summer months could not go fast enough as she so wanted to see Kirk again and kept wishing he could have come across to see her but the journey without a car was not straightforward. In one letter he did say he would try and get summer work in the Washington Valley and Samantha spoke to her grandfather to see if he could help.

Anna told Livinski how pleased she was with the work Samantha was doing at the store, she said people seemed to like her and the way she presented clothes to them. Sales in the North Conway store had never been so good. For her part Samantha enjoyed her work and no longer thought much about horticulture although she admitted to herself she would like to have a small garden of her own to look after.

Chapter 21

LEON AND JOSEPH

Livinski and Joseph, now both with time on their hands, often sat on the hotel veranda and talked of the past, mostly in English but occasionally lapsing into Polish.

"You remember Murphy's in Brooklyn?"

"I certainly do. I wonder if that waitress ever got away from there. I'm glad we decided to go."

"I can still taste the stew we had, how wonderful it seemed after all those weeks without proper food. And the walk over the Brooklyn Bridge to Manhattan and back, I would not like to have to do that now."

"I'm sure you wouldn't. I doubt if you could make it over the Jackson Bridge and back," Joseph said laughing.

If one could have heard what these two old friends talked about they would be amazed at how many times, albeit on different occasions, the same things were said. Perhaps this was a sign of the beginnings of old age or simply they liked to remember what it was like to be young, when everything was an adventure.

"We did well didn't we."

"Yes we did but we were lucky, ever so lucky."

They both agreed they had had a good life and there were no regrets about leaving Europe, far from it, for two World Wars later the Poles were back living under the control of yet another country.

Chapter 22

SAMANTHA AND KIRK

To the persons in our story the rest of the year in Washington Valley passed without anything unusual happening. The hotel had an average summer and the winter bookings were about the same as the previous year. Susanne continued to rule in the kitchen and Robert was comfortably managing the hotel without need of any help. Anna's stores had had a good summer and had been selling the winter stock fast with substantial orders having been placed for spring stock due to arrive in early February. Caroline's bookshop was ticking over with the sale of Margaret Mitchell's *Gone with the Wind,* as expected, topping the list, closely followed by Steinbeck's *Grapes of Wrath* receiving a boost from the success of the film starring Henry Fonda also released the previous year. Kirk was back in North Conway and had continued his close relationship with Samantha, leaving Livinski with plenty of time on his hands, wondering if they would marry and whether then he would have a great grandchild in the not too distant future. Caroline's children were growing fast – Daniel now fourteen was in the school's baseball and football teams, whilst his young sister, just ten, was showing in two small stage shows that her ballet lessons had not been wasted.

In Europe it had not been quiet, the nightly bombing of London and some other cities in the UK had continued. Then in May, Hitler launched Barbarossa, the name for his invasion of Russia, the British and her Empire now had an ally. The nightly bombing of London temporarily ceased, much of the Luftwaffe being transferred to the Russian front, but in North Africa the gains made against the Italians were slowly being lost to the new German general Rommel.

Chapter 23

Then on December 7th the unbelievable happened, the Japanese without warning attacked the American naval base at Pearl Harbour in Hawaii, and on the following day President Roosevelt formally declared war on Japan and her European allies. The shock and anger of all in Washington Valley was no different from that all over America. No one in America thought they would be at war and were thus completely unprepared both in the mind and in the ability initially to fight back.

Christmas followed all too quickly but the festivities were subdued. In the New Year men who had not already volunteered to fight were included in the draft just the same as men and women had been in Britain some years before. Kirk who was twenty-one volunteered in the first week at a recruiting station set up in Conway. He chose the Marines and was told to report for medicals and assessment in one week and assuming he passed these would likely be told to report to a training camp some six to eight weeks later. Samantha was devastated that her newly found happiness would likely end so suddenly.

However, directly after volunteering, Kirk asked her to marry him and she was once again over the moon. She told her granddad as soon as she came in the hotel after Kirk had seen her home from going to a picture show. Livinski too was happy for her and told her so.

"When do you think the wedding will take place?" he asked.

"We have not talked about it, he only asked me at the entrance to the hotel when he kissed me, and I said yes and came straight in to tell you."

"I think you better see him tomorrow and sort something out, I understand he is going in the Marines next month – are you going to wait until the war is over or get married soon? You better make up your mind."

"Would you mind, Granddad, if I got married soon?"

"My dear girl, it is not for me to decide, I just want you to be happy and of course I don't mind."

"Oh thank you so much, Granddad, I'll tell him I want to get married as soon as possible."

"Well if you do that, I'll start making arrangements for the wedding. We will have it here of course – what about his parents?"

"Oh I don't know, I do hope they will come. I think he said his dad was a fisherman. Do you think they will like me, Granddad?"

"Of course they will; everyone likes you. Anyway you are not marrying them. You better get to bed now."

It was well past eleven when Samantha went up to her room and Livinski, excited, was anxious to tell someone that his granddaughter was going to marry, but everyone except two or three guests in the lounge seemed to have gone to bed. He wandered about the hotel for a while and then picked up the telephone and rang Joseph, Anna answered.

"Hullo, Leon, what is the matter?"

"Nothing is the matter; I just have some good news to tell you and Joseph." He paused a moment, almost as if to give effect… "Samantha is going to get married."

"Do you know what the time is, Leon? It is almost midnight, Joseph is in bed asleep, I'll tell him in the morning. I am very pleased, I'll talk to you tomorrow, Goodnight Leon."

The following morning Samantha was up early and telephoned Kirk, hoping to catch him before he went to the ski slopes.

"Darling, I have told Granddad and he says we can get married in the hotel, he will make arrangements. I want to get married as soon as possible. You do too don't you?"

"Of course I do, but I must tell my parents and I would want them to come."

"I understand. Will you tell them today? We have so little time."

"Yes I will see if I can get in touch with them, our neighbour has a telephone. I will speak to you later."

Samantha went off to work and as soon as Anna arrived in the store she rushed up to her to tell her the news.

"I'm going to be married – he asked me last night!"

"I know, Leon rang me at midnight!"

"Oh dear I didn't know, he did seem excited. I am sorry."

"No need to be sorry it is lovely news, I told Joseph and he is pleased too."

The day passed slowly for Samantha, she could not wait to see Kirk. She would see him at the diner across the road from Anna's store where they had often met in recent weeks. With some half an hour to go before the store closed Anna told Samantha to go. Kirk had already come along to the diner and was sitting on a stool at the counter.

"I got off early, Anna told me to go. Where shall we go?"

"Have a coffee and something to eat first, let's go over to one of the booths. What would you like to eat?"

"I'll just have a piece of apple pie and some ice cream, how do you say it. 'à la mode'?"

"That's what they say in Canada – some say the same here."

He ordered another coffee and apple pie and they went to a table.

"Did you manage to get in touch with your parents?"

"Yes, it took me some while but I managed to speak to my mother. She was surprised but was happy for me and said she would of course tell my father. They would like to have good notice of the date of the wedding as Dad could easily be at sea as they were fishing up at the Banks."

"You'll have to tell me about the banks or whatever you said sometime, but I think we should think of when to fix a date – Granddad will organise it, I mean I know he will get a preacher and fix a date at a church. Are you any special religion?"

"I was brought up Episcopalian."

"I don't know what that is. I am Church of England."

"I think we are on the same side, my church is much the same as yours, that helps." The coffee and pie arrived. "Looks good, I could eat that." He asked the waiter for another piece and then, "You asked when you came in where we should go, I have an idea. How about we go to Jackson and talk to your granddad and see what he has to say."

"That's a good idea, he will be pleased to tell us what to do I'm sure."

Half an hour later they had taken a taxi and were at the hotel. They found Livinski in the kitchen talking to Susanne.

"You're back early; I was not expecting to see you tonight."

"We came to see you, Granddad, we want to talk to you about the wedding. I expect Granddad has told you we are getting married, Susanne?"

"Yes, I do know, I think he has told everybody," she said with a smile. "I am very happy for you."

"Shall we go into the lounge?"

Over the next hour most points were covered. First Livinski would speak to the Episcopalian vicar in North Conway and if possible arrange a date. Then when the date was fixed he would organise the sending out of invitations and make preparations for the wedding reception. Kirk would inform his parents of the date.

"If it is difficult for your parents to come all this way, I will arrange transport for them, so please tell them. We have then got to get you a dress, Samantha. But that should not be too difficult with Anna's connections in the fashion trade. How are you fixed for a suit, Kirk?"

"I have a good suit at home but of course did not bring it with me, I will have to go back to fetch it."

"No, don't do that, Samantha would not want you spending time going all that way to fetch a suit, I'll see you have one. Leave it with me."

Two days later the wedding date was fixed, Kirk had been measured for a suit and Samantha had almost certainly chosen her dress. The wedding would take place in the hotel on the 20th January. Kirk's father would be able to come as luckily the boat he sailed with was due for a complete overhaul of the engine which had been playing up on recent voyages, and the captain, not wishing to lose a good member of his crew, had decided this would be a good opportunity to get the engine fixed. He said they would make one more trip and be back, god willing, on the 18th of the month. Kirk told Livinski what his mother had told him and said they could be ready to leave then.

"Look, there is going to be little time for your parents to get here, especially if the boat does not get in early on that day, give me your address and I will make sure that a car is available to pick them up and bring them straight over. Can I get in touch with them?"

Kirk gave him the telephone number of the neighbour, who he said he had known all his life and who did not mind being called upon to contact his parents, someone he said who would have come to the wedding had it been local.

"What is the neighbour's name?"

"Janowski, he is a widower, he's Polish."

"How strange, I'll give him a ring and surprise him by speaking in Polish."

"Oh I don't know if he speaks Polish, he speaks the same as I do, there is no trace of an accent, like you, Mr Livinski, he was probably born over here."

Livinski was not conscious of his accent but was immediately reminded of his meeting in England with the Davis family and how they had detected his different American accent.

There was now barely ten days to the wedding and Samantha met Kirk each evening after work and on Sunday Kirk came out to the hotel early. They both wrapped up warm and went out for a walk on the hardened snow. It was a beautiful day and it did not seem right that everything would soon be spoilt by Kirk having to go away to war. Why were men so silly to have wars, Samantha thought, but she knew that this scene was being repeated all over America, just the same as it had been in England, and everyone hoping it would be over soon.

Livinski called Kirk's Polish neighbour and found the man could speak some Polish although born in America but he had not spoken for so many years, in fact since his parents died, that he took a while to get back to talking at any speed.

"I have spoken to a car hire firm in Camden and they will come to pick up Kirk's parents at one hour's notice, hopefully on the eighteenth but on the nineteenth at the latest. Would you mind telling them? I'll give you the car hire people's number, you probably know them."

Janowski took down the number and said he would have a word with Mrs Reynolds and warn her of the arrangements.

"Kirk mentioned you might have come along to the wedding if it had been local, why don't you come, I'll make sure there is somewhere for you to stay, you see I own the hotel where the wedding will take place."

Janowski said he would love to come along.

Kirk passed his medicals and the oral and written tests and was told he would be sent to officer training college in Quantico, Virginia. He told Samantha of what had happened and she at once proudly told her grandfather that Kirk was going to be an officer.

Samantha had known her grandfather long enough to know he was a good organiser and that he enjoyed taking control, so she left everything in his capable hands. She collected her dress and Kirk, after one fitting, collected his suit. The day was drawing near.

Over at Rockport everything worked out well for the Reynolds' family and Kirk's father sailed into port after a good catch on the evening of the seventeenth and directly he came in the door his wife went next door to tell Janowski they would be ready to go in the morning. Janowski then rang the car hire firm who said they would be round to pick up the family at ten the next morning.

Samantha would have one bridesmaid, little Abigail, who Anna had managed to get a dress to fit her which complemented that worn by the bride. Much to his relief Daniel was spared the job of being a page boy as he was too big and too old.

The Reynolds with Janowski arrived at eight that evening after having quite a hazardous ride over the last forty or fifty miles when it snowed heavily and the driver, with the help of the men in the car, was forced to stop and put chains on the wheels. Livinski met them in reception and got Robert to show them to the rooms set aside for them, telling them to come down to the restaurant where a meal would be waiting. He then spoke to the driver.

"I gather you had problems near the end. I don't expect you will want to try to get back tonight."

"No I would not wish to face that storm again. Could I stay here overnight?"

"Of course, I'll get the manager to see if we have a spare room, if not I expect he could fix you up in the lounge."

When Robert returned the driver was found an attic room that was empty and he had a meal with his erstwhile passengers.

Samantha did not meet Kirk's parents until the following morning over breakfast.

"Kirk has told us a good deal about you in letters he has written. It is so nice to meet you. I'm Emily and my husband here is Tony."

Samantha sat with them through breakfast and she seemed to get along well with both, although Kirk's father did not have much to say, and probably seemed a little shy. He was a big man, over six feet tall, with big hands and a strong grip, he had a good head of ginger hair going grey at the temples.

"Kirk tells me you are a fisherman, Mr Reynolds. I know nothing about fishing except what I have seen on the films. Kirk mentioned something about the banks – what did he mean?"

"Call me Tony. Kirk was, I guess, referring to the Grand Banks off Newfoundland. It's a popular place to fish but it takes three days for us to get there."

"Do you go there often?"

"No only once or twice a season, we go there principally for cod, but it takes two weeks and you cannot guarantee it will be worth it, although I must say sometimes you are lucky."

"Do the crew get a share in what is fished?"

"Oh yes certainly."

"This is a fine thing talking about fishing when your son is getting married," Mrs Reynolds, who had excused herself from the table shortly before, intervened.

"It was my fault, Mrs Reynolds, I asked your husband about what Kirk had said, something I did not understand."

Allowing Mr Reynolds to say something about fishing, which had been his life since leaving school, seemed to relax him and thereafter he began to join in the conversations on the table when they were joined by Janowski and the taxi driver.

"Have you ever been up to this part of the country before?"

"No, we haven't been many places, have we, Tony. But I did go to Boston once when I was young. We are not ones for travelling except I guess Tony does a bit when at sea."

Livinski joined them before they had finished breakfast and he filled them in on what would happen the following day. He explained that the marriage ceremony would take place in the restaurant which would be prepared by staff after dinner that evening when the tables would be moved to the ballroom above for the wedding breakfast to follow.

"Are you going away afterwards?" Mrs Reynolds asked.

"We haven't planned anything, it's been all so hectic."

Kirk came over to the hotel in the evening to meet his parents and have dinner with them and Samantha. Livinski hovered around but did not interrupt, leaving them, as he thought, to get to know each other. Kirk had brought his suit with him to save the journey back and forth from North Conway and Robert had found a room for him.

The following morning Livinski made sure that Kirk did not see Samantha at breakfast or for the rest of the morning and the first he saw her that day was when she came along on her granddad's arm to face the preacher. It is unnecessary to say she looked very beautiful, brides usually do, but Samantha did have a special air about her and Livinski was proud. The wedding breakfast and the speech that Granddad made went down very well and after the meal he told them he had arranged a honeymoon for them; they were to catch the night train to New York where they would spend two weeks in a first-class hotel. He also told them that at the hotel he had arranged credit for them to collect spending money for theatres etc.

"I hope you don't mind me fixing the holiday for you?"

"Granddad, it is wonderful – we had planned nothing and this is a wonderful surprise. Thank you so much." Samantha gave her granddad a big hug and Kirk added his thanks. Thus nearing eight o'clock, having packed for the journey, they were driven to North Conway and when the train arrived the conductor directed them to their own private suite; the train not due to get to New York until breakfast time.

Needless to say the honeymoon was a success and they were naturally not looking forward to returning to the real world and work; Kirk teaching on the slopes and Samantha working in Anna's fashion store. However, they were together and valued every day as they knew it would not be long before Kirk would have to go. Livinski gave them the use of his house in North Conway which he now seldom visited and had in mind that he might in the end transfer it over to them, but first would make sure that Caroline and Robert had no outstanding debts on their own house.

Chapter 24

IN THE MARINES

It was at the very end of February that the call-up papers arrived; Kirk had to report on 2nd March. Samantha saw him off at the rail station the day before he was due in Virginia as his journey would take more than a day. She shed a few tears when he left even though he assured her he would get some leave when his basic training had been completed.

At the end of April Kirk returned to North Conway for seven days leave before having to report to the Marines in San Diego. The week, as all leave from the forces, went all too quickly and there she was at the rail station again saying goodbye, only this time she had no idea when he would be back again.

Life in hotels in the Washington Valley went on as usual but with changes in staff. Our Robert McGregor, manager of the Wentworth, soon found it necessary to employ older men and women to take the place of younger ones who had volunteered to join the forces, but supply and demand meant that the market for these older persons was very competitive. Later on that year it was to ease somewhat when some store and small business owners finding their businesses failing through lack of orders, decided to cut their losses and seek employment. Then hotel bookings started to fall and a number advanced bookings were being cancelled. Livinski could see that the year 1942 was going to be a year of little or no profit for the hotel. However, he had built up substantial alternative investments and although some of these companies folded or became virtually worthless, others

308

improved beyond all belief with orders from the armed forces so that at the end of this first year of war our man from the small village in Galicia was fast becoming a multi millionaire. With all his wealth he made sure that family and friends shared in his prosperity and also he gave heavily to anything to help the war effort.

Caroline's bookshop continued to tick over but gradually with fewer new titles as less books were being published. Anna's stores also suffered with ladies initially trying to make do with what they had got and suppliers finding it more difficult to get fashion clothing manufactured. Joseph and Anna had themselves, however, also built up funds and could certainly ride the storm for some time and with Livinski, a major shareholder in the stores, keeping an eye on the books they knew he would always be there to help should they need it.

Samantha received several letters from Kirk and she in turn wrote many to him. In one letter he indicated by their secret code that he was about to be shipped somewhere and since he was in California it was almost certain that that somewhere would be in the Pacific. The American Navy of course had taken a pounding at Pearl Harbour and lost their battleships but fortunately its aircraft carriers had been at sea at the time and therefore lived to fight again. Early in 1942 the Americans had successes in the battle of the Coral Sea, and in April an audacious raid was made on Tokyo by Mitchell bombers, flown from an aircraft carrier; and although the material damage done was small, the damage to Japanese moral at home was far greater. Then in June American carriers, with an Admiral Nimitz in command, sunk three Japanese carriers in the Battle of Midway and now, so soon after, the heavy losses sustained at Pearl Harbour were being revenged. The next action of note was the landing of American Marines on Guadalcanal, one of the Solomon

Islands which the Japanese had occupied. There was big publicity of this landing and Samantha saw the newsreels of this at the cinema and wondered whether her husband had been amongst the Marines landing. She did not have a letter from him for several months and she made a special point of going to the cinema regularly really just to see the newsreels which showed continued fighting on Guadalcanal where she imagined Kirk might be.

Thanksgiving, Christmas and the New Year came and went and still no news, then in February – remember this was 1943 – the news stated that Guadalcanal was in American hands and the Japanese had been defeated on land for the first time. At the end of the month Samantha received three letters from Kirk who, although not saying where he had been, said he was well but had been cut off from writing, but now things were for the time quieter he hoped to write and receive letters. She surmised he must have been on Guadalcanal.

As for the war in Europe, Livinski was pleased to see that a new British general named Montgomery had defeated the Africa Corp under Rommel in a battle on the Egyptian border at a place called El Alemain, and that the British and Commonwealth troops were pushing the Germans back through Libya to Tunisia.

The diary that Samantha had started in the hotel after the visit to Billy Rose's Diamond Horseshoe in New York had been kept meticulously ever since and she noted with pride that her husband had been on Guadalcanal. However, she could have been wrong as while the fighting had been going on there, other fighting had been taking place in New Guinea and other Solomon Islands, with Americans capturing island after island and with the help of Australians holding on to the key island of New Guinea. Livinski followed all that was happening even though the news was naturally slanted to what the Americans were doing.

In Europe/Africa an American and British force had landed in Algeria and with a pincer movement with the British Eighth Army on one side had driven the Germans out of North Africa and into Italy where the Allies soon gained a foothold and moved up the boot of Italy on both sides. Italy surrendered but the Germans were putting up stubborn opposition, particularly at a place called Monte Cassino. In Russia the Germans had been stopped and were having to retreat.

Life in Jackson had continued as hitherto, but in no way did the war affect the people living there as it did in nearly all countries in Europe; of course they had the worry of sons and husbands being away and occasionally the sadness of learning that some poor person had been reported killed in some faraway place. Thus 1943 had passed and so into 1944 when came the big build-up of American, Canadian and British forces in England and finally the invasion of Normandy in June. It did seem to all that the war was nearing its end. Meanwhile the Americans were gradually moving towards Japan, taking island after island back from the enemy.

Samantha had the occasional letter from Kirk sent when he was able to write and when there were facilities for getting a letter in the post, but the great thing was that he had so far survived.

Chapter 25

It was in August that Livinski received an air letter with a Canadian stamp on it. He could not think of anyone he knew who would be writing from Canada and he slit open the letter carefully wondering all the time who it could be from. He looked at the end of the letter first, it was signed John, and he still had not guessed who it was from, but once he started reading he could hardly believe what he read.

Dear Mr Livinski,

I know you will be surprised to get this letter and it will test your memory to know who is writing. But I reckon you will remember an excursion to Clacton-on-Sea and a young 'know it all' boy – well that's me.

I have been training as a pilot in the RAF up in Canada and have some leave due to me after getting my wings and finishing another course and I wondered if there was any chance of coming down to see you for a few days.

As you will see I am at present on Prince Edward Island where I have just completed the course, and after my leave I report to Moncton in New Brunswick prior to shipping back to England. My fourteen days leave starts seven days from now and I would appreciate you letting me know if it is all right to come and perhaps giving me some directions.

Yours sincerely
John.

Livinski straightway looked for his atlas and maps, as he was not exactly sure where Prince Edward Island was in relation to New England. He saw that there was a railway line from the ferry terminal on the mainland that ran through Moncton, then on to St John where the line continued on across into Maine, the direct route to Montreal, and some way along a branch went south to Bangor and thus on to Portland. Livinski wrote at once to tell John the route he should take, explaining that when he got to Portland he should take the train to North Conway. He gave him the hotel telephone number and told him to ring from Portland saying the time of the train he was catching; he would be met at the station.

A week later John telephoned from Portland and was met at the rail station by Livinski in the Surrey driven by Thomas. They arrived at the station shortly before the train arrived and Livinski went through the booking hall to the platform to meet his young friend. The train stopped and the conductor lowered the steps and on to the platform came the young airman, resplendent in his RAF officer's uniform sporting his pilot's wings. John was certainly tall and handsome and it was difficult to see him as the young boy of the excursion. Livinski greeted him warmly and they walked to the carriage. Several heads turned as John got into the carriage and drove along through the town – no one, it would seem, had before seen an RAF officer, certainly not in North Conway, unless it was in one of a number of war films shown at the local cinema featuring the RAF.

John was quite overwhelmed by being met by a horse and carriage.

"This is very special, I never expected to be met by a carriage, makes me feel most important."

"We have kept up the custom of meeting special guests in the carriage, it makes them feel good and they get a better view of the town and where they are going. What sort of a journey did you have?"

"It worked out remarkably well, as I am sure you know Canadian Pacific have a concession to cross Maine as being the shortest route to Montreal from New Brunswick. This made it easy for me to get down onto the line to Portland, in all it took me eight hours to Portland, several of us had hired a plane to fly us to Moncton, the big RAF transit depot in Canada."

"How come you trained in Canada?"

"Since the war all pilots and many other aircrew are trained under the Empire Training Scheme, some in South Africa or Rhodesia, a few in America, even before you came in the war when the trainees had to wear civilian clothes, but most have been trained in Canada where the RAF opened many stations, mostly on the prairies."

"That is interesting, I am sure not many people over here know this. Would you be prepared to talk to a few of my hotel guests about it? I am sure they would all be very interested."

"Of course if you think it worth doing."

"People of course only know what they read in the papers or hear on the radio and I am all for them hearing first hand of other things. I believe you must have gone through the London Blitz, I am sure we would like to hear about your experiences."

By this time the carriage was nearing Jackson and John remembered Livinski telling on the excursion how Adam had proudly told them about the bridge.

"I remember you first drove into Jackson in a carriage and I even remember the name of the young man who drove you. It was Adam."

"Fancy you remembering that, yes that is right, Adam. Of course he is now a man in his sixties!"

"I also remember you describing the hotel."

The carriage reached the bridge and crossed and soon they were coming up to the hotel.

"My goodness, it is just as I knew it would be from your description. You know that story you told us has stuck in my memory like no other thing I remember in my life. You should write a book Mr Livinski, you describe things just as they are without any fancy words."

"Thank you, John, that is most flattering, but I fear I am too old now."

"My Dad says one is never too old, if you think that way you would not do anything."

There were plenty of rooms empty in the hotel and John was given one on the first floor. When he came downstairs he soon became the centre of attention, everybody seemed to want to talk to him – here he was an RAF pilot who so far had done nothing and yet everyone seemed to be treating him as a hero.

"I hope I can meet Joseph and Anna," he remarked to Livinski.

"You shall, Anna will be at her store today but Joseph should be around somewhere. Shall we go through the kitchen and see if he is in the yard?"

"I wonder if it is all as I imagined."

They walked across to the short corridor leading to the kitchen and opened the door.

"I don't remember you describing the kitchen but it is just about how I imagined it would be. This must be the table you all sat at to have breakfast."

"Yes, you are right."

"And this lady must be Susanne who took over from Martha. Fancy you still being here!"

"I don't know who you are, young man, but you are certainly a handsome one – all the girls will be after you, take my word."

"This is John, a young man I met on a train in England and who listened to an old man telling a story of his life. Anyway, shall we see if we can find Joseph?"

They went into the yard and into one of the garages that had been built when it seemed the automobile had come to stay. Inside they found a man working under the bonnet of a big saloon car.

"Hi, Joseph, someone wants to meet you."

Joseph stood upright.

"Please to meet you sir, I'm John, you won't know who I am but I wanted to meet you."

"I do know who you are, Leon here has told me about his story-telling and he said you would be paying us a visit. How do you think it is?"

"Everything is just as I imagined, I was telling your friend that he ought to write a book as he described things in a simple way which have stuck in my mind."

"Yes, he likes a good story, he told me the one about the Roman soldiers on the railway line, that was a good one."

"Yes sir, and quite true – at least to those who saw them."

The two weeks of John's stay soon passed. He had been taken around and shown the sites, visited the Mount Washington Hotel where earlier that year many senior politicians and finance men from all the allied countries had met to discuss what to do when the war ended, and who then had signed a very important document known as The Bretton Woods Agreement, taking its name from the village close by of that name. He was taken along the full length of the Kancamagus Highway and rode the famous Cog Railway. He had met Anna, Caroline and her husband and the two children, Daniel now seventeen and Abigail now a beautiful young lady of almost fourteen.

He had had a wonderful time, given a talk in the hotel, which was reported in some detail in the local paper, visited the house Livinski and Tanya had first built, where Samantha was now living, and also the two stores run by Anna which he knew about from the story told.

Everyone seemed sorry to see him go, and he left with many good wishes and was taken to the rail station by car accompanied by the story teller, Livinski.

"Thank you so much, Leon Livinski, I shall give your good wishes to my parents, and will do my best to keep in touch and hopefully one day after the war come and see you again."

Just before Christmas Livinski had another air letter from England, but not from John as he half expected it would be, but from his mother. In it she said she was sorry to tell him that John had been reported missing after his plane had been shot down on a raid over Germany. She thanked Livinski for looking after her son during his leave and hoped that he would write again some time in the future.

Chapter 26

THE VICTORS RETURN

As we all know the German war finished in May 1945 with the Russians smashing their way to Berlin and the British and Americans defeating the Germans in the West and entering Germany. Both Hitler and Mussolini were both dead. The Japanese were gradually losing the lands they had taken, by, as said before, the Americans island hopping and getting closer to Japan, whilst the British and Commonwealth forces were pushing the Japanese back in the jungles of Burma, and halting the Japanese in New Guinea and their advance towards Australia. The final end came when the Americans dropped two atomic bombs on Japan, causing them to surrender.

Kirk returned to the Washington Valley in 1946 to a hero's reception, having been awarded two medals for outstanding bravery in the field. He had indeed been on Guadalcanal for many months, for it took a long time to take the island and followed this with other beach landings and capture of those islands.

A year later Samantha gave birth to a little girl whom they named Tanya Anna. Livinski's wish had come true and not only that, the name Tanya would live on.

It was soon after Tanya was born that her uncle, Robert McGregor, became ill and found it necessary to retire early. Livinski had no hesitation in asking Kirk, who was then not settled as to what to do after leaving the Marines, if he would take over.

"I'll give you all the help you might need and I am sure you will make a success of it. We must keep it in the family –

first it was Edward, my son, then Robert, my son-in-law, and now I hope it will be you, my granddaughter's husband."

"I would be honoured to accept, sir. I know nothing about managing a hotel but I will do my best, but you must promise to tell me if I seem to be failing."

"You won't fail, certainly not someone who helped take Guadalcanal."

Yes the family would continue to run the business in which he had started work and which after a few short years he and Tanya had made their own. He had earlier given Caroline and Robert a share in the business and now he was about to do the same for Samantha and her husband Kirk, but of course he now had three grandchildren and they must share too. Thus after Kirk had accepted the job of manager he called his solicitor, revised his will, and gave instructions to transfer shares to both Samantha and Kirk.

After the solicitor left, Leon Livinski went out onto the veranda and sat in his favourite seat and he began to think. His old friend Joseph had already taken up his position on the veranda and was fast asleep. Leon's thoughts carried him back in time, he remembered arriving in New York and meeting the girls, he remembered Murphy's and the many times he had discussed this with Joseph, then there was that CPR poster and the way they had worked out how far they could travel. So many thoughts crowded his mind, the search in the library, then the Western Union man with the shades over his eyes, and of course the ride round Boston and finally arriving at North Conway. He could see the carriage and Adam telling them all about the bridge and hotel. Yes he remembered it all and would love to do it again. He suddenly felt lonely and wanted to tell someone how he felt but knew it was not the thing to do, it upset people and would do nothing to make him feel less lonely, if only Tanya were there he could tell her, he knew she would listen. Perhaps, he thought, if I close my eyes she will come and comfort me.

His eyes closed and he was soon asleep; for a time he dreamed and then there was Tanya and he began to feel better and drifted away. No more worries now, he had indeed had a good life and hoped he had helped others but he was now so tired.

Some ten minutes later Joseph woke up with a start and turned to look at his friend, he looked so peaceful – should he wake him? They had both promised to go over to see Anna in the store. He got out of his chair and walked the few steps to Livinski and shook his shoulder gently, but he did not stir. He tried again and then noticed his friend was not breathing. He called out for help but when help arrived he knew it was no good, Leon had left this world, and someone else would have to take over responsibilities for the Livinski family and business.

End